KATE GOODWIN

Every Step After

Copyright © 2024 by Kate Goodwin

All rights reserved. No part of this publication may be reproduced, stored or transmitted in any form or by any means, electronic, mechanical, photocopying, recording, scanning, or otherwise without written permission from the publisher. It is illegal to copy this book, post it to a website, or distribute it by any other means without permission.

First edition

*This book was professionally typeset on Reedsy.
Find out more at reedsy.com*

For my love
*I'm so glad I didn't have to wait
two decades to start forever with you.*

Chapter 1

"I'm sorry, there must be some kind of mistake."

The man across from me furrows his brow and strokes his doughy jowls with one hand, punching keys using a single, pudgy pointer finger. *Geez didn't this guy take typing lessons? Use all ten of those digits the good Lord gave you and speed it up!*

I grit my teeth and tell my inner judgy monologue—Margaret, I call her—to cool her jets. People always think that's my name, so it was the perfect moniker for the parts of myself I tried to keep under wraps. But my name is Meg. Just Meg.

My insides coil with anxiety as confusion fogs my brain. This guy is sweating enough for both of us. Droplets bead under the stringy strands of his graying comb-over. Patience, unfortunately, is not my strong suit. Definitely not Margaret's either. My financial future dangles precariously on the punch of those keys.

"Listen... Gary," I say with a saccharine sweetness, side eyeing the faux wood name plaque in the brass holder on his desk. "I just need to make sure everything is ok with our mortgage. My husband had it set up to auto-pay every month, but when I signed into the account online this week, I realized the payments haven't been pulling for the last six months. I have no idea how that happened. I just don't want our loan to go into default."

He grunts in response. The man behind the desk has grunted at me, his beady eyes never leaving the glow of his screen. Lovely. *He's well within arms distance. Reach over and give him a good slap. On second thought don't; he'd probably like it and ask for more.*

I stifle a laugh at my alter ego's joke and say instead, "I really need to know what's going on." Forcing my jaw to relax, I blow out a breath to add a little quieter, "I'm sorry, I have never managed our finances. It's been a lot to learn at 40, ok? My husband had always done that for us. Before. But now..."

Gary finally looks up, a glimmer of understanding sparking behind the coke-bottle glasses. The lenses make his eyes look even smaller—two shiny beetles examining me. I recoil from his pity. It feels greasy and turns my stomach. I shift my gaze to focus on the cheap watercolor print behind his head instead and clear my throat.

"Can I please speak to the branch manager? Like now? Please?"

If possible, the man narrows his minute eyes even more, pushing away from his desk with evident irritation, a squeal of protest from the chair wheels. Heaving his frame out of the leather roller, he works his way around the desk and edges by my chair to go out behind me.

I sigh in relief. The room is so much less oppressive without his oily presence. Resting my elbows on either side of the plastic and polyester chair, I massage my temples, willing the panicked thoughts bouncing in my head to please, for the love, quiet down.

I focus on my breathing and close my eyes, pretending I'm in my heated Flow class. The GI-Barbie instructor is my favorite. Five foot nothing with blonde hair curling perfectly down her back in a 94-degree studio, she loved barking out orders for us to get out of our heads. FEEL and BREATHE and DO NOT reach for that water bottle just to get yourself out of the discomfort! GI-Barbie would be so proud

Chapter 1

if she could see me now. Just sitting. And breathing. Practicing yoga, right here at the bank. How very Zen of me.

A shuffling behind me breaks my inner peace—if I ever had any—as a beanpole of a man walks in and rounds the desk. His silver hair glints under the fluorescent lights, accenting the kind, grandfatherly look to him. *He's gotta be better than ol' beady eyes Gary.*

"Mrs. Franklin, thank you for your patience. What Gary was attempting to convey was that you no longer have a mortgage with us. The loan was paid off months ago, and that is why the payments have stopped automatically pulling from your account."

The smooth baritone of his voice rumbles around me, but his words don't make any sense. We bought the brownstone about five years ago, on a 20-year note that's nowhere near paid it off. I'm certain we were still paying the PMI. We... back when I was a we. I suppose I am now just a me, though I think I'll need an auto-correct installed in my brain to make the switch. Add it to my widow to-do list.

"Ma'am? Did you have any other questions?" Mr. Branch Manager asks, not unkindly.

"Um, yeah!" I sputter, snapping back to reality. "Who paid it off?! We don't— I mean I don't— I mean who has that kind of money sitting around?!"

He smiles under his bushy gray mustache to open a nondescript file folder pulled from under his arm. The gold band on his left hand winks at me, boastful in reflecting the overhead lights.

"Looks like the full remaining balance was paid off on... ah. Right here. December 24th. A Merry Christmas to you all it sounds like! Same day the savings account was opened."

I vaguely recognize my jaw is hanging open like a big-mouthed bass, but I can't seem to snap it back shut.

"When you say paid off..." I realize how idiotic and repetitive I sound, but I can't seem to do anything about it.

He smiles again—a patient smile typically reserved for young and very naive child—and answers, "I mean that you now own your home free and clear. No more loan payments! Congratulations!"

I am truly flummoxed. We easily had another $400,000 on that loan. Where the funds had come from to pay it off, I hadn't the foggiest. And why had Rob not said anything? Something more flares in my brain then. Something else he said.

"Wait a second," I hold up a finger, thoughts churning sluggishly. "Hang on, what was the other thing you said?"

"No more payments?" he offers, confused.

"No, no," I shake my head vehemently. "You said something about the date. The date. That it was the same day… something else."

I snap my fingers at him, like I can draw the answer out with the sound.

"Oh, yes," he opens the folder again. "December 24th. It was the same day the savings account was opened for… let's see. Ah! Jared Franklin. Your son, I presume?"

"Rob opened an account for Jared? He never—I didn't—What's in it?" My mouth is open again. I can't help it. *Soon, you're going to break into a round of "Take Me to the River" if you don't close that trap.* Oh, shut it, Margaret!

"I believe it's one of our college savings accounts. He's coming of age for that soon, yes? Recently turned 18?"

My stare could bore a hole through this poor man's head. "Yeah… he graduates this weekend and is off to college this fall. P— uh, premed."

The bank manager chuckles, his whiskers dancing on his upper lip, "M.D. bound, eh? Well, that is going to cost a pretty penny. This account will certainly help."

He holds out a printed account sheet to me, and I take it with trembling hands. The numbers blur together, so I blink a few times to ensure I'm seeing this correctly. $750,000. Three quarters of a million

Chapter 1

dollars. Cash. Sitting in an account for our son to pay for college. What. Is. Happening?

"Thank you," I choke out, rising to my feet. The manager takes back the page from me, confused by my reaction. I stumble out of the office, beelining it for the glass doors, waving a hand over my head at the teller who calls out a "have a good day." At least I think that's what she says. I can't decipher anything over the loud buzzing in my ears.

The sun-soaked June air fills my lungs like that first gulp of breath taken after staying underwater ten seconds too long. I'm breathing more, sucking down air to replenish my depleted blood oxygen levels. Then, I'm breathing too much. Oh no, I'm hyperventilating. The traffic is loud, so loud. Horns honking incessantly, cabbies yelling out their open windows. It's too much. It's all too much.

My head swings right and left of its own accord, and I catch the briefest glimpse of blue. My feet run, I feel them pound the pavement, but I don't believe I'm the one controlling them. I hate running. Two more blocks and the buildings on both sides give way to a grassy knoll. My feet don't stop. They eat up the green space heading straight toward the water.

I slam to a halt at the edge of the concrete pier, pulling massive amounts of air into my lungs that leave me lightheaded. I think I might vomit. Or maybe faint. *Ooh or you could faint first, then die because you vomited lying on your back!* Ok, this isn't helping.

Sitting on a bench near the water's edge, I put my head between my knees. GI-Barbie elbows out Margaret, yelling at me to breathe with intention. Inhale. Exhale.

I've done pretty well holding the panic at bay since Rob died. I had to be strong for Jared. He was the one who had lost a parent, so I swallowed the rising tide of overwhelm every time it tried to break through. I guess today the swell was more than my battered mind could manage.

Ok. This is going to be ok. Let's try to reframe this. I have no idea what's happening, but the great news is most of the financial details I'd been freaking out over for the past year are now a moot point. With no mortgage payment and Jared's college covered, between the life insurance and my part time writing, I was set for a little while. Long enough for me to figure out the tangled grieving mess of my life.

That's something. That's huge. I used to tell Rob I'd kill him if he died before me. For many reasons but one of which is that I wouldn't know how to manage our finances without him. Maybe he took that seriously and made sure there was less for me to handle. Yeah, that was probably it. The man had been a thoughtful provider for almost 20 years. That had to be it.

So... he was a drug dealer on the side? He had a secret life you didn't know about. Amazing how you never suspected...

I shove Margaret away, but she had a point. Where did over a million dollars cash come from to pay the mortgage and set up that account? And had he really done it two days before he died? This made no sense.

We were comfortable enough in our firmly middle-class Chicago brownstone, just north of Hyde Park. The house was a steal, buying when the market was relatively stable from an older lady who thought pre-teen Jared was the most charming boy she'd ever met. Lake Michigan sat just a couple blocks from our front door. A dream really.

We'd struggled the first few years with Rob's law school debt, but I mostly worked now because I wanted to. Because I liked writing, and it put that journalism degree finished just before Jared was born to good use.

Rob had made some small investments over the years, dabbling in the stock market here and there. But he was no millionaire. The savings we set aside were modest amounts, really just enough for emergencies. And those had been burned through last year with the slew of medical bills from the barrage of tests and treatments they put him through.

Chapter 1

I force some more deep breaths, slowing down their cadence, willing my heart rate to calm as well. I may not understand what was happening but that didn't mean I should give the lakeside joggers a front row ticket to my mental breakdown.

Instead of focusing on what I didn't know, I switch gears to what I do know.

Number one, I don't need to worry about money right now. Don't ask questions. Just accept it for the moment and thank your lucky stars. Got it. I could do that. Pro-level compartmentalizer right here.

Number two, my one and only son is graduating high school tomorrow. I still had approximately 63 blue and silver balloons to inflate for the arch and 150 cupcakes to bake for his party after. Thank goodness he wanted pizza for the food. Might be best to head home now and get started on those cupcakes.

Number three, I am fairly positive I sat in fresh bird droppings when I collapsed onto this bench mid-mental breakdown.

Oh well done, Meg! Always a class act. I shoot an applauding Margaret a mental evil eye and pick myself up to walk home, avoiding the urge to brush off my backside until I can change.

Chapter 2

"Thank God you're here," I half laugh half sob, yanking Amelia over the threshold and closing the front door behind her.

I pull her in for a hug, needing to feel the strength of my big sister holding me up for a moment. As a rule, she semi-despises hugs. But she loves me. So, for now, she allows it.

"Woah, Meggers." Her use of my childhood nickname throws my aching heart off-guard in the best way.

Amelia presses her hands on my shoulders to gently escape the hug and hold me an arms distance away, her preferred comfort zone. "Probably still some spit up not yet dried on this shirt. Don't want to contaminate you."

"If it came from the mouth of my perfect nephew, I wouldn't mind," I argue, taking in her messy half up topknot and sure enough, spit up-stained tee.

It was fascinating seeing my sister uncomposed in this way. She'd always been the type A go-getter. Aggressively plucked and polished, climbing the corporate ladder to kick some egotistical old men off as she went.

We looked a fair amount alike in the shape of our faces and main features. But where her eyes were a cool gray, mine were a warm green. She kept her hair dyed a perfectly jet black, sharply angled at her jaw, while I barely managed to get highlights in my longer locks once a summer to add some dimension to my bland brown.

Though easily recognized as related, we were also opposites. She'd gotten married a few years ago, well into her late thirties. I got hitched at 21, still in college, and gave birth to Jared two months after graduation at 22. I lived in ironic, book-inspired t-shirts, cardigans and comfy shoes. She wore sleek black tops and spike heels to Whole Foods. But motherhood had changed her. First, in increments when Daisy was born. Then drastically more when Oliver came along a couple months ago.

The babies had made her sharp edges just a little softer, though she was still the fiercest boss babe ever. She'd traded 3 a.m. calls with Milan for 3 a.m. feedings, delegating more to her team. Her bi-weekly manicures were replaced by nails crudely painted by four-year-old Daisy. But she still wore her red lipstick like armor, even with the messy bun and puke stains.

She's my sister. I love every version of her.

"Earth to Meg... sis? Ok. What's going on? I know you have a blowout party to plan, and I have a quarter of a million cupcakes to frost, yet you're standing there staring at me like you haven't seen me in ages. Mark and the kids and I were just here last Saturday..." She looks me over, turning each shoulder a bit as if to inspect me front and back for visible damage.

"Have you ever wondered if Mark is telling you everything?" I blurt, the question surprising even me. "Just curious, that's all," I add, an attempt at casual.

Amelia's brow instantly furrows, her eyes narrowing as they meet mine. She adopts her steely head of corporate affairs tone with me.

"I'm going to ask you again, Meg Franklin. What is going on? What's this about?"

I freeze, unable voice my suspicions out loud. *Way to chicken out, Meg. Afraid of what she'll say are we? You know she'll be brutally honest.*

"No, it's nothing." I wave my hand to bat away the words I wished I could take back. "Weird dream I had last night. Left me unsettled, I guess. You're right we have SO much to do, what was I *thinking* inviting 80 people here?"

I gesture wildly behind me to the cozy but modern living area that led to the open concept dining with a doorway into the kitchen space. The walled garden beyond was my favorite part of the house. I was counting on no rain for tomorrow—more like pleading with the heavens to stay dry—so we could utilize the outdoor green space for overflow.

Amelia arches a brow and follows me. I can feel her suspicion burning a spot between my shoulder blades, but I have the benefit of our massive task working on my side. She lets the subject drop for now, thank goodness.

Dozens of unfrosted cupcakes are cooling on every surface of my kitchen. The blue and silver liners shine in the light coming in through the window above the sink. Amelia blows out an audible breath at the sight and picks up the icing gun, pretending to cock it.

"Alright, sis. Let's do this. Load me up."

We work silently side-by-side as our system forms. I load 12 cupcakes into one of the decorative boxes with a little insert to keep them standing. Amelia tackles icing them. She first tries icing a cupcake while I hold it, but I couldn't seem to get it into the box after without smudging frosting onto my palms. I don't know how those bakeries do it. This was tougher than I thought it would be. *Well, you are a chronic under-estimator,* Margaret points out unhelpfully.

Soon we find our rhythm. Unfortunately, the ease of familiarity opens a route for conversation. I feel her question building, ready to launch. Before she can bring it up again, I jump in to steer the topic

Chapter 2

away from myself.

"Still thinking you'll head back to the office at the end of next month? That's when your 12-week leave is up right?"

"Oh yeah, definitely," Amelia replies, not breaking her stride as she finishes the perfect rose swirl on the top of another cupcake. She's getting good at this. *Of course, she is.* Margaret rolls her proverbial eyes. She tended to be the jealous type. I hand my sister another box and take the full one to stack on the dining room table.

"Yeah, I couldn't do it. No offense, sis. You know I think you're super mom, but no way I could do the stay-at-home mom gig. I'd lose my mind! Plus, I worked hard to get where I am. I'm not gonna let some pasty-faced mustache replace me just because the dads are never expected to give up their careers. Oliver will love the daycare we picked out. Super small group sizes, very individualized attention. And they have a curriculum! For babies! Just think of how he'll get ahead for school."

She sighs contentedly, handing me another perfectly frosted cupcake.

Handing her a fresh box to start on, I say, "Honestly Ames, never thought I'd say this, but motherhood suits you!"

Her lovely face glows at the compliment. She has always been the prettier sister, but I didn't mind. From elementary days to now, Amelia always made space at the table for me.

"So," she says, setting down the frosting dispenser, ready for a break. "How much longer are you going to put me off with compliments and personal questions before you tell me what's going on with you?"

I try to laugh off the question, but it comes out a strangled cough instead. "It's just stress, Ames. Stress and grief, obviously. This is a lot. I've lost my husband. I'm about to lose my son to college across the country. I'm officially middle-aged, and I honestly don't know who I'm supposed to be without them. My family has been my reason for existing for so long."

11

I focus every ounce of my attention on placing more cupcakes meticulously into the next box. If I focus hard enough, I can almost forget the part I'm not telling her. Almost.

"While I know that's all been on your mind lately," Amelia says matter-of-factly, "I also know you're trying to distract me with your widow card. C'mon Meg. Something happened. I can feel it radiating off you! Jared's off gallivanting with his friends. It's just you and me. Spill!"

I never could keep a thing from her. I let out a huff of surrender and open the floodgates to tell her everything. Everything the bank manager said to me yesterday. (Nearly) every thought I've had since. I stop short of revealing every doubt, fear, accusation and denial boiling underneath the surface in my veins.

"I, um. I went through his nightstand… and his dresser last night," I admit, biting my lip and staring at the floor to avoid Amelia's eyes. "And his office desk. I hadn't had it in me to touch those since… you know. But last night, after Jared went to bed, I tore through it all. Every paper, every note, every receipt I could find."

"…and?" she prompts.

"And nothing! I don't know Amelia, I can't find a single thing!" I slap my hands down on the counter, nearly upsetting the bowl of frosting. *BREATHE! You don't want a repeat of yesterday's hysterics.*

"Mostly I proved he loves to golf a lot," I say, massaging the bridge of my nose. "I even checked his computer. Aside from a suggestive message in his Facebook inbox from a girl who used to work at his firm, which he completely ignored, not a darn thing! He was a steady husband and a great father to Jared. And now I feel like a raving lunatic, tearing through his things like the police comb through a house in a drug raid!"

"What was her name?"

"Huh?" I ask, scrubbing my palms down my face, collecting myself.

"The colleague messaging him. Her name." Amelia's voice is eerily

Chapter 2

calm.

"Oh, I don't remember, Chasity somebody?" She snorts. "Figures. The name never lies."

I stared at my sister torn between a laugh and a cry. "Amelia! Over a million dollars! Focus!"

"Ok, ok sorry! I was just trying to decide if we needed to go slash some tires. Sounds like it's probably overkill since it was a one-time offense, and he didn't take the bait, bonus points to him. Maybe if the opportunity arises..." She taps her chin, lost in imaginations before waving it off.

"Ok you're right. Now's not the time. Bigger fish and all that. Ok just gimme a minute to think."

Ooh, I love how her mind works. A little vandalism will teach that girl not to message her suggestive invitations on social media. Also slashing tires sounds like not a bad way to blow off some steam...

"Did you check all the financial statements? Go back through his tax forms?"

She is a wonder. "No, I guess I didn't think of that. Amelia, I don't run a corporate team like you do. I didn't handle our house finances! I'm not even sure where all he had accounts, honestly. Rob always did everything like that. Paid every bill, kept the lights on. I didn't have the guts to tell you before but in January, our power and water was shut off for a whole day. I—I didn't know when the bill needed to be paid."

My voice had dropped with each statement, ending in barely a whisper. I bury my head in my hands to hide the embarrassment and shield me from her pity.

"I was too proud to ask for help."

Tears fill my palms, spilling over as they multiply. Tears of grief, of hurt, of anger at myself and even at Rob for whatever secrets he was hiding. I feel Amelia's hand on my elbow. Turning me into her slightly sour-smelling shoulder, she rubs my back and speaks softly like she used to after the worst of the blowouts in our childhood home.

"Hey, hey, I'm sorry. I didn't mean to overwhelm you with the probing. Listen, your husband managing the money doesn't reflect negatively on you, ok? It's easier for one spouse to take that load in many marriages. You took the parenting load with Jared. He took the financial load. That's ok! There's no one right way to do things. It just means that now you've got a bit of a learning curve. But you are smart and capable! You've got this. It's ok to not know it all yet. We'll get there. I'll be here, and so will Mark. You know he's a wizard with numbers. Twenty-five years as a CPA ain't for nothin' sister."

She pulls back to tuck a hair behind my ear, unsticking it from a wet cheek. I pull in a shaky breath.

"Am I putting my head in the sand if I don't keep digging for now? If I just let it go because… because I'm not sure I can handle what answers I might find? I feel like I just need a minute." I barely meet her gaze from the corner of my eye.

"No, you're not putting your head in the sand," she answers firmly. "Let's focus on right now. Your son is graduating in just a few short hours, and this place will be hoppin' come tonight. One thing at a time, sis. What was that thing Rob used to always say? His little tagline. You know the one!"

A wobbly smile turns up the corners of my mouth.

"Take the next step forward, just one. And from there you'll be able to see the next one."

"That's the spirit! So let today's step be getting your son through his final stage of high school. Get him through graduation, then we'll figure out the next step from there. One at a time. We got this. Now go upstairs and put on that gorgeous little black dress that says 'yes, I'm a mother of a high school grad, but I've still got it.' You know the one!"

I give her a watery smile and turn towards the stairs laughing through

Chapter 2

the tears. She whips the towel at my backside with a "yeehaw" and turns back to finish the last few cupcakes. I sigh, allowing some of the weight to roll off my back as I reach the stairs, grab the handrail and take the next step.

Chapter 3

My hands have never hurt from clapping before, but they do today. I whoop and holler and whistle alongside Amelia, Mark, and Daisy. Even baby Oliver gives a victorious cry as my boy crosses the stage.

"We did it, Rob," I whisper, cupping my left hand over my mouth. "Just look at our boy."

I still wear my wedding rings there. I don't have it in me to take them off yet. Who would I be if not Mrs. Rob Franklin?

Jared pauses at the corner of the stage after receiving his diploma, his eyes searching, then finding mine. He blows me a kiss—which sets off the squealing girls in the front row—and switches the tassel dangling from his cap to the other side.

The blown kiss brings a massive lump to my throat as my mind flashes back to another one I received from him. A core motherhood memory. Jared, age 5, standing at the corner just one house down from ours, looking up and down the street waiting. His Power Rangers backpack is nearly as big as he is, weighed down with his packed lunch of PB&J, an apple and carrot sticks. He was so proud of that lunch because he'd packed it himself. As the bus pulls up and squeals to a stop,

Chapter 3

the doors hissing as they open, I can't tear my eyes away, unwilling to miss a single second. Without fear, he steps forward to board the bus, turning around just for a moment to meet my eye and blow me a big kiss before climbing the steps for his first time riding the bus to school.

I had driven him on the first day and walked him in to meet his Kindergarten teacher, find his cubby and unpack his supplies into the desk with his name taped across the top. He was all confidence in his voice and mannerisms but when he thought I wasn't looking, his hands shook a little as he lifted the lid of his desk and carefully placed the 16-count box of Crayola's inside. I'd offered to get him the 64-count at the store, but he'd shaken his head and told me, "That's more than I need mom. It's too many choices. I'll get overwhelmed!"

He was always wiser than his years. Still is. Maybe that's what was wrong with me now. With my husband gone and son leaving for college, a world of options lay before me. A blank coloring page and I'm holding the 124-count box of crayons. Expected to build a new life, but I didn't even know how to pick a starting color.

That wise little five-year-old winks at me from a young man's body as he slides into his place next to the other graduates. I am so proud of him it hurts. The hurt would be the good kind, except it's coupled with the pain that his dad isn't here to see it. *He knows though. He sees and he's proud too.* Huh, I guess Margaret can be nice occasionally. Good to know she's not all snark. I take that nugget and tuck it deep in my heart.

After the ceremony ends, Jared finds us without delay. While his classmates gather in circles together snapping group pics, my boy heads straight to me. I open my mouth to say something, anything to express all I'm feeling, but turns out I don't have to. He wraps me up in the warmest hug and stays there for a minute. My head only hits him mid-chest, the polyester acetate of his graduation gown scratchy beneath my cheek. A strange sensation considering he once had slept curled up on *my* chest, his entire body no longer than my torso.

He finally pulls away and looks down as I look up. We smile through the tears glimmering in both our eyes. I try again to tell him, to speak around the ball of emotion clogging my throat.

"Jared, we— I mean I— um," I falter over my misuse of the plural pronoun, tears threatening to spill over.

"I know, Mom," he cuts me off with the gentle reprieve to wrap an arm around my shoulder giving a comforting squeeze. "I know. Let's go home, ok?"

"Woo hoo!" Amelia shouts, making her way through the crowd toward us. "It's time to PAR-TAY!!! My favorite nephew everyone! Round of applause for the boy who should've been valedictorian. You heard me Principal Hallard!" She has her hands cupped around her mouth to magnify that last bit, and I roll my eyes.

"O-kay, favorite aunt," Jared laughs, pulling down her cupped hands to tuck one into his elbow. "Thanks for the shout out. I'm sure they'll take it under advisement."

He guides us to the double doors of the gymnasium where Mark waits, searching the crowds anxiously. Daisy strains at one hand, attempting to wrangle out of his grip. Oliver's car seat is in a death grip in the other hand. His relief is palpable as he catches sight of us heading his way.

"Hey, man! Congrats!" Mark says, looking like he wants to offer a handshake and shrugging when he finds no free hands.

Jared scoops Daisy up in one smooth move, eliciting a delighted squeal from her as he lifts her up onto his shoulders.

"Is it time for cupcakes, Jare-Jare?" she chirps, pulling his thick hair with both hands like a bareback rider grips a horse's mane.

"You betcha, Cupcake! To the party!" He goose steps out into the parking lot.

Chapter 3

I smile at the peal of giggles, and my aching heart warms as I follow the group. My people. My family.

* * *

"Ugh. I never want to see another cupcake AGAIN!" I groan into the arm of the couch. Every muscle of my body sighed once I'd finally sat down.

It's a quarter after midnight and the last of the party goers have bid their congratulations and said good night. My house can once more breathe.

"You sure I can't help clean up, Mom?" Jared asks, stifling a yawn at the bottom of the stairs.

I wave at him over the back of the couch, "No way! It's against the rules for the grad to have to work at their own party! To bed with you, sir! Besides, I've got my girls to help."

He chuckles and crosses to the couch to bend down and kiss my upturned cheek, "As you wish."

A collective "aw" goes up from my two friends who stayed behind to help me clean. He waves them off with a grin and climbs the stairs two at a time to his room.

I sent Amelia home a few hours earlier with a harried looking Mark. Oliver was fussy, Daisy sugar-overloaded and clearly the whole family needed their beds. It was just me and my book besties now, sprawled all over the living room couches.

Kristen, Cecelia and I have a very casual, non-structured book club who met whenever we found time, read whatever we wanted to read and shared our lists of "must reads" and books not worth the hype to guide one another's endless reading lists. We've been friends since our junior year of high school, there for each other through college, marriage and raising kids. Our kids were all teens and tweens now, and we found ourselves with slightly more time on our hands to read. Even so there would never, ever be enough time to finish our lists.

"Seriously, you and Rob did an amazing job with that one," Cece says, raising her water bottle toward the stairs after Jared's bedroom door clicked shut.

"It's true," Kristen yawns. "Janie barely wants to speak to me most days. She's all attitude, and mom just isn't on her cool list anymore. From everything I've read, girls are worse than boys in those teen years. NOW they tell me." She throws up her hands in defeat.

We grow quiet, thinking collectively about our kids, each just hoping to do better than our parents had. Cece props up on one elbow on the love seat to face me on the opposite couch.

"Be honest, how's Jared doing since Rob passed?"

I feel the sigh I let loose reverberate in my bones.

"He's doing better than I expected. I think having that year with him before he passed kind of helped… prepare him, I guess? Prepared both of us I think, if you can prepare for such a thing. We held out hope that he'd somehow go into remission. But Jared's a levelheaded kid. With his love of human science and medicine, he knew the odds. He understood what we were up against, perhaps even better than we did. He had already been leaning toward med school for his future, but once Rob got his diagnosis, it sealed the deal for Jared. He eats, sleeps and breathes pre-med now. He's beyond excited for college this fall."

"Columbia, right?" Kristen asked. "Gosh the Big Apple is a long way from here… How are YOU doing?"

These were my friends. I could be honest with them without them pushing me for details I wasn't yet ready to share. Details I didn't understand yet. *Better close that file back up for now.*

"Too many things," I answer. "Beyond proud. Unsure of what my life is now without the titles of wife and mom. Confused. Not sure I have words for all of it."

Chapter 3

"Did I hear him making summer plans with the Delaney boy? Something about California?" Cece stretches her arms up over her head and yawns into a shoulder, her jaw cracking.

"Oh yes!" I sit up. "That came up tonight during the party. Apparently, an uncle in Napa Valley owns a vineyard. He's invited Grant and a friend to come work for him this summer, and Grant wants Jared to come. We haven't really had a chance to talk about it but it sounded like he'd like to go. It would be a fun summer distraction and get him a little spending money for fall semester."

"I've always wanted to work in a vineyard ever since Keanu Reeves plucked a cluster of grapes in *A Walk in the Clouds*..." Cece sighs dreamily. "It sounds like a great opportunity for Jared, but what about you?"

I smile a little ruefully, "What's a mother's purpose after her child leaves the nest? I suppose I'm about to find out."

Kristen sits up, snaps her fingers and points right at me.

"Travel," she says confidently, jabbing her finger toward me for emphasis. "That's what you should do, Meg! Travel!"

Cece half sits to echo her agreement, and I wrinkle my nose at them disbelieving.

"Travel places by myself? I don't know girls..."

"No, no, listen she's right, it's perfect," Cece insists. "You could pick a place you and Rob had talked about but not visited and go! It could be a way to honor him. And also take a step toward experiencing more of life as a—well, as a single woman."

She says the last part gently, knowing that when she leaves here tonight, she'll be snuggling into her bed with her husband right beside her. I don't want to become the odd woman out in our group, but the fact is, it is a little awkward now. They are part of a unit. I no longer am. The dynamics have shifted, and we were still finding our footing.

I decide to tackle that thought another day and force myself into a standing position.

"Well, girls," I declare, hands on my hips. "I have made one important decision tonight, and that is the rest of these plates and cups and all this mess can wait til the morning. It'll keep. Let's all go enjoy our beds now. Besides, you two still have to drive home!"

After hugs, sleepy goodbyes, and a final wave off from the front porch, I close the door behind me and face the semi chaos of the first floor. I am exhausted but somehow the stillness, the quiet, the solitude has me avoiding the stairs and wandering to the office just off the kitchen instead.

Rob's desk is still a cluttered mess from my earlier vandalism. *You make a terrible thief. There's evidence of your break-in everywhere.*

Yeah, yeah, but what good is evidence when no one else is around to see it? I fire up my own laptop from the recliner in the corner. That was always "my chair" to sit and read or write while Rob caught up on client emails from his computer. It had been our little way of staying connected, even when work had him extra busy.

My Dell blinks on with a screensaver of some exotic scenery and a fun fact. I navigate to the search engine and my fingers hover over the keys, expectantly. When you can go just about anywhere, how do you choose? Back to the Crayola dilemma. I look behind me to the bookshelves where photos from our previous travels are placed sporadically in front of my favorite books.

Rio de Janeiro. Sydney. Tokyo. Milan. Edinburgh. We'd taken some amazing trips together once Jared had gotten a bit older. I can't help but smile over his magical, goofy grin riding Rob's shoulders, Cinderella's castle sparkling behind them.

I glance over to the steno pad on Rob's desk. He always kept one next to his keyboard to jot down random thoughts and to do items that came to him. The top page was the date of his last booked tee time. Under that, a word was written, underlined and circled. I lean over,

Chapter 3

nearly tipping out of the chair. Salzburg. He'd written "Salzburg" and "June" followed by a question mark. My eyes sting at the words. We'd always talked of going one day to do the Sound of Music tour. It was my favorite musical, and I dreamed of seeing the shooting locations around the historic city.

Do it, Meg. The hills are alive and right now, so are you. Do it for yourself and do it for Rob. Take the next step.

"Ok, Rob," I whisper to the room, typing into the search engine and clicking the first link on the list.

"Let's go to Austria."

Chapter 4

I never want this hug to end. But the announcements keep sounding overhead, reminding us that time is moving forward and so should we. Jared pulls back first, hands on my shoulders to look at me like I used to do to him, when he was still smaller than me. I feel a dampness on my cheeks as people stream around us. We're a rock, and they're the river current, parting and flowing past.

"You're crying? Aw, Mom, don't start or you'll make me cry too!" he says with a smile, wiping a wayward tear with one thumb. "Listen, this is going to be great for both of us. Dad never wanted us sitting around, sad and directionless. He wanted us to go on living! He believed we were strong enough. Let's prove him right, yeah?"

I smile at my wise boy, chest aching with love and admiration. How incredible is it to raise a child into an adult you can admire? I sniff up my emotions and laugh at my sappy self.

"Oh, you know how I get! Just ignore me. I'm so excited for you. I know you're going to have an amazing time in Napa. Don't forget your promise—one FaceTime call a week! I'll work around your schedule, whatever you need. You'll be a working man! I'm so proud of you, son."

Chapter 4

I go up on my toes to give him a quick peck on the cheek as he squeezes my fingers.

"Flight 2187 to Frankfurt is now boarding from Gate C14. Flight 2187 is now boarding," an announcement buzzes from a speaker somewhere overhead. That's my first leg.

"Take lots of pics, and don't forget to be in some of them!" he instructs, pointing a finger at me. "See you in six weeks!"

With one more quick hug, we turn opposite directions to head towards our respective gates. Jared had been more than supportive when I approached him with my idea the morning after his graduation. I thought it might help him feel more free to go away himself. We spent Sunday browsing flights and places to stay. He insisted on an adorable Airbnb apartment he found right in the heart of Salzburg so I could "make myself at home." Then we booked him a ticket to California, leaving close to the same time Friday afternoon. That way neither of us would be left at the house alone.

My boss at the tech news magazine I wrote part-time for had been relatively ok with me working remotely for the next month and a half. As luck would have it, a cybersecurity conference was occurring in Prague halfway through my trip. I'd be traveling by train to cover it in-person and spending the remainder of my working vacation in the Czech capital. The thought has me near giddy with excitement. With "mom" my full-time position, I'd never wanted to take the travel-required conference assignments in the past.

Theoretical technology is one of my favorite topics to write about, but cybersecurity is a close second. I couldn't write too many though because researching for those pieces has historically sent me falling down scary dark web holes. After one feature on the topic, I deleted all my social media, disconnected our smart home devices and was ready to throw my cell in a random alley dumpster before Rob talked me down.

I get to the gate just as boarding starts and pop into the closest ladies' room before joining the line. *You'll probably be directly in front of that mom with the baby and tantrum-throwing toddler for the entire eight-hour flight to Frankfurt.*

Margaret is probably right, but I won't let it get to me. I have enough nerves as it is. I've never flown anywhere by myself. My family didn't travel much growing up, though my parents were making up for lost time now, living as ex-pats in Italy.

My father had won a settlement after a serious work injury. He retired after that, and he and my mom bought a little place in southern Italy, using it as their base to travel Europe. Amelia and I heard from them occasionally, which is fine for both of us. We'd never been particularly close growing up and had grown even farther apart over the years. None of us really felt like putting in the work to pull us back together.

After I married Rob, travel became a priority for us. I even went on a few of his business trips with him when Jared wasn't in school. My heart gives a little squeeze, and I spin my wedding ring with my right pointer finger. A nervous habit. I don't know when I'll feel it's time to take it off, but I know I'm not there yet. Not today.

The line moves and I step up, phone in hand for the attendant to scan my digital boarding pass.

"Enjoy your trip, Mrs. Franklin!" she says cheerily, oblivious to the flash of hurt that crosses my face at the title.

Take off the ring if you don't like it. Easy solution. Instead, I take a deep breath and head down the gangway, taking the next step forward.

* * *

Stepping out of the airport taxi, I take my first full breath since last Friday. I spin a full circle on the sidewalk trying, and failing, to take it

Chapter 4

all in.

The city of Salzburg is a jewel nestled in the Alps with mountains all around. An honest-to-goodness castle looms high on the edge of the city. A fairy tale. Add that to my list of places to explore. I am equal parts exhilarated and exhausted from the overnight flight. For now, I need to figure out this whole apartment thing.

Unloading my massive suitcase and carry-on at the curb, the car and driver pull away, leaving me standing outside a lovely, historic-looking apartment building. I pull up the email from Alice—the host—and find the bit where she provides the key code access.

"2748, 2748," I mutter under my breath wrestling with my luggage up to the front entrance to punch in the main door code.

The door swings open with a click, revealing the most gorgeous entryway to ever exist in an apartment. Probably. The ceiling is vaulted in bell shapes, with accent beams crisscrossing in the centers. I am confident I will love it here!

I take the stone staircase up toward my indicated floor. The space is so narrow I have to turn sideways to haul up my luggage. Wrought iron sconces along the wall glow with a single candle-shaped bulb. The weight of a six weeks' worth of clothes has me grunting with effort.

Maybe if you'd packed less shoes... Probably true. At home I tend to wear the same comfortable flats daily. Fly me across an ocean, and I need no less than eight different styles of shoes to choose from. It makes perfect sense.

A friendly face pops around the corner of the next landing startling me. The bigger suitcase handle slips and bumps down a step.

"Brauchst du hilfe?" the woman calls down. A mess of brown curls forms a halo around her cheerful face.

Oh no, hang on. I know how to answer this, I just have to remember! Surely a full week on the Learn German app would've taught me some of these words right?

"Er, ich... spreche, um, kein Deutsch. English?" I ask hesitantly.

"Oh, ja English! American, huh? Wilkommen—welcome! Let me help!"

She bounces down the stairs with a literal spring in her step. An over sized sweatshirt emblazoned "NYC" in huge letters hangs over her cropped leggings. *A hoodie in June?* I smile at the little reference to home.

"Johanna," she says, sticking out one hand to me while grabbing the handle of the larger suitcase with the other.

"Oh, hi Johanna. Meg. Listen, that's heavy. You really don't have to..." my jaw drops as she yanks my suitcase up the rest of the stairs with the strength of a well-muscled man. *Okay then.*

"S'no problem," she replies with a smile, setting the bag onto the landing. "You are renting from Alice, ja?"

I snap my mouth shut and take the last few steps to join her.

"Yes! Yes, I am. For three weeks," I offer. "Listen, thank you so much, you didn't have to do that."

She's beaming at me with an interested but non-judgmental stare. Her eyes sparkle as she bounces on the balls of her feet in her Birkenstock sandals and white tube socks. *Wow, this lady is like sunshine and skittles had a baby...*

"Neighbors!" Johanna announces so suddenly and loudly I jump again. She points a thumb over her shoulder at another door that must be her apartment. I nod my head, unsure how excited I am supposed to be.

"Will let you get settled. If you want a friend for exploring adventures, knock on my door! I can show you the best spots, ja? Anytime. I never sleep anyway." Her smile is now stretched so wide I am surprised it's not touching her ears.

"Yeah, um, thanks Johanna. I'll—I'll let you know. Maybe. Ok, bye!"

I spin around to punch the code into the keypad. It beeps and flashes

Chapter 4

a red light at me. I chuckle nervously and look over my shoulder a bit to see her still watching me.

"Come ON," I mutter a prayer under my breath. "Aha!"

The door clicks and swings open to the studio apartment. I do a quick wave over my shoulder without looking and drag my belongings into the space as quickly as possible, letting the door swing shut heavily behind me.

"Whew!" I say, my back to the door as I survey the space. It's small but perfect for just me. The living and bedroom are one shared space with two overstuffed chairs situated by a floor to ceiling window. Scratch that, it's a door out onto a small balcony. So quaint!

The kitchen and bathroom are separated from the main living and sleeping space by doors. Very European. Very IKEA. A table in the entryway holds a welcome note from my host, including the Wi-Fi password and some information about the area—where to buy groceries, good coffee, etc.

You sure put that neighbor in her place, Margaret congratulates me. I instantly regret not being nicer. She was only trying to help. But I didn't come here to make friends. I came to try to figure out how I'm supposed to do life now, *by myself*. Without Rob. Without... anyone. Plus, a new friend would have "get to know you" questions. Questions I don't feel like answering. I came here for solitude. It's the right call.

The double bed is inviting with its tremendously plush down comforter. Maybe a few minutes of rest wouldn't hurt. I shrug off my shoes, ditching the light cardigan and flowy skirt I'd worn for the flight onto a chair. Don't want any airplane germs on my new bed.

I test the bed with a quick lie-down and oh my gracious, it is the definition of comfortable. Just a few minutes before unpacking and settling in will feel so good.

I wake up in total darkness and absolute confusion. It takes a moment to remember where I'm at and figure out why it's dark. My phone battery has a few percent charge left and shows 4 a.m. Alright, it wasn't just a few minutes.

I feel refreshed though and get up to unpack my things. Starting with the larger suitcase, I open it to see what's shifted where during the flight. No closets—it's Europe—but the large wardrobe will work just fine.

Rob always laughed at me for unpacking on trips. "Are you moving in or what?" he'd tease. But I liked settling into a space. It made me feel more comfortable. More at home. Perhaps that's part of what's bothering me so much right now. I feel unsettled in my own skin. Like this place with my stuff all in suitcases, my body doesn't feel like home anymore. Rob had been home. Jared was home. Yet here I was, off on my own. Maybe I wasn't ready for this trip after all. My fingers reach for my phone to check flight options back to Chicago.

Suck it up, Buttercup. Margaret mentally slaps my hand. *If you go back home, Jared will feel guilty about being in California and cancel his plans for you. You're a grown woman, for Pete's sake. Figure it out!*

My internal alter ego was such a judgy jerk. But also, a correct jerk. She'd been my mental companion these past six months on my own.

I finish the last of the folding, line my shoes inside the bottom shelf and close the wardrobe, satisfied. Grabbing my phone, a message from Jare shows on the screen. I open the text and smile at a picture of him with Grant, dramatically eating grapes reclined like Romans. I roll my eyes. *Teenage boys. Scratch that. All boys.* I thumb out a quick reply, laughing at his pic and letting him know I'm safe, but had fallen asleep before I had a chance to text my arrival.

The apartment is great. I add and pause. *Thanks for encouraging me to come. I think it'll be good for me.*

I hit send and toss the phone back on the bed. Grabbing a leather bound notebook and pen from my bag, I sit down to jot out a list of to-do's for while I'm here, starting with the most practical.

Chapter 4

1. Find somewhere nearby to buy groceries
2. Locate good coffee. Good pastries an added bonus
3. Visit that castle!
4. Go on *Sound of Music* tour (or is that too "touristy"? Never mind, I don't care. Doing it.)
5. Figure out what to do with the rest of my life.

I dot the last point a little aggressively before setting my pen down and checking the time. 6:30 a.m. Good enough. I throw on a soft floral dress, slip on some sandals and head out the door to accomplish number one on my list.

I pause on the landing, attention caught by the crack of light streaming out from under Johanna's door and scent of coffee filling the landing.

Bet over-zealous neighbor lady knows the best grocer around here. And she's already up!

Nope! I have to figure it out by myself. Straightening the thin strap of my purse and squaring my shoulders, I march down the stairs to conquer the day. It's groceries. How hard could it be?

Chapter 5

I return two hours later with sore feet—these new sandals were NOT made for walking—and zero groceries. In Salzburg, the markets are closed on Sundays. I hadn't even known today was Sunday.

Weary with defeat, I trudge up the stairs to see what I can scrounge from the bottom of my travel backpack. Surely there were some crackers or nuts I could snack on to hold me over until the restaurants open. That was an eternity away to my grumbling stomach. I had promised my travel budget I would cook at the apartment for all but one meal a day.

Before I can punch in the key code for my place, the door behind me swings open and the most delicious smells pour out in a cloud around Johanna's smiling frame.

"Guten tag, neighbor! You are an early riser, like me, ja? Already gone and back. You figured out you can't get any groceries today. Markets closed. Come, you will breakfast with me. Come," she reaches toward me to pull me into her apartment.

My brain finally catches up, and I open my mouth to decline. But my stomach chooses that moment to rumble loudly at the scents wafting from her kitchen.

"Ok," I find myself saying instead. "Thank you. Breakfast would be lovely."

Johanna claps her hands in delight and opens the door even wider for me. Stepping across her threshold, my eyes take a moment to adjust. It's a studio apartment, same layout as the one I'm in. But it feels half the size due to the overwhelming number of items she has in the room. Canvases and photographs cover every inch of the upper walls above the row after row of bookshelves absolutely jammed full of paperbacks.

That humongous smile still affixed, she waves me to the two-person table in one crowded corner.

"It's almost done! Let me get it. Tea or coffee?"

"Coffee sounds amazing, thank you, Johanna," I say, remembering my manners and shifting guiltily at her hospitality in the face of my absolute lack of desire to connect.

She bustles away through the kitchen door, humming a jaunty tune. Good grief, did this woman ever stop? *You could do with a tip or two on happiness from her, you know? You've been a bit of a grump.*

Well, excuse me for not exuding rainbows every moment since my HUSBAND DIED. Let's not forget that I've pulled it together every day for Jared's sake. But he's not here to see me now, and I feel the mask slipping. It started the moment I stepped on that plane by myself. *Yes, poor baby had her house and son's college paid for and had to take a dream European vacation. Sniff.* I couldn't even THINK about that mess right now.

"Here we are," Johanna announces cheerily, breaking me out of my increasingly hostile inner dialogue.

She sets a steaming plate in front of me. It smells amazing, and my insides rejoice at the prospect of eating.

"Tiroler Gröstl!" she says the name with a flair. "A traditional

Austrian breakfast of fried potatoes, bacon—oh, I do hope you like bacon—butter and onions!"

My stomach rumbles so loudly I can't help but burst out into laughter alongside Johanna.

"Oh, you poor dear. Let's take care of that, ja?"

After a few timid bites to test the flavor, I dig into the dish Johanna has set in front of me with vigor. A snack in the Frankfurt airport on my short layover Saturday morning was the last I'd eaten. No wonder I was starving!

"So," Johanna points at me with her fork and takes a sip of her black coffee. "You came to a foreign country. Alone. Yet," she shoves a bite in and talks around it. "I see wedding band on your finger."

Everything she says feels like when the TV volume is set to one or two clicks louder than normal. She leans back in the lime green acrylic dining chair and taps her lip with the tines, contemplating or waiting for me to say something, I can't tell. Today she's wearing rainbow striped overalls on top of a cropped pink tee and somehow kind of pulling it off. I take another huge bite to avoid answering her questioning statement.

"It is okay. You look... not ready to talk on it. No problem, I will not pry into your business. But I stand by my offer to show you around the city. Tomorrow, the markets will be open. I show you all the best stands to visit for good produce and fair prices. Some, they rip you off when they see you are tourist. I show you who to buy from. No problem."

She waves the fork in the air, and it's settled. I find myself nodding in agreement to what she's saying, without the conscious decision to do so.

"We go at 9 a.m. sharp tomorrow. I will pick you up, ja? And tonight, I will leave dinner outside your door by 6. Good? Ja, sehr gut. You will love. Promise." She finishes with a loud slurp of coffee.

Chapter 5

Her mug shows a map of the country on it and says, "I'm not yelling, I'm Austrian." It's perfect, and I suspect the growing warmth in me is from more than just the coffee.

After ending the visit with heartfelt thanks and reasons why I should get back, I leave Johanna's apartment, punch in the access code and step into my studio. The door clicks shut, sealing me into the much quieter, much emptier space. *Well. That was unexpected.*

* * *

Johanna was right—the dinner she dropped off last night was absolutely delicious, and I did love it. I think it was some kind of schnitzel. She also gave me the softest, fluffiest pretzel as a side. It definitely ruined my chance of ever enjoying a mall pretzel as much in the future.

I'm ready to go at promptly 8:45, having dressed and ate the muffin she made earlier. Sitting on the edge of a chair by the window, I keep smoothing my flutter-sleeved top down, as though it's going somewhere, and checking my purse for my wallet. Why am I so anxious?

Well, you never have been good at making adult friends. That's why your inner circle consists of the same two girls who befriended you in high school and your sister. Duh.

True, as usual.

A knock sounds at the door at exactly 8:57, and I cross the living space to open it. Johanna is on the other side, absolutely filling the doorway in a loose orange sweater and neon green jeans paired with hot pink platform sandals. Her style is interesting and completely befitting.

"Ready, neighbor?" she asks with that over stretched smile that shows every single one of her shiny teeth. She loops an arm through my elbow and pulls me down the stairs behind her, chattering all the way about the market located a few blocks from here. She outlines her shopping list for the week and which booths will have the best selections for what she needs and what I may want.

The day is perfect—sunny and warm. The streets are bustling with activity, but in a slower, more peaceful way than my hometown. Cars drive along without their drivers honking or shouting angrily out the windows. Cyclists pedal down both sides of the street. The air feels a bit cleaner, though I could be imagining that, and I don't find myself missing the Windy City at all for the moment.

Johanna points to different shops as we go—best place to get coffee, a hidden gem of a bookstore, a delicious bakery two doors down from a world-famous chocolate shop, and a souvenir shop with unique trinkets.

When we arrive, the market is every bit the lively, colorful place I had envisioned. Stand after stand of fresh, locally grown produce. Bread and pretzels still warm from the morning baking. Fresh and smoked meats. An entire stand devoted to cheese! Heaven.

Johanna calls out greetings to nearly every stand owner, calling them by name and asking questions about their latest crop, what's in fresh this morning or how their wife and children are. She stops at one stall filled with beautiful handmade soaps. The owner is hunched with age, hands weathered and spotted with swollen arthritic knuckles. After a few words exchanged in German, Johanna slips a paperback out of her purse and places it into the older woman's hands. The stand owner's eyes light up, and she jabbers something those five days on the app can't help me keep up with. She turns around and grabs a brown package tied in string, pressing it into Johanna's open hand. Johanna tries to refuse but the woman is insistent. She smiles and says "danke," one of the few words I do remember.

When the soap maker turns toward another customer to answer a question, I see Johanna subtly slip a bill into the stand's money box. I

Chapter 5

look away quickly before she catches me staring. *Hm, more to this one than meets the eye, it would seem.*

We finish our shopping for the week. Me with some fresh fish pulled from a glacier-fed lake near a mountain I can't pronounce. An assortment of fresh fruits and veggies. Some handmade dried pasta. Bread, cheese and smoked meats. Plus a few—ok maybe a dozen—strudels as well.

Carbohydrates. The food of the gods.

Dang right, girl.

As we head back to the apartment building, Johanna asks me about my plans for the week. I tell her about a few articles I need to write up and submit for eTech's online news site, and my hopes to soak in the city.

"What about you? What do you do for work?" I ask, genuinely curious at this point.

"Oh me? Editor. For a publishing house," she says casually, as if that wasn't the coolest career.

"Wait wait wait, you get to read books FOR A LIVING?" I half-shout at her, grabbing her elbow with my free hand. "That's a total dream job!"

She chuckles, "Ja, I've always been a bookworm since grammar school. It was a natural fit. I get to work my own hours from home. Our office went all-virtual. The reading and editing, piece of cake. It's the writers that present a challenge! My boss loves to send me the... how do you say, 'tough cookies.'"

"I bet you're the best, that's why they give you the hard ones," I say genuinely. Considering how she had me just nodding in agreement to all kinds of things I had planned to say no to, she must be amazing at her job.

When we reach the apartment, she throws an arm out, barring the door.

"Wait! Your phone," she says insistently.

"What?"

"Your phone! Give it. I'll take your picture. You have friends, family back home who will want to see where you're staying, ja? Plus, first trip to a Salzburg market!"

I hesitate. "But does it have to have me in it? Can't we just get a nice shot of the building?"

She rolls her eyes at that and holds her hand out expectantly opening and closing her fingers.

I sigh and hand it over. "I guess I did promise Jared I'd send pictures... including some with me in them."

Johanna holds up my phone, stepping back into the street to get an angle that includes a good portion of the building.

"Lachen!" she calls out, snapping a few shots, adjusting to include the building behind me, before handing it back to me.

"Super. Jared will love. Jared is... your husband?" she asks, as we enter the apartment building.

"Oh. No," I swallow the lump and head up the stairs first, keeping my back to her. "Jared is my son."

"Ok," she replies and doesn't ask me anything else. At the landing she announces that we'll venture out together again on Thursday to a place she's convinced I'll love and again, I find myself agreeing. She turns to put her key into her door, and I'm surprised to hear my voice calling her name.

"Johanna?"

She pauses and turns toward me.

"Thank you. I mean it. Thanks a lot," I say. And I do mean it.

"Bitte schön, meine freunden," she replies with a wink and a megawatt smile, then disappears behind her door.

I put away my groceries and grab my phone. Picking out my favorite of the photos Johanna took—she really has a great eye—I send it to

Chapter 5

both Jared and Amelia with the message, "Back at my apartment with fresh groceries from a real Salzburg market! I'm practically an Austrian citizen!" with some laughing emojis. Jared tells me emojis are so last decade, but I still love using them.

Hitting send, I pull up the group message with my book club and add the photo there too. To them I write, "You won't believe this but... I think I made a new friend. She took this pic of me in front of our apartment building. She lives across the hall." I end this text with the surprise and care faces and hit send, hoping my messages don't wake them.

Moments later my phone pings. It's a reply from Cece, the insomniac. It's a little after 4 in the morning in Chicago. "A friend?! You go girl! We're so proud of you. Knew you had it in you. Hope you're having an amazing time but not so amazing that you apply for residency, mmk? Kristen already said the book club would be too difficult to coordinate with the time difference! Hugs!"

I smile at the screen and put it away in favor of another screen. Powering up my laptop shows some new emails, assignments from Frank. He's been on me to put in more hours, come into the office and be "more part of the team" over the last month or so.

Honestly, I don't yet know how much I want to pour into this job. I like it but it doesn't... I don't know, doesn't fulfill me I guess. Maybe I'm just expecting too much from a job though. The primary goal of work is the paycheck, and I do need to start thinking more about what I want to do full time. Even with the house paid off, the insurance money won't cover all the bills for too long in this economy.

The house. Just the thought of it sends my stomach roiling. How could Rob have possibly paid off the house and opened a college fund for Jared? Where was all this money hiding? Where did it come from? Why wouldn't he have told me? None of this made any sense.

All the worry and doubts I'd tamped down with distractions this week rush to the forefront. I feel my anxiety growing legs to take me places I had no interest in going. After some deep breaths, I speak gently to myself.

"You don't have to figure this out right now. Maybe you won't have to figure it out ever, but definitely not right now. Just focus on work and let it go for the moment."

I throw myself into research for my next piece and eventually that doubt and niggling sense of betrayal eases within me. But I have a feeling I won't be able to put it off forever. At some point I will have to face this. And I dread the thought of what I might find.

Chapter 6

Just like she said she would, Johanna knocked on my door Thursday morning and directed me to change my heeled sandals into more comfortable shoes. She was not a big fan of public transport but a very big fan of pedestrian travel. We walked to the castle that day. I learned that Hohensalzburg was the largest, fully preserved castle in central Europe. Using the rare-at-the-time private toilet then was akin to utilizing an airplane bathroom now. There was a window, but otherwise it was quite claustrophobic. And no flushing. Contents deposited dropped straight out and down the side of the castle—bombs away!

Two days later, we strolled through the Mirabell palace and expansive gardens where Johanna made me skip through the leafy vine tunnel that Maria skipped through with the von Trapp children in the "Doe a Deer" scene of *Sound of Music* while she captured it on my phone. She also videoed me skipping and twirling around the Pegasus fountain, just like Maria and the children. I felt like such a fool at first. My cheeks burning, knowing I was in broad daylight, and PEOPLE COULD SEE ME. But the more she pushed and the more I relented, the more I realized I was truly having a lot of fun.

The following week, we drove over to the town of Mondsee in a car she borrowed from a friend. The church where Maria marries the baron, St. Michael's Basilica, is there. Johanna offered to walk me down the aisle, but the priest had just launched into his afternoon mass and no way was I interrupting that. She laughed and told me if I did a little jig down the aisle, it would definitely be the most interesting service this place has had in 200 years.

The town was absolutely beautiful, but it was the views on the drive over that really took my breath away. We passed by a town nestled into a valley surrounded by the mountains and on the very edge of a picture-perfect lake. The videos and pictures I took to send back home weren't even close to doing it justice. I wanted to bottle up the essence of what I'd seen of this beautiful country and take it home with me to cherish forever.

This week, we visited more coffee shops, bookstores, local stores and chocolatiers than I could keep track of. The chocolate—oh, the chocolate. I would never truly enjoy a American chocolate bar after tasting this chocolate.

This trip feels so different from all the places we had traveled as a family. I suppose I had always been "mom" on those trips. Planning, preparing, packing, ensuring everyone had everything they needed, is having a good time, has eaten and slept enough to keep away the tired and hungry crankiness that would otherwise ensue by late afternoon. Those adventures were amazing, and I would always treasure the time we had spent traveling as a family.

Now, my first ever trip alone, each day I found myself feeling more and more like... myself. Yet different somehow? *It's totally you, dummy. You've just been buried for a while.* I wanted to bite back at that thought. My family had not been a grave suffocating me. But I sat with it for a minute instead and decided maybe in a way, that not-so-small voice in the back of my head had a point.

Chapter 6

I had worn my titles of wife and mom proudly for nearly all my adult life. I couldn't have asked for better. But maybe in a way I had become only those titles. Maybe along the way, I'd lost Meg. I went to an office party for Rob's work. "Hi, I'm Rob's wife." Meet the teacher night at school or signing my kid up for sports it was "Hi, I'm Jared's mom!" I had my writing, but that was all done from behind a screen. My name showed up on a byline each week, but disconnected from the person who wrote it.

Maybe that's why I feel lost now. Because I'm not Rob's wife anymore. And though I'll always be Jared's mom, he doesn't need me like he used to. He's building his own life. I hope it has space for me, but I can't build my identity there anymore.

Maybe it's time to find Meg again. *I'm going to enjoy watching you figure this out,* Margaret toasts me with her imaginary cup of tea.

I tried to think back to who I was before Rob. We met in college, and I'd always thought we'd grown together through the years. Figuring out how to do life and raise a child together. Rob was steady. Rob was comfortable. But looking back, maybe only Rob grew, and I'd just molded myself to him.

A knock sounds at the door, breaking me out of my reverie. I glance at my watch. Johanna is exactly three minutes early. "Being on time is the same as being late," she had stated last week. "But being earlier than five minutes before time is rude to the other party, who may not be ready yet. Three minutes early is the exact time for optimal manners."

I tried not to laugh when she explained this to me, thinking about all the times Rob had complained about me taking too long to get ready and always running late.

I finish pulling the brush through my hair and cross to the door to find Johanna bouncing on the balls of her feet in the landing. I never know what to expect when I see her. Her style over the past three weeks has ranged from starving bohemian artist to homesteading hippie to discotheque girl to tonight's look of... quirky librarian?

She's in a brown plaid mini skirt with knee socks and clunky buckled shoes. A white button-down shirt has one half of the shirt tail tucked, the other out. Her French twist is secured with two pencils crisscrossed in the back. No matter what fashion she's in, she always exudes warmth and steel. Direct to the point of almost stern, but somehow also smiling and brimming with joy. She was full of paradoxes. I found myself drawn to her ambiance like a butterfly to a nectar-filled flower.

Back home, Cece and Kristen remained in awe that I had opened up enough to make a new friend. I tried to explain that it wasn't really a choice with Johanna, no more than a safe could choose to be cracked by the world's greatest thief. Bottom line—none of us really understood.

By now she knew all about Rob, the stage IV pancreatic cancer diagnosis and the year of fighting only to lose him anyway. She hadn't seemed surprised, like she had already sensed the loss in me.

I'd even found myself telling her about my shock and confusion over our financial mystery, something I hadn't disclosed to Cece and Kristen yet. I guess sometimes it's a little easier to tell the really hard things to a stranger. Someone who is further removed can listen without the clutter of prior knowledge and preconceived opinions.

Johanna had listened through it all, asking thoughtful questions, probing my feelings far more gently than I would have imagined she would be capable of with her loud mannerisms. For my mysterious funding, she gave some advice I'd been percolating on ever since.

"Listen, Meg," she'd said while we sipped tea at a cafe in Mondsee. "If you're a person who can accept this as a blessing without knowing the how, then do it! That's the right thing for you. But if you're the person who this is going to bother, the doubt planting in your mind, growing roots of suspicion that poison your memories of Rob, then you need to dig this out. That's the right thing for you to do. So, figure out which person you are, then do the right thing for you."

Chapter 6

I swear I'm trying.

Tonight, her eyes have a special sparkle as she takes a step into the apartment and waggles her thick eyebrows at me.

"For our final night of fun before you leave for Prague, I'm going to take you to a hidden *local* gem. It's the real deal!" she says, motioning for me to grab my purse off the chair and come along.

I pick up the purse but narrow my eyes in suspicion at her emphasis of the word "local."

"You're not taking me to McDonald's are you? Because while I get the humor in that, I would be SO ticked if my last dinner in Austria was a freaking Big Mac."

She waves a hand, dismissing my suspicions, "No no no, silly. I am funny, but I am not cruel. No, you will love. You trust me."

It wasn't a question. It was a fact. A weird, confusing fact. I didn't trust all that easily, but she was right. I did trust her. I shrugged at the oddity and followed her out the door.

After a few blocks, we arrive at a quaint little business at the end of a long strip of buildings. It has the traditional Bavarian architecture of white walls, intersected by exposed framing of dark brown beams. The leaded glass windows glow with a warm light from within as the sun sinks behind the row of new and old businesses. A little sign hanging over the door read "Das Einzig Wahre."

"The Real Deal" Johanna says, pointing and translating the sign. "See? I told you I'd take you to the real deal!"

She chuckles at her own humor and pushes the heavy wooden door open. My eyes take a minute to adjust to the dimness of the space. I'm overwhelmed by the delicious smells. It's familiar. It smells like…

"Johanna!" a ruddy faced man with a walrus mustache calls out. He's shorter than me with a belly that made him nearly as round as he was tall. Waddling to the host stand near the door, the man gives my friend a big hug, which she bends slightly to receive.

She returns his embrace heartily before pulling back to include me in their moment.

"Antonio, this is my friend Meg, all the way from America! Meg, meet Antonio!"

"Italian!" I blurt, my brain finally catching up to my olfactory senses. "It smells like Italian food!"

Antonio lets out a big rumbling laugh, two meaty red hands splayed on each side of his belly.

"That's right! Best you'll find outside the borders of Italy herself! Come! I will give you my loveliest table. Any friend of Johanna is family here," he says in a heavy Italian accent, leading the way to a cozy corner booth that feels both inviting and intimate.

We sit down and I look around expectantly for menus.

"Ah, no menus here, bellisima! My wife, Daniella, will peek from the kitchen, take a good look and fix you what you need. Amore mio always knows. Always knows what the heart needs," he says tapping his chest with a sausage-shaped finger.

With a wink and a smile, he slips two glasses of water I hadn't even seen him pour onto the table. Setting down a lemon wedge next to mine, he winks and disappears. *I think this place must be magic.* I feel a tingle of it in the air as I reach for the short-stemmed glass.

"So?" Johanna asks me over the rim of her glass. "Did I disappoint for our final hurrah?"

"You've done nothing but surprise me since we met. You couldn't disappoint me if you tried. Well, except if this HAD turned out to be a McDonald's. Then maybe."

We laugh together and slip into a moment of comfortable quiet, soaking in the atmosphere of this little place. With the smells coming from that kitchen, my mouth is absolutely salivating, and my stomach rumbles too.

"Meg," she says sitting down her glass in mock seriousness. "It's been

Chapter 6

almost three weeks. Have you figured out who you are yet?"

"Hey, now! It's not that simple!" I squeak at her defensively as she rolls her eyes and crosses her arms. "You're so sure of yourself, you've probably never gone through a self-discovery process like this."

When I thought about it, I really didn't know that much about Johanna's past. She had a way of giving short, non-informative answers to the things I'd asked her and steering the conversation back to me every time. I hadn't really realized that until just now. *Self-absorbed much?*

"OK, let's get to work then. You need my help," she says matter-of-factly, bringing me back to this conversation. "Tell me about yourself in high school. You met Rob in college, ja? So, let's go to before that."

"Oh, high school, ugh," I say blowing out a breath. "First of all, I was a hot mess back then. My parents had moved us from a quiet suburb in northern Wisconsin to Chicago for my dad's work the summer after my sophomore year. I'd just turned 16. Talk about culture shock. I was so backward it's amazing I could walk a straight line. I hid behind my bangs for most of the year, yet somehow managed to still make two friends, which are still my best gals today. So, I guess in that regard, it wasn't a total fail."

"Hm, I see. And Rob. He was your first love, ja?"

"Oh uh...," I start to answer yes, but snap my mouth shut when I realized that really wasn't true. *She sniffed you out like a bloodhound.*

"Oh ho," Johanna's eyes light up. "He wasn't! Ok, girl. Ah, what's that phrase you Americans use? Spill the tea!" She sets down her glass again and leans forward, steepling her fingers in front of her.

"I mean... Rob was the first love I ever had as an adult. I don't know, does it even count if you're too young to vote?"

"Meg," Johanna says my name truly serious this time and reaches out to take my hand across the table. "Just because you were young does not make your love any less real. Old, young, love is real and matters at every age."

I swallow the sudden lump in my throat. "In that case no, Rob wasn't my first love."

Daniella chose that moment to appear at the table, just as short and round as her husband. The two were the perfect match. Her dark, graying hair is swept up into a high bun while a white apron covers her solid tea length dress. A lace collar peeks out above her apron. She's holding two bowls in her hand, piled high.

She sets a bowl down in front of Johanna and says bluntly, "for joy." She sets my bowl down stating, "for healing." Then she spins on her heel and marches back to the kitchen. I turn back gaping at Johanna but she merely throws me a huge smile and digs into her bowl with vigor. I waste no time and do the same.

When that first noodle hits my mouth, I think my eyes roll back into my head. *Yep. Magic. It. Is. So. Good.* The flavors are rich and deep, yet familiar. I swallow that first bite, and I can feel the moment it hits my stomach. It settles into me, wrapping me from the inside out in a soft, warm blanket of comfort. The nostalgic bliss of your best childhood memories in food form. It feels like home.

I open my eyes and find Johanna staring at me, knowing laughter dancing in her eyes.

"The real deal, right?" she asks with a grin.

"I think this might be the realest experience I've ever had with food!" I reply, twirling another hearty bite onto my fork.

Without a doubt, I was eating this whole bowl and quite possibly will lick it clean too. *After all, you wouldn't want to miss out on any of the healing.* We enjoy several minutes of fork twirling and noodle slurping and savoring every bite. While my flat noodles are covered in a rich creamy sauce, Johanna's bowl contains a variety of noodle shapes covered in a lighter sauce. I smell a bit of a tang wafting from her side of the table. I add a thick mushroom slice to the end of my forkful of

Chapter 6

pasta while she spears a sun dried tomato. Daniella is a goddess of the kitchen.

Johanna watches me eat for another moment before pointing her fork at me to say, "Alright, let's hear it. You didn't think I would forget, did you?"

I roll my eyes playfully at her and shove another huge bite in my mouth, taking my time to enjoy chewing before answering.

"Ok so yes, there was someone before I met Rob," I finally tell her, pausing for a drink. "Back in Wisconsin. I was a freshman; he was a sophomore. Dreamy blue eyes, longish near-black hair that he was constantly flipping out of his eyes. He wasn't one of the cool kids, I was never really the type attracted to the star of the football team. He was quiet, didn't stand out aside from the fact that he was taller than most of the guys in our small school. Strong shoulders. And his hands. Girl, he had beautiful hands. Long fingers that looked strong enough to protect but gentle enough to interlace with mine…"

My voice had taken on a dreamlike quality, and I'm staring off to the side of Johanna with my fork hovering in mid-air. *You are an absolutely hopeless sap.* I clear my throat and focus on my bowl and the next bite I'm twirling.

"Um, yeah. Yep, that was him. We took a poetry elective together and it was an instant connection, though it took some time to draw him out of his shell. We were paired up for an assignment the first day. I dropped my pencil and when he handed it back to me… I swear it was like a movie scene. Our eyes locked and his finger brushed mine… Whew. Still gives me a tingle to think back."

"Ja," Johanna's eyes sparkle at me over her bowl. "Then it was same with Rob when you met?"

I frown for a moment. "Well. No. With Rob it was more of a friendship that developed into a steady, comfortable love. Still love. But it was different."

She waves her fork at me, sauce flinging from it onto the crisp, white linens. "Never mind. I interrupted. Continue."

"Anyway, he was literally the sweetest guy I had ever met. He thought deeply and dreamed big. Super good with computers too! He'd built his first computer by himself in middle school. Even dabbled in hacking, just to prove he could, never did any damage. But he was also intense in his feelings, fiercely protective. And yeah, I really did love him.

"But at the end of my sophomore year, my dad accepted a job offer in Chicago. The type of construction work he specialized in had been drying up in our area for a while so he took the job without hesitation. We had no warning. Just like that, my family was whisked away. We tried to keep it going for a bit, long distance, but…" I shrugged. "Life. You know?"

"Wow. I knew you were holding out on me. Listen to you! Such a romantic," Johanna says with a chuckle. "So, what's your genius doing now? Big dog at Google? Head developer at Amazon? Ooh, dark web criminal, ja?" She wiggles a conspiratorial eyebrow.

I laugh, "Honestly, I have no clue! We had a big fight a few months after I had moved away. And that was that. We drifted apart, and I never heard from him again. I tried looking him up once…" *Ha! More than once!* "Ok, more than once, just out of curiosity to see where he had ended up. I always thought he was destined for great things, but I couldn't find any info on him."

I shrug and return to the fast-approaching bottom of my bowl, but Johanna's brow furrows as her eyes widen.

"Wait, now. Your computer genius ex is off the grid? This just got more interesting. Hold on, we're going to find this guy. I'm pretty good at this. I always dig up all the dirt on potential debut authors before we sign them. Be sure there aren't any skeletons in the closet before we put our name on their book, you know? What's his name and date of birth?"

Chapter 6

"Oh, that's silly," I blush. *Oh, come on. You know you want to!*

"I... well, ok, guess it wouldn't hurt. I have always wondered what happened to him. It's Sebastian. Sebastian Sylvain. Um, birth date. June 18, 1982. We went to Superior High School together, up in northern Wisconsin."

Johanna's face is illuminated as she punches the information into her phone. I find myself leaning forward, holding my breath for what she'll find. After several long minutes and even longer sighs, her brow furrows deeper.

"Hm..." she says, scrolling with her thumb and tapping at the screen a few more times. "This is too weird. I can't find a single thing on the guy. No Facebook, no Twitter, no Insta, no TikTok, no Snapchat, not even LinkedIn. Hold on, I'll check the obituaries for the last 20 years and-"

"Oh. I hadn't thought of that..." The breath feels stolen from my lungs.

"Nope. Not dead," she shakes her head and oxygen returns to my brain. "Nothing there either. In this day and age, this is truly impressive. Everyone has a digital footprint. But not this guy."

She looks up at me and says definitively, "Your man must truly be a computer genius. That's the only explanation. He doesn't have digital records because he doesn't want to have them and knows how to wipe the slate clean."

Johanna locks her phone, tucking it back into her skirt pocket as we return to our respective bowls. Johanna's opened the neatly closed box in my heart that held all things Bash. I'm having a hard time getting the lid on again.

Having both just taken our last bites, Daniella appears out of nowhere again at our table. This time she says nothing, just slaps a plate of tiramisu down on the table and stalks back toward the kitchen, back hunched and head jutting forward. Across the table our eyes meet, and we burst out laughing. Picking up the two forks, we dig in.

Leaving the restaurant, I feel beyond stuffed and more peaceful than I've felt since I took Rob for his first CT scan after the doctor didn't like the way his blood work was looking. Johanna and I walk with arms linked, enjoying the hint of cool on the summer evening breeze.

"I too lost my husband," she reveals suddenly, without missing a step. I stop dead in my tracks. She has no intention of stopping, so I jog a few steps to catch back up.

"It was 18 months and three weeks ago my Jakob died. He was the light of my life. My one. My only," she says, without slowing her step.

"Wait, what? Why didn't you tell me? You let me go on and on about Rob, without even telling me you were going through the same thing?" I ask, stunned and reminding my feet to keep taking steps forward as I absorb this new information. I feel betrayed. Hurt bordering dangerously close to anger. *See? This is why we don't make friends.*

She shrugs nonchalantly.

"Because I could see that you needed me. Someone, a dear friend, had walked me gently through my darkest days after Jakob died. When I first saw you in the stairwell, I could see the same pain in you that I knew so well. I wanted to be that person for you. I waited to share my story because I didn't want our limited time together to be about me," she explains in that completely no-nonsense Johanna way.

"In truth," she continues, "before the day you arrived, I hadn't left my apartment in two weeks. Sometimes, you'll find that even though you're mostly better, the dark days still come back for a bit, knocking the wind out of you again. The day you arrived I'd spent the entire morning giving myself a stern talking to in the mirror about not locking myself away. 'The world needs you, Johanna. Enough wallowing. Get off your couch, change out of those two-day old clothes and go live!' That's what I said, and that's what I did. I'm a good listener when I want to be."

Chapter 6

"Sounds like Margaret talking," I mutter to myself, still taking in this revelation of my new friend who I didn't know much about at all. "But you seemed so happy, so joyful when we met! I never would've guessed you'd been suffering."

She shrugs, "Turns out you were what I needed too. In our deepest hurts and longest suffering, helping someone else makes us remember why we're truly here. No man is an island, and all that. This world needs you. And it needs me. We're allowed to hurt, to mourn, to grieve. But we can't stop living. We don't stop mattering."

We've arrived outside of the apartment building, my head still spinning. My heart warms looking up at the place, knowing it's the last time I'll see it illuminated in the deepening twilight by the streetlamp out front. That same heart warms even more when I meet the gaze of the woman standing next to me. My friend. I reach out for her hand, pull out my phone and snap a selfie of us under the streetlamp, the apartment in the background.

"Johanna, I don't know how to thank you. You've changed my life. For the better. I... I think I'm going to be ok. Maybe not this week. But some week in the near future."

She smiles her extra-wide smile and pulls me into a hug so tight its nearly uncomfortable, but I savor the squeeze. She whispers—the first time I've heard her speak quietly, "I know you will be!"

"How can we keep in touch?" I ask, pulling away. "You know I don't have Facebook."

"You know," she says, pulling away, "I believe that some people come into our lives just for a moment. I think this was our moment. You needed me. I needed you. If we should meet again, we'll know for certain we were meant for more than just this moment. In the meantime, keep living Meg. Keep living for more than just you."

We link arms one more time to climb the stairs a bit awkwardly together. I wouldn't have it any other way. She's already promised to wave me off at the train station tomorrow morning, but I can feel this is our true moment of farewell. The ending of our chapter.

We both reach our doors, and I look over my shoulder one more time as she fits the key into her lock.

"Thank you, Johanna," I say one more time, then I enter the apartment and close the door behind me. It's the first night since December that I get into bed and fall asleep without crying.

Chapter 7

Arriving at the hotel in Prague, I feel like I'm entering a glass house. The entire building seems to be made of windows overlooking the Vltava River. My cab driver told me on the drive over that it's a pretty easy walk to Old Town and just a little longer to Prague Castle. After the conference, I'd have almost two weeks to explore before returning home.

The room is clean and modern with crisp white linens, a freshly tiled bathroom and a lovely view of the river. While I can't complain about the accommodations, I'm already missing a certain studio apartment and the friendly face waiting with breakfast across the landing.

Part of me feels disappointed that I didn't get her phone number or email or SOMETHING so we could stay in touch. But also, long distance relationships of any kind have always been tough for me to manage. I never know when to reach out or how often. I have no natural flow for this type of thing and end up feeling either guilty for not reaching out or worry that I'm annoying.

So maybe Johanna is right. It's ok for it to have been for just that particular moment in both our lives, when we needed one another. I learned a lot from her in the three weeks we spent in one another's company and know I'll cherish the memories we made together.

The train ride from Salzburg took a winding path east then south, through Vienna, then back west toward the Czech Republic's capital city. The cybersecurity conference I'm here to cover starts Sunday and runs through Thursday. Bit of a long one really, but it's the big one for Europe this year. Frank had been salivating for someone to cover but didn't want to pay the cost of travel. That made me the perfect candidate.

It's early evening when I settle in. I could go out and explore a bit tonight, but I'm wiped from the long train ride. I had fully intended to finish at least one of the books I'd brought with me, but the scenery kept distracting me. I found myself rereading the same sentences over and over.

Instead of leaving the comfort of my space, I order room service and fire up my laptop to check out the itinerary for tomorrow, decide which talks to attend, review the interviews I'd already scheduled and compare it to the list of named presenters. The previous week I managed to get a few sidebars set up with some big names in the business, but I liked to keep my eyes and ears open for any attendees that could add more interest to my stories. Frank had hemmed and hawed so much over me being remote for six weeks that I had to make absolute certain I sent back a good solid piece each day of the conference.

Finished prepping for the conference, my mind turned again to the savings account and paid off mortgage. *Paid for with blood money.* No, Margaret. *Drug money? Does that sound better?* Rob was not some kind of mobster. I know he couldn't be involved in anything violent. No way. But something less black and white? Something white collar that "didn't hurt anyone?" It doesn't feel impossible.

Rob had grown up with a single mom who worked two jobs to support him and his four sisters, two of which hadn't made it to 25.

Chapter 7

Drugs. That's how I felt certain he wouldn't have gotten mixed up in that. The other two seemed to be getting by ok, just didn't have much interest in keeping in touch. I'd seen them at the funeral but there hadn't been a call or a text since. Their mom had passed a few years back.

With his history, Rob was proud of the life he'd built for himself. For us. His stellar academics and a pretty decent short stop arm got him a full ride to the University of Chicago, where he worked on his bachelor's in business while I got my degree in journalism with a minor in creative writing thanks to some grant money and scholarships. He was a year ahead of me, with plans to go on to law school. Somehow getting married as soon as I finished school had sounded like a good idea at the time.

We had a good life together. Rob started at a low-level, ambulance-chaser type firm for a few years before snagging an associate position at a corporate firm. He worked his way up to full partner three years before his death. He didn't talk much about his childhood but strove to build a life for Jared and I that was far different from both of our upbringings.

He worked long hours for his clients and often traveled for them too. Sometimes he invited us to go with him on the longer work trips. Now I can't help but think back to the ones he didn't invite us to go on. Was he really traveling for the firm or was there something else going on? Is it actually possible he had another life I didn't know about?

Opening a new browser tab, I log in to our main bank account page and toggle over to the loan page Gary had shown me, clearly annoyed at my ineptitude. There it is. Our mortgage loan. The account still shows for now, displaying a $0 balance. I click on savings, but then remember the college account had been setup in Jared's name alone. That wouldn't show on my profile. I click back to the mortgage page and select the link to open the last statement. There it was, plain as day.

A payment for $403,526.38 posted on December 24th. Two days. The mortgage was paid off just two days before Rob died. One day before he left the house for the last time by ambulance after he'd collapsed at the bottom of the stairs.

I can feel my heart rate starting to pick up and force myself to click "X" on the window before closing the screen. I can't look at this right now. I'm still getting too worked up and that's not going to do me any good. Tomorrow is the start of a few big days. I hadn't ever attended an event like this outside of one that occurred in Chicago about 4 years ago. I feel rusty and nervous.

After washing my face, I apply my thick layer of anti-aging cream. *Ha! What a scam... I don't think those crows' feet around your eyes got the memo.* I root around in my travel cosmetics bag until I find the melatonin I packed in case of emergency. I really hate taking anything, even natural stuff, but tonight feels like the kind of night I'll have to. I can feel my mind racing, just beneath the layer of thoughts I force toward my bedtime routine. Routine is good. Routine is safe. *Routine is BORING.* I chew up two of the gummies and head to bed to huddle under the covers and wait for the tears to come.

***

It takes twenty minutes just to choose an outfit for the first day of the conference, even though I'm limited to what I packed. *You know you over packed. Half your closet is here! Who are you trying to impress?* Myself, I decide.

I settle on a black sheath dress, opting for simple with elegant undertones. I pull on a red cropped sleeve suit jacket, my favorite, going for a professional daytime look that can transition easily to night. My black wedges are secretly super comfortable while looking

Chapter 7

dressy. A swipe of mascara and a touch of blush and I feel... almost ready.

You know who really channels confidence and makes the room pay attention? Amelia. You need to channel her.

No one says no to Amelia. And I need all the courage I can get. I pull out a red lipstick tube from the inner pocket of my cosmetics bag. Amelia had given it to me a few years ago to take on our anniversary trip, telling me to put it on and drive Rob wild. So, I did. Once. That was the first and last time I'd used it.

Tears blur my vision slightly as I swipe the red lipstick on. It's not really me, but right now, burdened with grief and confusion, I don't really want to feel like me anyway.

Go get 'em, Tiger. I take a breath and wink saucily to myself in the mirror, like Amelia would. Tucking my trusty notepad, phone and favorite pen into my pockets—*gotta love a dress with pockets*—I leave my room to head down to where the conference will begin.

Five hours later my head is literally buzzing from information overload. My phone battery is low from all the talks and conversation snippets I've recorded, hand cramping from trying to speed write the notes I could manage. I have no idea how I'm going to condense each day's materials into a concise, well-structured article. Yet, in some ways, I sort of welcome the challenge. I hadn't thought of... well, the other things in my life since the bathroom this morning. And that was something.

Grabbing a diet soda, I head into the next talk I'd earmarked to attend. This should be the last one for today. The topic was on penetration testing, encouraging companies and governments facing today's hackers to hire cybersecurity firms to test their vulnerabilities by trying to break into their networks.

I settle into a seat near the back in case I doze off and set up my phone to record. A young man with slicked back blonde hair and a bold teal suit takes the stage, clicking his pointer toward the screen behind him. His company name flashes up—a firm local to me—and I jot his name below it.

The woman in the next seat, also wearing a "Press" tag at the end of her lanyard turns toward me and asks, "Guardian Securities? You know where they are based?"

She has a lovely French accent that matches her polished pantsuit and silk blouse.

"Oh! Yes, I wrote an article on them a few years back. They're in my hometown—Chicago."

"Ah, Yank, oui?" she holds out a manicured hand to shake mine. "Chantal DeBourjac. Pleasure."

"Chantal, very nice to meet you! I'm Meg. Meg Franklin."

A man in the row ahead of us shifts, blocking my view of the stage. I crane my neck around him to jot down the points of the presentation so far.

A shiver runs down the back of my neck. I shift, feeling for a stray hair tickling me. Finding nothing I return my attention forward. Next it's my stomach. A quiver of anxiety? Anticipation. The feelings put me off-kilter, and I sip at my soda to try to quell the sensation. *It's probably the caffeine, duh.*

I stop drinking and pull a packet of saltines out of my jacket pocket to try those instead. My Gram had taught me to always take a pack of crackers if they're put out with lunch. Never know when you might need them later. One small way I kept her with me.

I'm so consumed by what I'm feeling that I don't notice the presentation is already wrapping up. A glance at my watch confirms it's been over an hour, and I somehow missed the majority of it. Hopefully, my recording picked up enough to pull any important bits from. I close my notebook and stand as the room erupts in polite applause.

Next to me Chantal huffs, "Hey, Meg. Right? I missed the speaker's

Chapter 7

name. Did you happen to catch it?"

"Er, let me see. I just put away my notebook, hang on a sec," I say, juggling my can to reach into my pocket.

"Aaron Thomas," a deep voice comes from in front of them. The rumbling sends a tendril of sensation down to my toes and something flickers in my brain. Recognition.

I raise my head and our eyes lock, suspending time. My breath whooshes out of me, and I can't find another. I know those eyes. I could never forget the way they had always looked at me as if I were the whole world in one body. The same way they were looking at me now. I drop the can with a clatter.

"Sebastian? What are you, I mean, I didn't know—I haven't. It's you!"

While he looks pleasantly surprised to see me, his reaction doesn't come close to matching the absolute shock ricocheting through my body. He looks the same, and yet so different. He's even taller—6'4" if I had to guess. His narrow high school boy frame has filled out and the cut of his clearly tailored suit shows he's taken good care himself. His hair is worn a little shorter now, mussed on the top instead of hanging down for him to flip out of his eyes like he used to.

He laughs a little, a warm sound from his chest, and says, "Well hello there, Meg."

Then he just keeps staring. Smiling. Standing there. Alive. *Woah. I did not see this coming.* Next to me Chantal's mouth hangs open, pencil still poised over her paper.

He nods toward her without taking his eyes from mine, "Aaron Thomas. You got it?"

"Oh!" she blurts. "Oui, yes, thank you. I got it. Well, I'll just be, ah, I'll just be going then."

Fumbling with her bag she says under her breath, "Meg? CALL ME. Let's do breakfast. Room 621."

She squeezes around me to exit the door behind us, but I can't seem to get my feet to move. My eyes roam over his face, both remembering and re-learning. His hands grip the back of his chair as he leans toward me, his fingers just as long and as strong as I remembered, but more tanned and a little lined. I trace the veins with my eyes until they disappear under his cuff-linked sleeve. The same, yet changed. Older.

I'm suddenly self-conscious of the wrinkles around my eyes and between my eyebrows. I attempt to relax my forehead to ease the lines, squeezing my core to tuck my tummy in a little.

"Don't do that," he says abruptly, reading my mind. Then adds gently, "You're even more beautiful now than you were in high school."

My cheeks flame so hot I imagine they'd sizzle if touched. I realize I am in fact touching my cheek and pull my hands down to twist my fingers together at my waist.

"So…" he says, waiting to see if I'll say anything. My mouth is broken. I can't. He gestures to my lanyard and Press tag and says, "Here for work?"

"I thought you were dead!" *Meg. Oh. My. Gosh. IDIOT!* I slap my hand over my mouth, too late, then try to explain. "I mean when I looked, not that I was looking. I wasn't googling you or anything, but wow, Sebastian, I haven't seen you! In forever!"

His blue eyes dance, obviously finding amusement in my stammering attempts at conversing. "It has been forever—almost 24 years," he says, his tone taking a serious dip. "But here you are. And here I am. Let's catch up. Dinner at 8:00?" I nod, mute.

"Meet in the lobby. I have a meeting to run to, but I'll find you."

He holds my gaze so intensely I forget to breathe. And then he's gone, and I'm standing in the meeting room alone. The spotlight on the stage clicks off. *Sebastian freaking Sylvain. Did that really just happen?!*

* * *

Chapter 7

I'm in the lobby at 7:57. Johanna's influence lingers. Nervous energy radiates off of me, bouncing around the cavernous lobby. The hotel has six different restaurants, and I have no idea which one we're going to. I changed my outfit four times before putting the black dress I had been wearing earlier back on, wanting to look like I was not trying too hard. *Taking 95 minutes to get ready is not trying too hard?* This is NOT a date. I am newly widowed. I am not dating, nope. No way. But... I also wanted to look good. So, I had showered and freshened my hair and face in a way that I hope looked like I hadn't. I was just magically more radiant. *Sure, Meg. Just keep telling yourself that. Our little secret.*

I feel him before I see him. That same shiver runs down my neck, skating down my spine, and my stomach somersaults inside me. Sitting on the edge of the velvet-covered chair I'd chosen, I coach myself to not turn around. I'm frozen ramrod straight, my face stiff from the effort to maintain a calm, neutral expression as I internally freak out. He's here. He's definitely here. *Yep, this is what a non-date feels like.* Sarcasm. My greatest coping mechanism.

"Good evening, Meg," he says from somewhere above my left shoulder. My name in his mouth is familiar, solid. I feel the heat from him standing behind me on my bared arm, my blazer ditched in the room. I wish I had it now so I could pull it in tight. The nervous habit made me feel protected. I turn, feigning surprise and open my mouth to say hello but find my voice gone yet again, lost in the blue of his gaze.

"I hope whatever article you turned in tonight has a bit of a higher word count," he teases lightly, offering me his elbow. "I thought we'd adjourn to the rooftop restaurant for dinner. If that's alright with you. I took the liberty of reserving a table."

He seems undisturbed by my utter lack of language. We head toward the elevator where a man in a gray sweatsuit holds the door for us. He holds a pizza box and wears a gold ring on eight out of ten fingers. He nods toward us as the door slides closed, then opens the box to slip a slice out and dig in on our ride up. As a line of grease drips from his chin to his sweatshirt, I try desperately not to watch, but I can't block out the smacking of his lips and chomping of his molars together. The sound has me cringing. Hard.

"Oh, you guys want one?" he holds out a fresh slice toward us, mouth stuffed with the first one.

The food sounds coming from him make me want to crawl out of my skin, but I manage to answer, "No, thank you."

Beside me I see Sebastian shaking in silent laughter. I smack him with my clutch purse, subtly, although clearly our elevator companion only has eyes for the pie in his hand. The doors finally, blessedly open at the 7th floor, and he grunts a goodbye to us as he gets off. As soon as the doors close behind him, Sebastian bursts out with laughter.

"You seemed to find your words for him just fine! I'd almost forgotten how grossed out you get by chewing sounds. That was a treat to watch," he says, delighted.

I whack him again with my purse and bite back, "Yeah well you try to not be grossed out when you can practically feel the grease flicking off his tongue onto your shoulder! I was worried for my dress! It's the only black one I brought."

We're both laughing as the doors ding open again. I find my heart has eased a little of its clenching somewhere between the ground and top floors. I feel almost comfortable in his presence again already.

The hotel's rooftop restaurant has both indoor and outdoor seating. Sebastian leads us through the thick crowd, turning sideways to squeeze through. One hand stretches out behind him slightly, almost as if he's reaching back for me. The movement feels so familiar. So protective. So him.

We make our way out a set of glass doors. It's a gorgeous night and the views from here of the city and snaking river below are breathtaking,

Chapter 7

calling me to the railing. The full moon shines off the river, rippled in its reflection. A single fishing boat chugs along down its center.

Turning back, I find Sebastian, hands in his pockets, ignoring the view to stare at me. He's lost his tie, and the top two buttons of his crisp white shirt are undone. The black pants cling to him just right while the jacket accentuates his broad shoulders, cutting in at the waist. He's enchanting in the moonlight. Margaret mimes snapping a picture in my mind. I tell her to print an extra copy for me.

I smile at him a little and he makes a sweeping motion with one hand towards the perfect corner table with plush chairs to sit back and enjoy the view. A small "reserved" placard is placed at its edge.

"Your choice," he says, following my lead.

I choose the further seat to settle into, leaning forward with elbows resting lightly on the table.

"So..." I chuckle, suddenly nervous again. "Two decades to catch up on... where do we start?"

He settles into his chair comfortably, inviting me to do the same.

"Let's start with now and go backward. However far you want, whatever you want to share. I want to hear anything and everything you'll tell me. I'm listening. I arranged for a bit of everything to be delivered to the table so we don't have to worry over orders and could speak uninterrupted. I hope that's alright."

It was... thoughtful. Classic Bash. Like magic the first of the hors d'oeuvres is brought to the table. A savory tart filled with creamy mushroom and topped with crispy bacon. After that first bite, it's like my voice finally decides to show up and a tidal wave of words rush out. I start talking, and I can't seem to stop. I tell him about Jared, where we live in Chicago, why I'm in Prague, that I've just come from Salzburg. I tell him about Rob, how we met and married while I was still studying journalism, the cancer, his passing. I tell him about my amazing niece and nephew, my parents moving to Europe.

Margaret keeps piping up in my brain to *SHUT UP*, but I can't. I can't stop the words because it's Bash! My Bash. He's here and he's the same yet different. I want him—no, I need him to know. I need to tell him everything. Well, almost everything. And, because he's Sebastian, he sits there the entire time, listening. Nodding and asking questions, his eyes rarely leaving mine.

I'm not exactly sure how I went from thinking my first love could be dead to spilling my guts to him in a corner booth of a magical European city, but here we are. Evening has deepened into night by the time I finish. The realization of how long I've been talking has my cheeks on fire again.

I drop my forehead into my hand and let out a self-deprecating laugh. "Oh my gosh, I'm so sorry. We've been here for hours, and I've done nothing but talk about myself. Why would you let me do that?! You must think me the most self-absorbed person on the planet."

He gives me a half smile and reaches across the table to take my other hand. The warmth of his fingers is felt all through my body, in my very soul. Like a cherished memory, half-forgotten and now resurfaced.

"Meg," he says gently, and waits for me to look up at him before continuing. "I'm just thankful you found your voice again! No, really, you seem to forget—I love listening to you talk."

Oh, my heart. He used to say that to me late in the night when we were lying in our bedrooms, whispering into the phones cradled against our ears long after everyone else had gone to bed. "I love listening to you talk."

The rush of feelings overwhelms me, and I take a long drink from my glass to hold myself together. My eyes dart over to the glass of the indoor area of the restaurant, still full considering the lateness of the hour. I laugh nervously, emotions bubbling. *PLEASE stop giggling and hold yourself together like the middle-aged woman you are.*

"It's just—it's so good to see you. Really good. Please, please tell me

Chapter 7

about you! I want to know everything, too. What are you doing here? Work I assume, but who do you work for? Where do you live now? Are you... are you married?" I ask the last question quickly and swallow hard, unsure I really want the answer but needing to hear it too.

I take a few bites from the dessert set between us and listen attentively as he answers each one.

"Yes, I'm here for work. I work with Aaron actually, the one who was presenting this afternoon? Guardian Securities." He pauses and takes a sip of his water.

My heartbeat stutters, missing a beat. "Wait, you work for Guardian? In Chicago? You work—and live—in Chicago?"

He smiles, like I'm finally grasping what he already figured out. "Yes, turns out life blew both of us to the Windy City. I've been there since I finished my grad program at MIT."

"But I've never seen you there!" I blurt. *Idiot.*

"True," he says amused. "I suppose in a city of 2.7 million our chances just weren't high enough."

I sit back, thunderstruck. *He hasn't answered that last question though.*

As though reading my thoughts again, he answers looking me directly in the eyes, "And no. I'm not married. Perpetual bachelor I suppose, much to my mother's chagrin."

I release the breath I hadn't known I was holding and cross my fingers under the table that he didn't hear it whoosh out. I mean good grief what am I thinking anyway? I'm in no way fit for any type of romance at the moment. My heart and life are in tatters, shredded by loss and confusion. I'm not sure I've even made eye contact for more than a split second with a man since Rob died, before today. Before Bash was suddenly there, back in my life.

Stop thinking. Just be here in this moment. Be present. Chalk up one more positive point for Margaret, I guess. The space seems quieter, and I realize the restaurant and rooftop have just about cleared out. A glance at my watch shows it's a few minutes before midnight.

"Oh wow," I laugh. "I had no idea it was this late! Bash, I feel like I still don't know anything about you! And I really, really want to. Is it too much to meet again tomorrow for dinner? I have some interviews lined up throughout the day between the sessions I need to hit, but I'd really love the chance to reconnect more."

His brow furrows a bit, and my stomach twists. I'm about to be let down.

"Ah. I'd love to. You have no idea how much I'd love to. But I have to get back. I was only here for today, some meetings that had to be carried out in person. My flight back to Chicago leaves at 6 a.m. tomorrow. I'm so sorry. If I'd known…"

I wave him off with a forced laugh, trying desperately to hide the disappointment welling up inside, "Oh don't be silly! How could you know?! We haven't known where one another was for decades! Not your fault."

My voice feels a few pitches too high. He pulls a card from the interior pocket of his jacket with a pen and jots something on the back of it, handing it to me.

"Here's my email, and I added my cell number to the back. Please, Meg. Don't let another year go by without me hearing from you. Ok? Preferably not even a month. This week—tomorrow—would be my first choice, but I won't push. I know you've been through a lot. But I'm here."

I take the card without looking at it, unable to break away from the intensity of his stare. As we leave the restaurant together, he insists on walking me all the way to my room on the sixth floor. When he stands in the hall, waiting to hear the click of the security lock, I know it will take a sheer force of will to not call him that very next day.

Chapter 8

Turns out busyness really does keep one on the straight and narrow. The rest of the week in Prague is beyond busy. Multiple interviews, so many talks, dinners with Chantal to discuss what angle we were taking for that day all on top of the actual writing and submitting stories to our respective magazines for online publication the next morning. I barely had time to even think about contacting Sebastian.

By the end of the conference, I was so ready to come home. I called the airline and changed my ticket to return Friday instead of staying the extra time after. It was strange, walking up the steps to the familiar brownstone, putting my key in the lock, feeling its familiar stick before unbolting and opening the door to this place that has been home for years. It should feel comforting but instead it's... empty.

Jared is still in California for another few weeks. I didn't tell him I was coming home early. I didn't want him to come home too, so I wouldn't be alone. He's a young man now. He needs his own life, and so do I. I owe it to him and myself to figure this out.

I have always prided myself on my independence since I learned to tie my own shoes at age three. Somewhere along the line, I think I'd lost that part of myself. Settled in with Rob, I found ease in him always taking the lead. And look where that's left me now. Floundering to take any definitive steps forward. Johanna had asked me who I was before Rob. Surely that girl was still in there somewhere.

I go to bed early that night and wake up to spend Sunday morning unpacking and airing out the stuffy house. Cece and Kristen are coming for Book Club—*more like post-trip gossip session*—tonight at six. I still need to pick up snacks.

On one hand, I absolutely cannot wait to tell them who I ran into. They had never met Sebastian. But goodness knows they'd heard enough about him from me pining and moping over him the entirety of our junior year and part of senior too.

On the other hand, I feel nervous to tell them. I want to say I don't know why… but I do. I know. It's because of Rob. Because having one single butterfly in my stomach over seeing Sebastian again felt like an absolute betrayal. I loved Rob. I still love Rob. Kristen and Cece loved Rob. How can I even mention anyone else?

No way I could keep it from them though. After so many years spent as best friends, they read me more clearly than the novels we devour. They'll see it all over my face. I guess I'll just have to trust that they won't judge me too harshly. *Good grief Meg, you ate dinner with the man, not walked the aisle! Stop making such a big deal out of everything!* It's so easy to be my harshest judge.

My doorbell rings a few minutes after 6. I smile to myself and open the door to my two squealing best friends who wrap me up in hugs, despite the dishes in hand and bag-laden arms.

We completely cover the coffee table with our goodies and pile our plates high before snuggling into our familiar seats on the couches – Kristen on the opposite end of the couch from me, and Cece in the wingback chair near the window.

"Ok!" Cece starts in. "Spill!"

Chapter 8

"And don't leave anything out! You know I don't get to travel much with my brood. Give every detail that we may live vicariously through you, the first woman ever of our group to travel SOLO. Sounds incredible! At this point I'd settle for a trip to the store by myself!" Kristen's laugh is muffled by the lemon tart filling her mouth.

I give them the full scoop on Johanna. They were as shocked as I was that she too was recently widowed and that I didn't find out until our last day together. I think I saw Cece—the group empath— wipe a tear when I told them about the day we met, how Johanna had just pulled herself up out of a deep episode of depression. I tried describing the culinary magic that was "The Real Deal" but I know words could not adequately express that meal. They too determined the owner's wife must be some kind of kitchen witch, brewing up recipes for emotional fulfillment.

I knew I was stalling when I attempt to paint a picture of the train ride from Salzburg, anticipation already fluttering in my stomach as I thought of what came next. I think they could sense it too. Kristen made a "go on" hand motion, and they both leaned toward me from their seats.

When Sebastian's name dropped, Kristen gave a little half-scream and covered her mouth while Cece smacked the arms of chair and jumped to her feet.

"No way, you are lying! Sebastian?! THE Sebastian?! The Sebastian you spent nearly TWO YEARS of high school mooning after?!" Cece yelled, pacing the floor. "This is… wow. I mean, this has got to mean something right? How do you feel?!"

I tuck a strand of hair behind my ear nervously.

"I'm still trying to figure out how I feel. But guys, that's not even the craziest part. He lives HERE. As in Chicago. He's been living here all this time!"

Now it's Kristen's turn to jump up, "Here?! Are you serious? What does that mean though? I'm with Cece, it MUST mean something!"

"Geez, ladies, sit down before I freak out too! I don't know, ok? I'm still processing! He gave me his phone number, but I don't know. Rob only passed seven months ago. I don't want a rebound relationship after two decades of commitment. It's a betrayal to Rob. Isn't it? What will people think? I don't even know what I think!"

I bury my face into my hands, overwhelmed by the war of emotion in my head and heart. Both women come and sit down, one on each side of me, Cece scooting me over to squeeze in next to the armrest.

"It's not too soon, I say. Not like this. This is not some random guy flirting in a coffee shop. It's Bash! Remember when you believed he was the love of your life? I know Rob has been that for all these years. But who's to say you can't have two great loves? As long as they're not at the same time, there's no rules about this. Only YOU can decide."

Kristen nods and adds, "I agree and who cares what anyone else thinks! What do YOU think Meg? Maybe you don't know that yet, but you're the one who gets to decide here. Rob loved you. There's no way he wanted you to spend the rest of your life alone, denying something that could bring you a lot of joy and love to your life. Maybe not today, but you don't have to dive full-in on this. Just keep the door open maybe and see what might come through it. Slowly. You know?"

I feel tears slipping down my face at their love, their acceptance, their care for me. I wipe at my cheeks with the back of my hand, sniffling a bit.

"You guys are the best, you know that? Last week seeing Bash again, it wasn't like it took the place of the feelings I still carry for Rob. More like it rekindled other feelings, from the past."

Pulling in a shaky breath, I continue. "And for a moment, I felt... cherished. Bash always had this way of making me feel that, even when I was an insecure, confused 15-year-old girl. I'd never felt that before from anyone—certainly not my parents—until him. I hadn't really known what I'd been missing until he came into my life. Didn't know love like that existed."

Now we're all three a bit misty-eyed. When we look at each other and realize it, we can't help but laugh at ourselves.

"What a bunch of saps we turned out to be!" Kristen chuckles, wiping at her eyes with her sleeves. "I blame the pre-menopausal hormones. Not that I'd ever admit that to my husband. Well ladies, it's past 9 and I promised the kids I'd come kiss them in bed before they fell asleep. I want them to feel what you said, Meg. Cherished."

"They do," Cece assures her and pivots to me, "Listen, we can't tell you what's right for you. But don't let worry over how something looks hold you back. You know your heart, your intentions. Take the next step that's right for you. See how you feel from there before you decide what you want to do, where you want your life to go. Ok?"

We manage a little group huddle hug of sorts before my friends pack up their leftovers and wave goodbye. Closing the door behind them, I consider everything that was said tonight, shaking my head that our "Book Club" did not discuss one single book tonight. So typical. We all loved to read, but we loved to gossip even more. I wander up to my room where I've mostly unpacked my suitcase, running two loads already today.

The clutch I'd brought for evenings at the hotel was on the dresser. Unclipping the top, I reach in, past the red lipstick—mental note to tell Amelia she was right, it *is* powerful—and run my finger along the thick edge of a high-quality business card.

I pull it out and study the front. It's embossed with "Guardian Securities" and "Sebastian Sylvain" followed by an office phone number and email address. That's it. On the back, his handwritten cell number makes my breath catch a little. I think I'd recognize that handwriting anywhere. Like his hands, his writing was beautiful. Slanting and elongated, it scrolls elegantly across the back of the card.

I tap it against my chin for a moment. *Oh, just do it already! You know you're going to!*

But not tonight, I decide. Darkness has a way of messing with my mind. I'd decide in the light of day what step I wanted to take next, then pray it was the right one. I change into a lightweight sleep set to combat the summer heat that accumulates every summer in the second story of the house. With a long look at our bed, I turn and leave the master to sleep in the guest bedroom. Only a handful of tears sneak out on the white cotton pillowcase before I fall asleep.

* * *

I'm still avoiding the decision when the bank calls Thursday morning. The voice identifies himself as Gary, though I could've guessed that since his first word was a grunt.

"Mrs. Franklin, the manager wanted me to call and ensure that you understood that the account for your son is over the FDIC insurance limit."

"Sorry," I reply, "I'm not sure I understand. We've never had… this much in the bank. What's the problem with the account?"

"Well, ma'am, technically you're not on the account so I can't say much to you, but the manager was concerned that you seemed so confused last month when you came in. Clearly you still are. *(Grunt.)* Accounts are insured by the FDIC up to $250,000 per account owner. Your son's account is sole ownership, since he is 18. However, if he'd be willing to add you as a joint owner, it would be insured up to $500,000."

His voice is so droning even a box fan sounds more interesting.

"Ok, yes, I think I understand. So, how can I be added?"

"*(Grunt.)* Your son would need to come into the bank with you and sign a new account agreement to add you. NOW do you understand? *(Grunt with a cough.)*"

Chapter 8

I thank him, holding back from grunting at him in closing, and hang up the call. I check the calendar. Jared isn't due to come home from Napa for one more week.

I'd caved and called him Monday to let him know I was back home. He tried to insist on flying home that day, convinced something must be wrong. But I assured him I had just worn myself out working the conference and missed the comfort of our own four walls. It took some doing, but I talked him down to stick to his original plan.

We'd built up our open and honest communication skills during the year Rob was sick. But I had no clue how to broach *this* topic with him. How could I explain where the money had come from if I didn't know myself? The thought of tarnishing his memories of his father made me ill.

I wander into the master bedroom to strip the sheets in there. Merely out of habit, I suppose, since I haven't slept in there since returning from Europe. Pulling the gray duvet off the bed sends a whirl of air moving and a flutter of movement catches my eye. Sebastian's business card slips off the dresser.

I pick it up, my eyes roving across the embossed name again. Guardian Securities, Chicago's top cybersecurity firm. In the top five list of the country's top cybersecurity firms and top eight globally. Decision made.

* * *

Sebastian was cool confidence and zero surprise when I called, as though he'd known I would. I'd intended to ask him to meet me for lunch sometime next week, but he insisted he was available today, speaking to my twisting anxiety when he asked, "why wait?" Two hours later, I'm walking into a corner bistro famous for their sandwiches and soups to meet him, a jangling bundle of nerves.

He's already there, sitting in a corner booth—one arm stretched across the back of the bench, the other draped over the table, holding a coffee mug. A navy suit jacket is tossed over the back of the bench, the blue paisley tie loosened from around his neck to leave the top button opened. *The man knows how to wear a suit. Gotta give him that.*

I want to take a moment to breathe before heading to his table, but he looks up as if sensing my presence, and our eyes lock. Tightening my grip on the manila folder I brought with me, I make my way between the tables and bustling servers of the busy lunch hour.

"Hi," I say, arriving at the booth. He'd stood as I approached, so I wave my hands in a sit-down motion, both pleased and embarrassed by the chivalrous gesture.

"Hello, Meg," he replies, taking his seat across from me. "I was so glad you called, although I had hoped it would be sooner, if I can be honest."

"Oh, right. Well, I really wasn't expecting you to meet today. I'm sure you're very busy," I say, tucking a stray piece of hair behind my ear, even more self-conscious now to be sitting across from him.

"Never too busy for you," he says, steepling his fingers in front of him and eyeing the manila folder I've set on the table. "I thought we could order first. It looks like you had something specific you wanted to discuss. This place is known for their sandwiches. There's a chipotle chicken one on the menu. It made me think of you."

"I—," *He remembers. He remembers after two decades what kind of food you like...*

"Yes, that sounds perfect."

The waitress looks about Jared's age. She pulls a pencil from her curly pouf to jot down our order on a pad of paper. The chipotle chicken and water with lemon for me, a Reuben and a refill on the black coffee for Bash.

And then she's gone and it's just us. Bash waits—watching, patient.

Chapter 8

I'm convinced he's the most patient man on the planet. *At least for you he is. Now stop stalling.*

I clear my throat and tap the folder on the table anxiously, "It's a little hard to know where to start with this."

"Take your time," Sebastian says, sipping the fresh coffee the waitress brought while smiling and fluttering her eyelashes at him. He didn't seem to notice.

Gather your wits about you and let's do this. You need help. Here it is. I pull in a deep breath.

"Ok, I went to the bank a few weeks ago, before my trip to Europe. I have never managed our family's finances, so when Rob died... it was a lot to process. A lot to figure out. I didn't notice until June that our mortgage automatic payment wasn't pulling from our checking account anymore. I was worried about fees and my credit, so I went to the bank," I pause to squeeze the lemon into my water—a slight tremor to my hands—and take a fortifying gulp from it.

"I don't understand how, but they told me our mortgage loan was paid off two days before Rob died. There was just over $400,000 left on the loan, and he paid it off. We were comfortable, but we did not have money like that. I don't understand where it came from."

"And that bothers you, not knowing where it came from?" he asks calmly, as I feel my face flush and my heart rate pulse in my fingertips.

"Yes, it bothers me!" I snap, before remembering we're surrounded by the lunch rush crowd and force myself to lower my voice. "I feel—I don't know, I feel like my husband had some kind of secret life where he made tons of money that I didn't know about! And it's not just the mortgage either. There was also a college savings account set up in Jared's name..."

I lower my voice to a hissing whisper, "With $750,000 in it. So, we suddenly have over a million dollars to pay our house debt and our kid's way through college and med school?! None of this makes any sense! I'm hoping you can dig into this and find some answers. Was my husband some kind of criminal?"

My throat is so tight the last question comes out as a squeak. Bash reaches across the table to cover my hand with his own. Instantly some part of my brain sends a wave of calm over me in response. I close my eyes to gather myself.

"Of course, I'll help you," he assures, his voice steady. "You know with my line of work I'm able to dig fairly deeply into financial transactions. It's one of the many services we offer our corporate clients, even some government contracts too. I'd tell you more, but I'd have to kill you," he adds with a wink. "Is all the account information in this folder?"

I nod and push it toward him across the table. He slips it into the satchel half hidden under his suit jacket on the booth's bench. The steel grip of anxiety on my body eases a bit with the knowledge that he's going to help me—even if I don't particularly like asking for help. It's comforting to not be in it alone. This time I reach across the table, to give his hand a squeeze. He lifts one eyebrow a little in surprise.

"Thank you. Seriously, thank you. Now, since all we did in Europe was talk about me, today all I want to talk about is you! How did you end up here in Chicago? How are your parents doing? I'd love to see your mom again, it's been ages. Rebecca?"

His eyes sparkled at the mention of his little sister, just like they had whenever she was around back in high school. She was six years younger and had the special gift of lighting up every room she walked into.

The waitress appears with our sandwiches and sets the plates down in front of us. Mine looks delicious—the avocado perfectly ripened atop well-seasoned chicken. She hovers over Bash again smiling. He thanks the girl without looking, and she turns away, visibly deflated.

"Oh, Rebecca," he says with a chuckle before a flicker of sadness sneaks across his face as he cuts into his Reuben. "Well, she really went

Chapter 8

through some hard times in high school and had my niece during her senior year. But Rebecca can take any situation, any struggle and make something beautiful. She got her GED, then her bachelor's in business through night school. She now runs her own business, creating art from discarded materials. Raised Scarlett on her own—with some help from our parents of course—but she's an incredible mother. She's based here, but currently in Milwaukee working on another piece for a museum there with found items from old buildings torn down or being renovated around the city."

He takes a bite of his sandwich and swallows, throat bobbing, before continuing.

"And Scarlett?" his smile grows even more. "She is the most incredible teenager. Outgoing, funny, beautiful, and so smart that she makes her old uncle seem simple minded. She's president of the Student Council, and her mom says she's a shoo-in for homecoming queen. But the cool part is that she doesn't even care about stuff like that. See what I mean? Smart AND lovable."

Watching him talk about his sister and niece with so much pride has my chest warming. He really had been the best big brother back then, and clearly that hasn't changed. He never chased her off or made her feel unwanted when the two of us were hanging out at his house. Instead, he welcomed her in and found ways to involve her in our fun. Eventually his mom would call Rebecca away to do something else "to give you two some time," she'd say with a wink.

Barb had been cool like that—unlike my own mother who screeched "that's close enough!" anytime we sat too close on the couch. That, among other reasons, was why we rarely hung out at my house.

His phone buzzes suddenly, and he picks it up quickly before I catch the caller ID on the screen.

"I'm sorry, I have to get this. Should be quick," he tells me apologetically, swiping across the screen to answer.

"Sylvain. Yes. Hm. I see. What of the—No. No that's unacceptable," his brow furrows and his eyes harden. He pulls the phone away for a moment to murmur to me, "I'll be right back."

He stands and crosses the crowded restaurant in a few strides, putting the phone back up to his ear when he reaches the door. I can see him through the window, though I'm trying to be a little surreptitious with my spying. He looks tense and swipes his hand through his hair before gripping the back of his neck tightly. After an abrupt nod, he hangs up the phone and looks up. I busy myself with my sandwich before he comes back in, pretending I didn't just watch his whole conversation through the glass.

"Everything ok?" I ask nonchalantly as he returns to our booth.

"It will be. Sorry about that," he says, sliding back into his seat, tucking the phone away neatly into his jacket pocket. "Where were we?"

I eye him a moment to see if he'll say more about the call. *Quit being nosy,* Margaret snipes, as though she isn't just as curious.

"Partway through Sylvain family catch up time. Tom and Barb? How are they?"

"They're great! Fantastic, really. They retired down to Florida. Destin area so mom could be near the ocean like she's always wanted."

His parents had been everything Amelia's and mine were not. Encouraging, supportive, THERE. Truthfully, I'd been a bit jealous at times. But they'd only ever been kind to me. Even offering to fly me from Chicago on long weekends to visit when they found out we were moving. But that was before... before everything fell apart.

"And Chicago? How'd you end up here?"

"Ah, right," he replies, wiping his mouth with a napkin. "Well, after I finished at MIT, I took a cybersecurity analyst role at a company here in Chicago. No one was really doing remote work then, so it seemed like a good place to settle with plenty of big firms in the area."

Chapter 8

"But not Guardian, right? They've only been around the last 10 years or so. I wrote a feature article about the company."

"Is that so?" He arches a brow with a smile, and I flush a little.

"Well, as much as I could write anyway. It's a very tight-lipped company you're at! Even the C-suite team is a mystery. I couldn't believe that. Never seen a company keep its leadership hidden. I get that it's a secretive business, cybersecurity, but still, it's odd. I don't suppose you'd like to give me the inside scoop…"

I wiggle my eyebrows at him conspiratorially and he laughs.

"Would that I could, Meg, because that *would* be quite a scoop! Alas, all employees are required to sign binding NDA's that don't ever terminate, even on resignation. And those suckers are iron clad, so if I value my life and livelihood…" he mimics locking up his lips and throwing away the key over his shoulder.

"Fine," I say, feigning a deep sigh and flipping my hair over one shoulder. "But if you ask me, being gainfully employed is over-rated. Speaking of which, you'd probably best get back to work. I have to go in too. I'm due for some face time in the office myself. Even though I'm very part time, they'd like to see more of me. I'm just not sure how much I want to give to this job. I love writing. But I don't know that this is 'it' for me, you know what I mean?"

He nods and pulls out his wallet to drop a fifty on the table before I can reach for my purse.

"When can we do this again?" he asks, straight to the point.

A surge of nerves hits hard, my stomach knotting around the sandwich I just ate. I grab my bag and put a little more space between us as we head towards the exit.

"Oh, I'm pretty busy these next few weeks. Jared will be coming back, and we've got to get him ready to leave for college. He wants to get there before the first semester starts, give him some time to get his bearings. He's a planner, that one!"

"Family first, I completely understand. So, you'll call me after you get Jared settled then?" he asks without pushing. A straightforward question that I know I could say no to if I wanted.

You don't want to say no. She's right. I don't want to say no. Instead, I say, "Sounds perfect. Until then, Bash."

"Until then, Meg," he replies, and we step out into the hot summer sun to head opposite directions.

Chapter 9

"That's the last of it, Mom!" Jared hollers over his shoulder, slamming the rented Jeep's trunk hatch down and brushing off his hands on the back of his jeans. He's always done that after completing a task. The first time I saw him do it, he'd just put the final block atop a tall tower he'd been working on. He stood back to survey his work and wiped his hands on the back of his 2T romper. He'd been doing it ever since. My little boy—my grown son—all packed up and ready to move off to New York City.

Columbia had a top-notch premed program. The day his acceptance letter came, we were so proud and not at all surprised. I'd always known he was destined for great things. I just didn't know Rob wouldn't be here to see him do it. But maybe he was seeing it. In a way, I think he knew. And at least he'd been there to celebrate the acceptance with us last fall.

"Mom!" he calls out again, waving his hands to get my attention. "You ready?"

Was I ready? Heck if I knew but what choice did I have anyway?

I smile and reply with a phrase I must've called through the house a thousand times through the years, "Ready or not, here I come!"

I lock the door behind me and climb into the passenger's seat. Jared insists on driving the first leg. That puts me in charge of the music. I connect to Bluetooth and crank my favorite late 90's/early 2000's playlist. I choose to ignore when I hear Jared mutter "oldies" and sing along quietly as he navigates us through traffic and out of the city. Once we hit the open road, it's pretty much a straight shot east on I-80 all the way to New York.

Traffic eases about an hour outside the city, I reach over and turn down the music a little.

"So…" I start hesitantly. "We didn't get a lot of time to talk last week with me at the office more and you busy packing. And, you know, sleeping til all hours of the day," I add teasingly, elbowing his arm on the console between us.

"Hey now, I was trying to stock up! Starting college with premed intentions means I probably won't sleep for another 10 years or so. Thought I'd better get it while I can! Nothing wrong with rollin' outta bed at 2 p.m., I say. You should try it sometime, Mom! Nobody will be home to bother you!"

His joking smile falters as what he said registers. I reach over and give him a reassuring pat.

"Don't let those thoughts build a nest, son. I'm gonna be just fine! Shoot, I'm practically excited to have the house all to myself! I probably won't even clean every week. You know? Walk around in my underwear and that kind of fun stuff. Some Risky Business slides in my tube socks. You have no idea how fun your old mom can be when left to her own devices."

"Uh huh, sure Mom, I'll believe it if that weekly cleaning schedule on the side of the fridge disappears. You know, the one you've been living by for as long as I can remember!"

"Ok, you caught me. I'll probably still wash your sheets, but lessen it to once a month, so they'll be fresh JUST IN CASE you decide to come

Chapter 9

home unexpectedly. I wouldn't want you sleeping on stale sheets, Jare! But you don't know everything. You've never known me as an empty nester. I might leave a dirty dish in the sink overnight! You can't tell me who to be."

We share a laugh, then Jared groans, spotting the exit sign ahead. Right on cue I burst into song.

"Gary Indiana, Gary Indiana, Gary Indiana. That's the town that knew me when!" I belt out in my best Broadway voice complete with jazz hands.

"Some things never change I guess!" he rolls his eyes playfully. I made him watch The Music Man with me once every summer until he turned 16, and he finally put his foot down. That didn't stop me from torturing him with my singing, however.

I let a few miles go by, watching the white lines pass by beneath us. If I don't focus on each one, they blur almost into a solid line. Looking back, the years of Jared's childhood were like that. Sometimes the days felt so long, but really, they were rushing by, disappearing so fast that most days were barely distinguished from the next. I hope I did enough. I know I loved him enough because I couldn't possibly love him more. But I hope I loved him the right way, the way he needed.

Rip the bandaid off, mama. Clearing my throat, I decide to face the elephant in the room.

"So, Jare, be honest with me. How are you feeling about everything I told you last week? About… about the money. Whatever you're feeling, it's ok. No judgment. I'd just like to hear your thoughts."

He's quiet for a moment. Taking his time to think before he answers, instead of quick and breezy answers like his dad. Rob had a way of rushing into things without giving it full consideration. *Jared is all the best parts of both of you.*

"Well, part of me is just overwhelmingly thankful, Mom. I can't tell you how many sleepless nights I had after Dad died, wondering how on earth I was going to pay for college. Knowing I would never put that burden on you. I had every intention of figuring it out, that's why I applied for so many scholarships. And jumped at the chance for this summer job. It wasn't really just a fun thing to do. I wanted the money for school.

"Another part of me is... I guess confused? Maybe even a little angry? It feels weird to be angry at Dad for providing for us. But why all the secrecy? It just feels pretty suspicious. Where did he get that kind of cash? It's kind of hard to let myself carry negative thoughts of him now that he's gone. As though I shouldn't because he's not even here to defend himself. I feel guilty for thinking it, but how can I not be doubting with the limited evidence at hand?"

I listen quietly and nod in support at everything he's saying. It pretty well mirrors most of what I've been thinking and feeling myself.

"I wasn't sure I wanted to tell you, but I think you should know. I've asked someone—an old friend—to look into it for me. See if they can figure out where the money might have come from."

You said "they" instead of "he." Very sneaky. My hands twist nervously in my lap as I wait for him to respond. He's quiet again. Processing.

"Sure. If you think that will help, I trust you. Promise me that, no matter what your friend finds, you tell me. Ok? Promise. I don't want you carrying any of this alone."

I smile and take his hand for a moment. "Of course, I'll tell you anything that turns up. Pit stop?" I ask, pointing to a sign indicating a gas station and a Starbucks at the coming exit.

After a quick break, I grab a venti caramel latte and we switch drivers. I shouldn't drink this much coffee. We'll likely have to stop again in two hours or less. But Jared convinces me to get what I want. There's no rush so we can stop as much as I need.

When we get back on the interstate, Jared tips his seat back for a little nap. I queue up an audio book from my app. About five minutes

Chapter 9

in I realize I am in no mood for any more mysteries and switch to a fantasy with romance instead.

I settle in and let my mind wander over the story, mooning over the strong male love interest and mentally yelling at the female protagonist to get it together and just realize he loves her already. It's a pretty swoon-worthy story, and I just hope it doesn't have a third act miscommunication breakup. I hate those.

At some point I stop listening as Jared's sleeping form catches my eye. If I wasn't zipping along at 81 mph, I'd spend the day memorizing his face. It's mostly a grown man face now, but traces of the boy he was still exist, especially while he's sleeping. The way everything softens in sleep—his mouth hanging slightly slack—he looks every bit the innocent 13-year-old boy who came to me anxiously for advice on asking his crush to the Valentine's Day dance. He grew out his chocolate brown hair a little this summer. It has a more tousled, free look to it. Liquid caramel eyes are hidden under his closed lids, with dark thick eyelashes that made every girl, including me, jealous. *Does he look happy?*

Jared had looked up to Rob for everything he did. Rob had played baseball, so Jared played baseball. Rob liked the Yankees. Jared rooted for them vigorously. Rob hated vegetables, Jared ate the ones I insisted he try at dinner begrudgingly and with much commentary, though I swear he did like some of them secretly.

But career-wise, Jared had a heart for medicine from the start. It must've been kismet when Aunt Amelia bought him his first doctor kit at his second birthday. I played patient at least twice a day, every day for the entire year. Then he moved on to doctoring his stuffed animals. Each one had a different malady to be treated by Dr. Jared. I had saved a few of his most beloved stuffies and each one still had a gauze wrapped leg, bandaged cheek or an arm in a sling.

When Rob was first diagnosed, Jared was nearly as informative as our oncologist. He researched as though he himself were responsible for coming up with a treatment plan. I worried a bit about him taking it on himself that way, but I also understood the enormous pressure, the desperate need to *do* something. Anything. He attended as many of Rob's appointments as he could and often came to the infusion center after school to sit with him for rounds of chemo.

After the clinical trial failed to show any improvement and the PET scan showed more activity in yet another lymph node, Jared had begged Rob to get another opinion. In truth, Rob already had multiple opinions. His doctor was a friend of a friend and had sent his scans to two other oncologists, one at the renowned Mayo Clinic. It was too late, there was nothing to be done. Rob knew before that though. He told me he felt it in his bones, that his time was coming.

We celebrated that last Christmas together and it was nothing short of magic. The undercurrent of grief was there, but Rob felt better than he had in months, and it lifted all our spirits so much. For that one day, we almost felt like a normal family. But then that very night, we were rushing to the ER and one day after… It was surreal, to go from such a high to gone forever.

I was already dreading the holidays this year. Jared promised he'd be home for both Thanksgiving and Christmas. I promised myself I would not be a burden on my son but honestly, I know I couldn't face those days without him. After the "firsts" though, I swore to myself I'd never make him feel like he had to be there because I needed him. Only if he wanted to.

For the rest of today, Jared and I go back and forth taking turns driving. We sing some old and new favorites, we chat, we laugh and we reminisce. And the 13-hour drive turns into a healing balm for my soul.

We pull into our hotel well after midnight and crash hard. After sleeping in a little, we head to the campus to find Jared's dorm. He

Chapter 9

pulls up the email to get the info and navigate us in the right direction. The campus is fairly quiet for now, classes still a week from starting. But Jared isn't the only student looking to get settled in early. A handful of others mill around, heavily freshmen and most with parents. As we carry the first load of boxes to his assigned building, Jared holds the door open with his foot for a waif of a girl with long dark hair and huge green eyes. She looks up to give a shy thank you. He flashes that famous Jared-grin at her, and I see her melt a little. She tightens her hold on her bag and hurries down the steps, turning toward the dining hall, glancing back from a few yards away.

Jared continues to hold the door for me, completely oblivious. I roll my eyes and shake my head chuckling.

"My my, is this a co-ed dorm?! You're gonna have to be careful, you know? That megawatt smile of yours is likely to break a lot of hearts here around campus."

Jared laughs and replies, "Oh geez, Mom, only you would think that! Besides, I'll be too busy to even notice a pretty girl soon. I wouldn't really want to start anything right now anyway. Feels pretty selfish to expect a girl to wait around on you for 8 years while you finish med school."

He pushes open the door marked Jared F. and Doug M. It looks like we beat Doug here. The double room is fairly spartan: twin beds pushed up against opposite walls, a nightstand beside each, desks and wardrobes on the opposite walls, on either side of the door.

A shared jack-n-jill bathroom runs between this room and the one next to it. That ought to be interesting—four freshmen guys responsible for one bathroom. I unpack the caddy of bathroom cleaning supplies and set in a very visible place, congratulating myself on the foresight to teach Jared to clean his own bathroom years ago.

Still thinking about what Jared said when I return to the bedroom and start making the bed, I tell him,"While you're not wrong, you will be busy, don't write love off altogether. You never know!"

He pauses, holding a button down on a hanger in front of him, "Hey that's right, you and Dad met in college. I'd almost forgotten about that." He laughs, "I'm pretty sure I'm not ready to find 'the one' just yet. No worries there."

After we hang his shirts, we walk back to the Jeep together to grab another load. He doesn't have too much, since he'll be buying his books and some supplies here. Jared's never been the material type either.

As we dive into the next box, he pauses and studies me a moment.

"What is it?" I ask, tucking a loose strand back into the high bun piled atop my head.

"You're going to be ok, right? I mean, you're not going to go back home to an empty house and… I dunno fall apart or anything right?" I almost laugh at the question but stop when I see the seriousness in his eyes.

"Well son, I don't really know what to expect quite honestly. I've never done this before. Dropped my only child off at college. Been a widow. Kinda new territory, you know?"

I shrug and continue unpacking as I answer, giving my hands something to do by way of folding sweats into the drawers of the wardrobe.

"But you know me," I say, sending a wink his way. "I'm kind of a tough old bird."

Jared doesn't smile back. Dropping the bundle of cords he'd been untangling, he crosses the small side of the room and grabs both my hands.

"Mom," he says forcing my attention to him and away from the clothes. "Just promise me you won't stop living. That isn't what Dad would have wanted. He loved life, his family, adventures. He would be heartbroken if all your joy died with him. I know you've been grieving, and part of us probably always will be grieving. But don't stop living

Chapter 9

when you're not the one who died. Ok? One more promise?"

He lets one hand go so I can wipe at the tears trickling down my cheeks. I sniff loudly and lean in for a hug, soaking up this beautiful, kind boy Rob and I brought into the world.

"A wise friend recently told me the same thing—to keep living. I'll have some hard days, sure. And I've got to figure out my place in this strange new world. But I will. I promise, kiddo. Now let's get all your stuff just how you want it before Doug shows, yeah? That way he can't try to crowd your space. I hope he's not a snorer!"

We return to our work, finishing up the last few boxes. I grab a notebook from my purse to jot down a list of items to grab from the store for Jared's room before I head back home tomorrow, toilet paper at the forefront of my mind. Boys never think about buying toilet paper but it's absolutely the first thing they'll miss when it runs out.

The first page brings a smile to my face. My "to do" list from Salzburg. Looks like I had done all of them except number five: figure out what to do with my life. But hey, I managed to complete the first four, with a little help from a friend. I had thought I needed to do it all on my own. But maybe I was wrong. Maybe I could figure out number five too, with help. Maybe there was someone else who was back in my life now, for this moment, that is just the right person. Maybe it didn't have to be the rekindling of something from the past, but something fresh, something new, something different. Something for this moment.

I finish the dorm supplies list for the store and flip back to the first page. I cross off the first four, relishing the dopamine boost. I add a little number six to the bottom and next to it write "call Bash."

Chapter 10

The phone rings suddenly in the quiet space of the kitchen. The accompanying vibration sends it skittering a few inches across the counter as the chime dings. Wiping my hands on a dish towel, I smile at Amelia's face lighting up the screen, tapping to accept the FaceTime call.

"Hey hey hey!" Amelia sing songs through the screen. She's still in her white tie-neck blouse, from work, but the bow is half out, her classic red lip a bit smudged, and her sleek angled bob mussed on one side. But she's holding my adorable nephew and smiling, and life seems altogether messy and beautiful.

"Hi there, Oliver! Are you trying to grab Auntie Meg's face through the phone? Oh, I wish I could hold you too my little man! Yes, I do! Auntie Meg loves you Olly Oliver, I sure do!"

Amelia swings him to her other hip, outside the camera angle and clears her throat loudly, "Hi, I'm here too, Meg! HELLO TO YOU TOO SISTER! Geez Louise, have one cute kid and suddenly I'm chopped liver!"

She turns away from the screen and calls over her shoulder, "Mark! Hey, Mark! Come get Oliver so my sister will actually speak to me in

Chapter 10

an adult voice! Her baby voice is completely OBNOXIOUS."

"Hi, Meg!" Mark waves from the doorway as Amelia passes him the baby. "Bye, Meg!"

Amelia rolls her eyes and laughs, "He's such a doofus. He's my doofus though, and I love him."

"He's one of the good ones, sis!"

"Yeah," her eyes go dreamy for a moment, and I smile for the joy she's found in life.

"He really is. So is—was Rob." She gives me a half smile. "How's empty nester life treating you?"

I sigh loudly and look around to contemplate just how it is going.

"Well, it's 8 on a Thursday night, and I'm surrounded by two dozen cupcakes that I have no idea why I made or who's going to eat them. My house is spotless. Laundry is done. I guess I just needed to do… something. Anything. I don't know Amelia. What am I doing?"

Amelia crosses her room to close the door behind her before flopping back on her bed.

"Give yourself a break! Your life has changed drastically this year! There's gonna be a lot of that, I think. But also, what do I know? I've never done what you're doing now. Never been through it. I hate that I can't fix this for you, that I don't know how to help." She shrugs helplessly as her brow furrows with concern.

"You're here. That means a lot."

I abandon the half-frosted cupcakes on the counter and go to flop on the couch. Legs splayed over the arm, the camera angle is definitely giving me a double chin, but I'm too weary to care.

"Have you… heard anything back from Sebastian? About… you know," she asks quirks an eyebrow up and down in a cartoonish way.

I sigh again, "No. I haven't. But I did kind of tell him I needed some time to get Jared moved into his dorm and all before we met again. So, I think he's probably waiting on me."

"O-KAY," she draws out the syllables. "Jared's been settled in his dorm for almost three weeks now... Why haven't you called him? What aren't you saying?"

I avoid the screen to stare at the texture on the ceiling above me. There are no ceiling lights in the living room. That always bugged me, having to light the room with lamps only. Why would architects ever design a room without lights? *Nice stalling. Quit avoiding and be real.*

"I almost called him from LaGuardia while waiting on my flight home from New York. Then I almost called him on the cab ride home from O'Hare. Then... you get the point. I've *almost* called him every day. I pull his contact card up, stare at his name for 12 minutes and 38 seconds. Then I chicken out, lock my phone and chuck it somewhere far away from me. It's become a lovely little evening ritual really. Very logical. Very adult."

She arches one perfectly waxed brow, pencil slightly smeared at the end, and waits silently for me to continue.

"Amelia," I sigh heavily. "I don't know what you want me to say. I've been a widow for less than a year. Don't you think it's too soon?"

"Too soon for what, sis? To marry him? Yeah, it's too soon for that. But too soon to talk to him? Too soon to get to know him again? Too soon to see if you still have feelings for the guy who was your entire world during high school until he broke your heart and I almost drove up to northern Wisconsin to commit murder? Nah, I don't think so. Not too soon for that."

She's breathless from her run-on sentence monologue, and I chuckle at the memory. After the breakup, I had been crying on and off for days when she came home from college for the weekend and found me curled in a ball. I heard Mom tell her I'd been like that for two weeks. I remember being surprised Mom had even noticed. Amelia marched upstairs, looked at me a moment, then slapped her hand against the door frame and cried, "That's it!"

Chapter 10

She grabbed her car keys and hollered, "I'll be back by tomorrow night!" before I realized what was happening. I ran out to the driveway, my bare feet sticking to the thin layer of snow, to stop her from leaving. We sat in her car for a long time, talking about everything. I felt a lot better after that and only spent *some* of my evenings in the fetal position for the rest of the year.

"Meg, you can't stop living because Rob died."

"Oh my gosh, you've got to be kidding me. Yeah, I've heard! Is everyone in some kind of group text planning what they'll say to me next?! I GOT IT, ok? I'll go live! Fine! And if you say, 'Promise me Meg' I will hang up this call right now."

I roll my eyes, and we laugh it off together. We chat for a few more minutes about how work is going for her, balancing being a mom of two now with a demanding corporate job. She's a wonder, my sister. I tell her often, but she still doesn't believe me. She fills me in on the kids' latest doings. Oliver has been rolling over back to front now, and Daisy has started Pre-K which she absolutely loves. I tell her about Jared's first couple weeks of classes and how his roommate Doug has a girlfriend doing a semester abroad in Tokyo who calls at weird hours of the night. They also seem to fight a lot, so Jared doesn't think it'll last long.

I can hear Oliver wailing in the background and a glance at the clock says it's past his bedtime. I give my love to her and the kids and we end the call.

Just like that the house is quiet again. So, so quiet. Maybe I need to get a dog. *A dog? That's your big life idea?* I groan at the thought of potty training a puppy. Most of the house is hardwood, but the big area rugs are definitely not ones I could ball up into my washing machine.

I pull out my laptop and google "best dogs for a woman alone," then backspace that out to ask "easiest dog to potty train." The breeds range from Toy Fox Terrier to Bernese Mountain Dog. Quite a selection.

An email alert pops up. Ugh, Frank. After getting Jared settled at school, I'd started going into the office three days a week. I probably should transition to full time. No reason not to. Writing is definitely a passion for me but cybersecurity isn't. I'd thought I wouldn't have a choice. Bills to be paid, and all that, but with Rob's mystery money I had time to think. Maybe too much time.

Going in to the office more had me firmly in Frank's sights. He was constantly popping up in my inbox with questions, story ideas for me to research and pitch at our weekly meetings. I roll my eyes at his latest, completely unnecessary email and minimize the mail window. He could micromanage me the days I came into the office, not while I was at home after hours. No, thank you.

Opening a second tab in the browser, I type "How to live after the death of a spouse." The internet has all the answers, right? An list-style article with 12 tips pops up second in the search results. I'm pleased to find I've already accomplished some of the items. I've consistently been getting up and getting dressed. Pat on the back for that.

Take a road trip. Ha! I'll do you one better than that! I did an international flight! Suck it, list. *Yeah... not sure you're really understanding the spirit of the list here, Meg.* Whatever, a win is a win.

Exercise and meditation. No problem. Weekly Flow with GI-Barbie. Check.

Give of yourself. Hm, that one jumps out at me from the screen. In years' past, I never had to look for an opportunity to volunteer my time. Between Jared's school and Rob's law firm, the opportunities fell into my lap. I'd baked like Betty Crocker for bake sales, made dishes for office lunches, helped build stud walls with Habitat for Humanity, Jared and I even traveled to Mexico once to help with the construction of an orphanage. I suppose now I'd have to find somewhere to give of myself by myself.

What is it that makes your soul sing? I don't know.

Chapter 10

An email notification pings, causing me to jump a little, and pops up in the bottom right corner of my screen. *If it's freaking Frank again, I'll tell him where he can send his next unnecessary email,* Margaret threatens.

But it's not Frank. My heart leaps into my throat when my eyes land on the sender's name: S. Sylvain. I swallow that vital organ back down into my chest as best I can before clicking the notification box to open the message.

Hello, Meg. I hope this email finds you well. Wow, I can't believe I just typed that. Feels like I'm sending a note to someone in HR. Or worse, I AM HR. So, let me try that again.

Hi Meg! Oof. Exclamation point right off the bat. Too much, right? Hang on. I'll get this right.

Hey, Meg. I really enjoyed our lunch a few weeks ago. And running into you in Prague, of all places. Who would've thought? I kept waiting for you to call. I believe Columbia started classes two weeks ago. I may or may not have Googled that information, but I'll never tell. You haven't called yet. So, I'm going out on a limb here and making first contact. I hope that's ok.

Fact is, I've changed over 20 years and so have you, but somehow when I'm with you I feel like that awkward 16-year-old computer nerd all over again. To be clear, I'm still a computer nerd. Just a little older now and slightly better at hiding it in public thanks to the development of (some) social skills, though Rebecca would argue otherwise. The cool confidence is more of a corporate persona I've adopted, but I digress. I'm still more comfortable behind a computer screen and probably couldn't have said all of this to you in person. I'm sure you remember; I guess maybe I haven't changed that much.

I'd love to see you again, no expectations. You've been through a lot recently, and I'm not asking for any kind of commitment from you. It's just that now that I've seen you, I don't want to waste any more time <u>not</u> seeing you. So, if you would like to see me too... when can I see you again?

Always, Bash

I giggle like a schoolgirl at his words, breaking the quietness of the empty house. My heart feels like it's beating out of my chest expanding as I read his message again. It's so... Bash. He'd felt familiar, but also so aloof when we had lunch together. I'd kind of forgotten how he was when we'd started talking. The attraction was undeniable, but he was so closed off at first. It took a little time to break down his walls. But once I had, the view was beautiful.

I fiddle with the place my wedding band had been, forgetting momentarily I had taken it off after dropping Jared at Columbia. I shake out my hands and hit the reply button.

Hey, Bash! Yes, I am the type to use an exclamation point in a greeting. I'm a writer, and I call that part of my creative license. Sue me.

If we're in the business of being honest, I've almost called you about nineteen times since I left Jared at Columbia. It's...complicated for me right now. I appreciate you clarifying your offer without expectation of commitment. I could, however, use a friend right now, if you're available.

Don't laugh but I was doing some Googling myself, trying to figure out what I'm supposed to do next. I'm deciding between finding a charity to volunteer with and adopting a dog that will likely ruin my house and what little sanity I have remaining. Any thoughts?

Yours, Meg

I stare at my message for a few moments, then highlight the "yours" and tap delete. Old habit resurfaced I suppose. When we'd passed messages back and forth, often slipping notes in each other's lockers, and that was our signature lines. He signed "always" and I signed "yours." I had typed it this time without thinking. Felt a little scary. Definitely not ready for that.

I click send with "Meg" as the close, and return to the kitchen to finish frosting the last of the cupcakes for heaven only knew who. It's barely been two minutes when my laptop is chiming again. A new email alert. I drop the frosting bag and race back to the living room,

Chapter 10

slipping a little in my fuzzy socks.

Meg! There. I did it too. Guess I can borrow your creative license when I want to. I think I have the perfect thing in mind. Are you free Saturday morning?

Always, Bash

The smile stretching across my face is probably the definition of the term "ear-to-ear." I tap out a quick "yes, free for what" response and hit send. His reply takes less than 60 seconds.

That's for me to know and you to find out. Pick you up at 10. Wear something comfortable.

Always, Bash

Cupcakes finished, I head upstairs to do my nighttime over 40 skin care routine—*Getting older sucks*—brush my teeth, floss to make my hygienist happy and head to the guest room to sleep. The smile lasts long after my head hits the pillow.

Chapter 11

The doorbell rings at promptly 9:55. My thoughts immediately go to Johanna, bringing a grin to my face. She would approve. I put a final pin into my messy bun—*for a style that's intended to be "messy" you sure spent a massive amount of time on it*—and run down the stairs to open the door.

Bash leans against the porch railing in jeans, his arms crossed over a black Henley, the top two buttons open. The shirt is well-fitted, and I have to shove Margaret and her definitely NOT just-friends commentary back down to smile brightly at him.

"Hey! I just need to grab my purse and throw on some shoes. Do you want to come in for a minute?"

The words are out before I really think about them, and the next thing I know Sebastian Sylvain is standing in my living room. In my living room, in the house I shared with Rob and raised our son and now live in alone. And I… don't know how to process what I'm feeling. A nervous laugh bubbles up as he steps further into the room, hands in his pockets. I disappear into the kitchen to grab my purse before I say anything completely idiotic.

I return to the living room, bag on my shoulder, and find he's moved

Chapter 11

over to the fireplace where family portraits line the mantle. He's paused in front of a wedding photo of Rob and I. It feels like a lifetime ago. It *was* a lifetime ago.

"I, uh," I sputter, looking for something, anything to say. "I haven't gotten out my fall decor yet."

Literally could have said anything but that. I resist the urge to hide my face, cover the burning of my cheeks. Or just run away from this embarrassing scene altogether. Change my name. Move to another country. Everything is currently on the table. Or the mantle. *Wow Meg. This is going to go swimmingly.*

He smiles a half smile, like he knows exactly what I'm thinking and is enjoying watching the reel of panic playing in my head.

"Me either," he says easily, giving me a reprieve from myself. "Are you more a pumpkin spice latte lover or are you still a tea girl?"

I smile back, thankful he's chosen to turn my idiocy into valid conversation. "You caught me. I won't say no to a good latte, but tea is still my first love."

He nods knowingly, "I thought so. Shall we?" He angles his head towards the front door I left standing wide open.

He waits while I lock the door behind us and leads me to a sleek black sedan idling at the curb in front of the house. *He's holding open the car door for you... try not to swoon!* I climb into the passenger's seat carefully avoiding brushing his hand on the door frame.

The interior is dark. Windows tinted heavily and seats covered in a smooth black leather, the car smells... spicy. He climbs in and reaches across the console to hold out one of the two to-go cups from the holders.

"Chai tea latte," he says, handing me the warm cup. That was the smell. I bring the cup up to my face and breathe it in. Autumn crackles along my senses. I open my eyes to find him watching me before he turns his attention to the street and pulls away from the curb.

"What's in the other cup?" I ask.

He grins slyly and answers, "Pumpkin spice latte."

I give him a playful punch on the upper arm, "And here I thought you remembered my favorite drink! You were just guessing!" *Woof, I'd like that arm wrapped around me tight. That thing was like a rock!* Enough, Margaret!

He smiles and rubs said bicep as though I've wounded him. Then adds quietly, "I did remember. I just wasn't sure how much you'd changed, so thought it best to hedge my bets. Business tactic."

"Surrrre," I reply and switch subjects, steering us safely away from anything too serious. "Speaking of business, how are things at Guardian? Your business card is very 'international man of mystery' and doesn't even have a title on it. What's that about?"

"I'm sorry ma'am, that's on a need-to-know basis and you simply do. Not. Need. To. Know," he slides on a pair of dark aviators like some kind of crime scene detective. "Ah, I'm just kidding. I manage a group of cybersecurity analysts and engineers. Hackers, but turned legitimate. You know the type."

He navigates us through a few more blocks of traffic, and I realize I still have no idea where we're going or what we're doing. I'm also surprisingly fine with that. My usual M.O. as family planner is to know every detail of every outing. It's kind of nice to sit back and not worry about the agenda for once.

"Quite frankly, my job isn't that interesting. At least not the parts I can share. So why don't you tell me about your work writing for eTech? I'm not one bit surprised you became a writer. I knew it from the first poem you shared in Mrs. Heinman's class. You mentioned possibly taking on more?"

I let out a huge sigh, "Yeah, writing has been the only thing I've ever really been good at it. Aside from being a mom. And I do love it, usually. I'm just not sure I love where I'm at. I don't really feel like I'm doing

Chapter 11

anything productive, you know? Nothing that's making any kind of real difference." I bite my lip, self-conscious from what I've shared.

"Oh, ignore me, I've been on a bit of a ramble lately. Losing Rob and sending Jared off to college. Not really sure who I am without them."

I pick absentmindedly at the cuticle of my thumb, stealing a glance over at Bash. His eyes are on the road, but I can tell he's listening. He has a concerned look and is nodding seriously.

I motion out the windshield, "Hence my request for helping me find some purpose in life. I thought about asking the club—sorry, my book club—but Kristen had a two-day dance competition with her oldest and Cece is out of town with her husband for their anniversary."

Ok Queen of Babble, that's probably enough sharing for now. Or for the week. Maybe the year.

I grimace. "Ah, there I go talking too much again. Sorry, Bash. You'll be sorry you ever picked me up!"

He shakes his head, "Need I remind you? I love hearing you talk. The ride would be boring if we both just stare at the city traffic."

But then a lull does settle on us while I work up the nerve to ask him if there's been any progress on the money I asked him to look into.

Keeping his focus solely on the road he answers, "I wish I had better information for you. So far, all I've been able to determine is that the money came from an account in the Cayman Islands. It gets a little tricky to nail down the details with those offshore accounts. Tight security and all. Most use ID numbers instead of names."

He must sense my disappointment because he reaches across the console to squeeze my hand. "Hey, it's ok. I'll keep digging into it, alright? I've been a little swamped at work so I haven't put as much time into it as I should have. Just… try not to assume the worst. Seems like Rob must've been a pretty good guy if he managed to snag you. Yeah?"

I keep my gaze in my lap and nod, not really in agreement. My mind goes back and forth between thinking I must be the most naive woman on the planet—unwittingly married to a criminal—and reaching far for unlikely explanations like a long lost wealthy aunt died suddenly, and he just didn't get a chance to tell me before he died.

We've pulled up outside a warm and welcoming old building that looks like it might have been a house long ago. The front entry door is engraved with swirls of clouds and ivy intertwined, a square pane of glass gleams just above eye level. Large terracotta pots on each side boast colorful arrangements of fall flowers with English ivy spilling out and down the sides.

Bash parks right in front and before I realize what he's doing, is opening my door again, offering me a hand to step out. His hand is warm. Comforting. Solid. We walk up to the building. The glass on the door has an artistic outline of an angel on it. No signage is visible. I stop and look at Bash expectantly.

He nods his head toward the building and explains, "This is Angel House. A safe place for women with or without children to come when they need to get out of a bad situation."

"Oh, a women's shelter?"

"It's more than just a shelter," he says. "The staff here works with them to brush up their resumes, build computer, money handling and life skills, get setup with healthcare and financial assistance, establish the children in daycare or school, participate in group counseling, and, when they're ready, moves them into affordable housing in a safe neighborhood with all the necessities. Or, if the situation is really severe, even move to another state."

"Wow, that's a lot. You've worked here before then?"

He nods, "Yeah, I help out when I can. Twice a month I teach a computer course, trying to help make those without any prior office experience more employable. I called ahead yesterday and Tasha, she's the head 'mother' of the house, said she could use your help with a

Chapter 11

creative writing class they're offering this month. I thought it was a great fit for you."

"Oh," I say suddenly nervous. "I—gosh I've never taught a class before! I wouldn't even know where to start. Can't I help out with cleaning or something? I'm great with a toilet brush!" I laugh self-deprecatingly.

He turns toward me and places both hands on my shoulders to look me in the eyes. "These women have been through a lot. Most of them since birth, quite frankly. They don't usually come from loving, middle-class families to end up in these situations where they have nowhere else to go. Some of them, but not most. The writing course is intended to be one of the many ways to help these women process the pain, the horrors they've been through.

"I know I'm calling it a class—which probably sounds scary since you haven't had time to prepare—but think of it more as leading a discussion on why they should consider writing or journaling to help them process. They also offer therapeutic painting classes. However, I'm realizing that I've kind of sprung this on you… which isn't fair. I didn't think this all the way through. If you don't want to do it, I can make an excuse to Tasha, and I'll take you home right now. No judgment."

I swallow and think for a minute. I've been seeking a way to help someone besides myself. Now an opportunity falls in my lap. How can I say no to that? I'm unprepared, not uncaring. I nod that I'll do it, hoping I can find the right words to be of some kind of help to someone. I take a deep breath, and Bash pulls open the door.

Taking a step into the entry, we almost trip over a young girl—red faced and arms flailing—chasing a slightly older boy with a bundle tucked under his arm. She squeaks to a stop when she sees us and lets out a wail, throwing herself at Bash—wrapping arms and legs around his leg.

"Oh 'Bastian," she sobs. "Thomas took my dolly you gave me, the one with the yellow curls like mine! He took her and he won't give her back! Make him give her back, 'Bastian, pleeeease!"

The little girl is looking up at the man next to me with blue eyes so wet with hurt and desperation that my heart does an unexpected flip flop.

Bash gently detaches the child from his leg and kneels before her, taking both her hands in his. "Annie, sometimes us boys aren't so nice. Even though Thomas loves you, he is still learning too. Sometimes he makes the wrong decision. Let's go find him and talk this out. He's your brother. You two have to stick together."

An older woman, approaches from an office doorway off to the right of the entry. Her light V-neck cardigan is a calming blue color. Worry creases her brow but disappears when she sees us and adopts a welcoming smile. She sticks a hand out to introduce herself.

"You must be the writer! We're so glad you're here. I'm Tasha," she adjusts her gaze to Sebastian and nods toward the boy now peeking out from a set of double doors further down the hallway. "Mr. Sylvain, it appears you have more pressing matters to attend to. I'll take her from here. She'll be done by noon."

I glance helplessly at Bash, who gives an encouraging smile and waves his hand in a shooing motion. We head down the hallway while he follows Annie into a room that appears to be a cozy library with row after row of reading materials, broken up by reading nooks of one or two chairs.

"Thank you so much for offering your services to us, Ms..." Tasha paused uncertainly.

"Franklin. Meg Franklin. I didn't actually know what I'd be doing today, was just wanting to help in some way. Give back, you know? But honestly, I'm no teacher. I've never taught any kind of class, much less a writing class! I'm a little nervous..." *A LOT nervous!*

Chapter 11

At the end of the hallway we reach a wall of glass with double doors leading out into a lush, green courtyard. Tasha pushes one open and leads me out. The building runs all around us, a large square, with this little paradise smack in the center.

"Oh wow, I was not expecting this when we pulled up!"

"Yes," Tasha smiles. "It's our own little slice of peace in the middle of a chaotic city. A place of kindness and refuge when life has been cruel. I'm sure Sebastian told you about what we do here?"

"He summarized as we arrived. He said he comes twice a month to teach computer skills to the women, to help them get jobs."

Tasha blinks. "That's what he said?"

Confused, I ask, "Er, yes, I think so... is that not correct?"

She waves a hand and leads me to the center of the garden space. "He's too modest. He does more than teach computer skills. Well, here we are!" she says, gesturing to a semi-circle of chairs that face a fountain, its bench area cleared for a speaker.

"The women will be assembling here over the next five minutes. Why don't you sit and collect your thoughts for a moment. The main idea of this exercise isn't to create the next Jane Austen. It's just one of the many outlets we offer to help the women process their trauma. Art therapy, writing, music, oh! And here comes my favorite now!"

A beautiful golden retriever bounds across the grass toward us. Tasha kneels down to receive his sloppy wet kisses and rewards him with a scratch behind the ears.

"George is our therapy dog. And as you can see, he's very effective. After a very stressful morning, I feel loads better already."

Indeed, the woman's face carried a true smile now, replacing the one she'd pasted on when greeting us at the door. "I'll leave you to it then! The women will come prepared with blank notebooks, a sturdy pencil and wounded but healing hearts. See what you can do for them. You may surprise yourself."

She glances at her phone and the worry lines reappear. Turning away, Tasha walks briskly back toward the building. I'm left alone for the moment in this paradoxical paradise. I can hear the sounds of the city, the roar of engines, horns honking, construction sounds. Yet, I can't see any of it. In here the noise fades to the background, and it somehow feels quieter. The greenery, pops of color from the flowers, a gurgling fountain in the center, it all works together to make this area a place of peace.

I pull out my phone and shoot a text to the Book Club, telling them where I am, what they're expecting me to do and asking for good vibes, promising to fill them in on the details later. Kristen responds before I put it away.

Maybe you've never been quite in these ladies' shoes, but Meg, you do understand loss and heartache and are literally learning to rebuild your life in the aftermath. You aren't a stranger to the concept.

Cece's reply pops up right after. *Agree, you got this! Just speak from the heart!*

I send a heart emoji in response and silence the phone, tucking it into my purse so I won't be distracted by it buzzing in my back pocket.

A small-framed woman approaches the chairs. She is so hunched that on the street I would've assumed she was much older. Her light brown hair hangs in her face. When she glances up, a pang goes through my heart. She can't be more than mid 20's. She lifts one side of her mouth in a half smile and drops her eyes again quickly. Tugging her long sleeves down, I catch a flash of yellow and green, old bruising, and a collection of scars.

Meg. You are in way over your head.

I don't have much longer to think before more show up, but I know that I have to try. These women have been let down by enough people. I won't turn away, even if I feel less than worthy to stand here.

The rest of the group files in. Eight women in total. Though features

Chapter 11

vary, just over half of the group look the same as that first woman. Heads bowed, hiding behind their hair. Three of the women carry themselves differently. They make eye contact and smile, touching the hunched women gently on the shoulder, offering a seat next to them. The women who have been here longer, presumably, who are further on their journeys of healing. I make a mental note to look to them for cues on how it's going.

It's then I realize all the chairs are full and the group of women now sit expectantly. Waiting for me... *Don't screw it up, Franklin.* I move to stand more centrally in front of the women, crossing my arms, then uncrossing them not wanting to seem closed off.

"Hi," my voice cracks. I clear it with a cough and try again. "Hi, I'm Meg. I've been asked to come today to help with a creative writing session. I, um, I'm a writer. I write news articles. But creative writing, that is, writing from the heart has always been a passion of mine. Writing got me through some tough times growing up. Writing can be a tool we use to help us process our feelings, get them out in a tangible way. You know? Have any of you ever tried writing out your feelings? Story, song, poem, a letter? Maybe taken a creative writing course in college?"

A young girl who couldn't be more than 19, with jet black hair and combat boots jeers from the seat she's slumped into, "Lady, do we look like we been to college?"

A fire burns in my cheeks red hot as I realize my error. "Um, sorry, I mean, I—"

One of the older women who'd met my gaze and given a tentative smile upon arrival turns to say, "Pipe down Brit!" Turning back to me she smiles again and says, "Thanks for not making any assumptions about us based on our current life circumstances. You were saying?"

The anxiety constricting my throat to the point of near closure eases a little. I nod and give a shaky smile in return.

"All I meant was it doesn't really matter if you've ever had a class on it or not. We're not here to worry about grammar or correct phrasing. Any writing we practice today should come from the heart. Does anyone have any examples of a time they tried writing out some feelings? Please share if you do, and tell me your name, if you don't mind. I'd like to get to know each of you."

After a moment of nauseatingly awkward silence, the woman who'd told Brit to "pipe down" raises her hand. "Rita. And yeah. When I finally had enough and gathered up my courage, I wrote a letter to my ex. Left it on the counter for him when I walked out. Not really sure the bastard can even read. His only skills seemed to be drinking and gambling away my hard-earned tips. Oh. And he had a real solid right hook."

The ladies around her nod in agreement, a sisterhood bound together by the violence and maltreatment borne at the hands of men.

I swallow the pity that wants to surface and nod encouragingly, "Yes! Rita, that's a great example. And how did it make you feel to write that out, to put your feelings on paper?"

Rita chuffs, "Felt good! Real good actually. Didn't fix anything from the past. Still had to walk away from a wasted 15 years of my life with nothing but my name and the clothes I could fit in a Walmart sack. But that letter felt like the first real thing I'd said in all those years."

Another young woman raises her hand, "I'm Penny and when I was a teenager, I used to keep a journal. It didn't stop my step-dad from coming into my room at night after my mom fell asleep, but it helped to be able to tell someone. Even if that someone was just the notebook I hid under my mattress. It always believed me when no one else did."

I nod vigorously, unable to say anything around the lump rising in my throat. *Don't cry, Meg. Do. Not. Cry. These women need empowering, not pitied.*

One more raised her hand, then stood up. Her dark brown corduroy overalls were accented by a bright orange turtleneck underneath. "When the police made me write out a report of what happened to me, they filed it away, safe. My family wouldn't speak to me afterwards. They cut me off, but I knew what I'd written was true. And not even they could take it away. It was recorded forever." She started to sit, then stood again. "Oh, and Amanda. My name is Amanda. They couldn't take that from me either."

"Ladies—Rita, Penny, Amanda—thank you for sharing. This is what writing can do for us. It gives a voice to our feelings, tangibility to our past experiences. It helps untangle the web of thoughts in our minds and can apply a healing balm to the hurting heart. It shines a light on the deepest, darkest places inside us and, even if no one else ever sees it, we see it. And we can begin to heal.

"That's what this class is all about. Not about becoming the next best selling author. It's not about writing the prettiest or most profound words. It's about baring your soul, telling your story. Because secrets have power. Secrets destroy. And when we hold our secrets inside, they maintain control. But when we dig them up and shine a light, they lose a lot of that power. The hurt may remain but hurt can heal when we regain control of our lives."

All eyes were on me now, and something was welling inside of me that I couldn't name. *Time to wrap it up. You've opened the gates, now let them come through themselves.*

"Ladies, you've got your paper and you've got your shovel—in this case, a pencil. Let's dig to uncover the hurt inside, so that healing can truly begin. Don't even think too much. Just put pencil to paper and write. Start with your name. I am Meg. This is my story. And flow from there."

The women before me looked down into their laps, opened their composition books and began. Some wrote their intro as instructed and kept on writing. Others wrote the opening line and stalled. I knew the feeling. I wasn't worried. I could see in their eyes a spark of something. They just needed time.

Checking my watch, I'm shocked to find most of the hour is already gone. And here I had been so worried over how to possibly fill the time. About 10 minutes later, I feel that tingle. It was quickly becoming familiar. I glance around the courtyard and find Bash standing just outside one of the doorways, leaning against the frame in that casual, devil-may-care kind of way. He grinned at me, and I felt it all the way down to my toes.

Tasha pushes through the door a moment later and approaches our group.

"Alright ladies, I think that's all Meg has time for today. I hope you've found it helpful in your healing journeys. As you—yes, Brit?"

I'm shocked to see that particular hand, chipped black polish and all, in the air.

"Yeah, uh, when is she coming back? You know, to read our assignments?" Brit asks, motioning to her composition book where she's already filled two pages.

Tasha turns toward me expectantly as I feel my eyes widen. "Oh, ah, yes if you'd like to share, we could do this again? Tasha, I don't really know the schedule here..." I flounder.

She turns back to address the group. "Meg will be back in one month to revisit with you and see your work. Ok? Alright everyone, it's now lunch hour. Let's head into the dining room. Chop chop!"

A moment later I'm standing alone near the fountain. Well, nearly alone. Bash has come up quietly beside me, his hand brushing my lower back and sending a spark through me.

"So," he states evenly, "from what I could see, that went extremely well."

I turn to him, bubbling, "Bash, oh my gosh, I can hardly believe it but it did! I was so terrified; I had no idea what to say to these women.

Chapter 11

Honestly. And first I thought I'd really bombed it, but this one lady, Rita, really came to my rescue. Then we started connecting. I was really connecting with a few of them. And when it was time for them to write, so many of their pencils just flew across the page. The words were just bubbling inside of them. It was incredible! I feel... I don't even know how to say how I feel but it's amazing. Really amazing."

My smile is so wide I think it might crack. Sebastian smiles back, knowingly. "I thought you might like it here." He reaches for my hand, and I take it—without thinking. In that moment, it just feels right. Like we've done this thing together, but also, my heart swells knowing I did something on my own.

The doubt creeps in a moment later, deflating me like a balloon as I remember the gravity of the situations these women have faced. "I mean it was just a writing class... it's not like I saved these women or healed their trauma. They've been through so much. Maybe I didn't even help them at all."

He lifts my chin with his free hand so that I meet his eyes. So. So blue. "Don't do that. Don't minimize your contribution. No one can do everything for these women. A lot of it they have to do themselves. This place, anyone who works or volunteers here, just gives them the tools and support to do it. But only if they want to. They have to want it too. We can't put the will to heal and work through their hurt in them. This is just one of many tools, and today, you handed them a shiny new shovel."

We walk back through the building to exit out the front. I can hear the sound of silverware clattering on dishes and happy banter between some of the women, a whine from little Annie about Thomas stealing her roll. Going back out through the heavy wooden door, the noises and busyness of the city really crash back in.

"Out here is the real challenge," Bash says, heading to open the passenger door of his sedan for me. "In there, they exist in a peaceful, protected environment. But they can't stay forever. The real challenge is helping them be healed enough and strong enough to face the outside world again. A world that has repeatedly hurt them, beaten them down, stolen their hope and joy. It's—" he blows out a breath. "It's not easy. And it doesn't always work. Sometimes the women leave here and end up right back in the same bad situations they were in before. Sometimes even worse."

The burden that falls on his shoulders as he speaks is visible as he stands waiting for me to get into the car. I reach out to place a hand on his arm.

"Hey, the work you're doing here. The work Tasha and the others are doing. It matters. If out of every ten women that come through here, only one is able to build a healthy life, then it was worth it for that one. If one child comes out from this place knowing that a better life is possible, then it was worth it."

His gaze locks with mine, weighing my words. "I know you're right. I just… I just wish there was more we could do."

I give his arm a squeeze and slip into the cool dark interior of the car. The autumn air has a crispness to it today. Bash slides into the driver's side, starting the purring engine with the push of a button. He reaches over and turns on my seat warmer, his forearm brushing my hand settled between us. I shiver—not from the cold—and smile as he pulls away from the curb.

"Lunch?" he asks with a grin.

"I'd love nothing more," I answer.

Chapter 12

The book club gathers the following week on Sunday night, per our usual once a month routine. The happy chatter sharing our kids' news drops off more quickly than usual. Looking at my two friends gathered here, I find them both staring, waiting expectantly.

"Hey... what's going on, girls?"

Kristen pipes up first, "Don't play coy with us, missy. We want to know what's going on with YOU and a certain someone whose name starts with S, E, B, A..."

I laugh and wave her off rolling my eyes, "Yeah I know how to spell it." I feign a heavy sigh but can't stop the smile that plays across my lips.

Cece points at my expression and singsongs, "Called it! You're a goner. We knew it." She exchanges a smug look with Kristen.

"O-kay you two, don't gang up on me now! I thought this was a supportive group!" I laugh chucking a throw pillow at Cece.

Kristen adds, "Oh we support you alright. Now give us the deets so we can be well-informed in our incredible support." Both lean in toward me eagerly, and I feel like a monkey on display at the zoo.

"Keep your shirts on, ladies," I say taking another sip of my pumpkin spice latte. Definitely a second favorite. "You guys know about the women's shelter already. And yesterday we had a picnic lunch on the Southbank Riverwalk. It felt… nice."

"Nice?!" Kristen questions accusingly. "That dreamy look in your eye suggests it was better than nice!"

"Ok, ok, it felt like… something. Like it could be a thing, you know? But you guys know how I feel already. I just don't know if I can do this. He wants to take me on a little day trip this Saturday to, I don't know look at leaves or something. When we're together, I feel like he's holding back. Like he's waiting on me to make the decision if we can be an 'us' again. It's a lot of pressure!

"Plus, we've been down this road before! It didn't work out for us. You guys were there last time. You remember the fallout—the year of heartbreak. I don't want to go through that again. I can't go through that again. I've been through enough."

I can't meet their gaze after laying it out like that so I study the mug in my hands. Cece and Kristen leave their seats to come sit on either side of me, forming what we've dubbed as our "club huddle."

"It's ok to be scared, Meg," Cece breaks the silence. "Your feelings are completely valid. We just don't want to see you alone forever. I know it feels soon. There's no way you could've predicted Sebastian would show up in your life again like this. I think you owe it to yourself, if you even think you may want it, to give it a chance."

Kristen's hand rests on my shoulder as she says, "You don't have to sign away the deed to your heart to give it a chance. It's been amazing these past couple weeks seeing you smile again."

A little crack in my armor shows when a tear slips through. "You guys are the best, do you know that? Thanks for being here, like you've always been here."

I grab a tissue and dab at my eyes, "Now let's get back to our regularly

Chapter 12

scheduled event, yeah? Cece, how was your latest small town romance? Did that rough cowboy win the town florist's heart? And Kristen, I want to know what you thought about that suspense you just finished. Did you see the twist coming or was this one a total surprise? We can't exactly call ourselves a book club if we don't talk at least a little about our books!"

We launch into a lively discussion over our latest reads and upcoming releases we're all adding to our TBR lists. By the time our evening ends, I feel a flicker of hope. A faint glimmer of "try." And I think I'm ready.

* * *

Sebastian's promptness doesn't surprise me when the doorbell rings this time. I open the door wearing what I think is the smile of a woman excited to spend the day with an old friend. But he must catch something in my eyes because the first words out of his mouth are, "What is it, Meg?"

I laugh nervously, waving him off. "What a way to greet a person! Geez, Bash."

But he doesn't waver. "Sorry for skipping the niceties but it's written all over your face. Something's up. What is it?"

Literally, the man is a mind reader. I fiddle with the ribbed hem of my sweater. "I, well, I was going to wait til you dropped me off. I didn't want to start our day together with it. But I guess you're a little too sharp for that so follow me."

I turn from the entry and head to the office, keenly aware of his presence behind me. The room is cool and dark. The curtains have stayed drawn as I've been avoiding coming in here too often. Picking up a letter from the desk, I hold it out to him.

"I—I got this letter just yesterday. Well, technically Rob did. Anyway, it was about an account. A checking account. At a different bank from the one we usually used. They sent a notice because the account was close to going dormant with almost 12 months of no activity. It doesn't have much in it, a few hundred dollars. But..."

Sebastian had been studying the letter, but his eyes flick up to mine at my hesitation. He doesn't push though. Just waits for me to continue, calmly holding my gaze. I grip the corner of the desk to steady myself and continue.

"So, I tried logging in to the bank's website. After a few guesses using our regular passwords with Rob's email address, I got in." I try to breathe through the pounding in my ears.

His blue eyes hold mine steadily. "You're feeling anxious because you didn't know about this account?"

"No, I didn't know about it. But that's not what's upsetting." I run my hands through my hair and pace a few steps behind the desk. *Just say it. Put it out there. It's not protecting you to keep it in.* It erupts out of me in a flurry of words.

"It upset me because I don't understand what I saw. Every month—as far back as the online history would go—$2,000 was deposited, then a wire transfer went out at the end of the month. Like clockwork up until last December. I tried calling the bank, but they wouldn't give me information on the wire transfers. I guess that's secure, and I'm not on the account. They closed the account now, because I told them Rob had passed. They're sending a check for the remaining balance to his estate.

"But what was this money for? I checked our regular checking account. I can see the money hit this account on the same day his paychecks went into our account twice a month. So he must've split his direct deposit. But where was it going? Who is he paying every month? What is happening? Who was I married to?"

I realize my voice has reached a fever pitch, raising with each

Chapter 12

question by the time Bash's arm comes around me in a blanket of warmth and reassurance. I lean into him, thankful for something to anchor me in this moment.

He pulls back to place both hands on my shoulders—his go to move to stabilize me. His eyes are sober but without judgment. "Thank you for bringing this to me, Meg. We haven't made much progress on trying to track the Cayman Islands account. We've got the account ID number, but linking that to an actual face is tougher. That's the allure of these accounts. But wire transfers are a bit easier to look into."

He pauses for a moment. Letting that settle.

"I know it's easier said than done, but leave this with me for now and let's try to enjoy our day. That is, if you still want to go?"

I pull in a deep breath, less shaky than the one prior, and nod. "Yeah. I mean yes, I do want to go. Honestly, I think I could use the distraction."

"Alright," he says, taking my hand and leading me to the door. "Let's do this."

Five minutes later, we're merging onto the interstate, the soothing sounds of a string quartet covering popular songs drifting through the speakers and settling the anxiety I'd unleashed earlier. I still didn't get where we were going, but I was just happy to be anywhere but at home with my thoughts.

"So, you're taking me somewhere you've been before? What's with all the secrets anyway?"

Sebastian's eyes slide from the expressway to me with a grin. "Nope, I haven't been. But I'm hoping it will feel familiar to you," he answers.

"...even though you don't think I've been there before," I state, puzzled.

"Correct. I mean it's possible, I don't know everywhere you've been for the last 20 years," he shrugs.

That stings a little—how long we'd gone without knowing anything about each other. I have no regrets because I loved Rob and without him, Jared wouldn't have existed. Yet, I'm learning that conflicting feelings can often co-exist. I'm trying to adapt, although my first instinct is to resist. I don't like messy. I like clear, black-and-white feelings. Unfortunately, those seem few and far between these days. *Or maybe life has always been more complicated and you just didn't want to see it.* Maybe.

We've been driving on the interstate for close to an hour chatting about the season, Jared, Scarlett and Rebecca, and the hobbies we've developed over the years. Primarily reading and writing for me with a little crochet thrown in when the weather gets cool. Boating for him in the summers and, much to my delight, he was still an avid reader.

"I still can't believe you have a boat now. When I was a kid, anyone who had a boat was the absolute coolest to me."

"That's still true, we are the coolest," he says teasingly with a wink. "I'd love to take you out some time. It's getting too cool out now but maybe if we hit a warm sunny day and bundle up."

My heart jumps into my throat at the idea of making future plans with this particular man, and I swallow it down before answering. "Yeah, I'd like that."

A billboard for a lawyer catches my eye and my mind leaps back to Rob and my confusion over the growing, multi-layered mysteries now surrounding his death. Bash must sense my shift in thoughts because he reaches across the console to squeeze my hand. "Hey, where did you go?"

I pinch my lips together and shrug. Not wanting to talk more about it for now. My thoughts are all over the place and the imagined scenarios in my mind now were stretching into even more dark schemes with the money going out of the secret account each month. Voicing them, I'd probably sound like a lunatic. *If the shoe fits...*

Bash must sense my need for silence in this moment because he doesn't push, shifting to merge the car smoothly off the interstate onto

Chapter 12

a state highway. I haven't the foggiest idea where we're going, because most of my married life travel was done outside the state, or even outside the country. This late October day is perfect for a drive. The leaves are transforming from green to rich red, vibrant yellow and deep orange. It's lovely, and I'm intent on enjoying it.

About 20 minutes later, we've arrived. A quaint sign reads "Woodstock, established 1844, population 25,646."

"Woodstock? You're taking me to Woodstock?" I pull a stoned face and hold up two fingers in a peace sign for emphasis.

He laughs, "Well, not *THAT* Woodstock. That one's in New York. But yes, A Woodstock. I can't make any promises, but from what I've read, I think you'll like it."

He follows signs to the town square, and I pull in a breath. I've definitely not been here before, yet it does feel somehow familiar. The town square is the definition of quaint with its brick paved roads, old-fashioned lamp posts, small businesses, and the center park-like setting with paved paths and trees in varying stages of turning to red. A gazebo stands in the very heart of it, lights strung up around it and into the trees—unlit in this early afternoon hour. Sebastian parallel parks along the square, a skill I never quite mastered, and we get out to breathe in the crisp, sun-soaked air.

"Feels like you've been here before even though you haven't, right?" he asks from behind me. He's close enough that his breath skitters across my neck and down my spine. I grab my sweater from the car and wrap it around me tight. *As though the shiver was from the autumn air. Right.*

"Yes!" I answer a little too exuberantly. "It's like when you have a word on the tip of your tongue but you can't quite access it to say it." I rack my brain a moment, then turn toward him. "Ok, I give up. What is this place?"

He holds an elbow out to me, and I take it, matching my stride with his as we walk by the shops. It happens so naturally I refuse to read too much into it. I can feel the warmth of his skin through the thin knit of his charcoal gray sweater. I'm beginning to suspect that he only owns black, gray, and dark navy clothes as that's been all I've seen him in so far.

"Two reasons I thought—and maybe hoped—it might feel familiar. First, Groundhog Day was filmed here. Not in Pennsylvania. This is the real Punxsutawney." He gestures his free arm around us.

"Second, and the real reason I brought you here is because I read this town is considered the Midwest's real life Stars Hollow."

My feet stop on the pavement and my jaw drops. Eyes snapping up, his earnest smile melts me.

"You acted like you hated watching Gilmore Girls with me!" I squeal, smacking him on the shoulder. "Oh my gosh, I KNEW you secretly loved it. Oh, you are something else. Where should we start then? Wait. If it's Stars Hollow, then the obvious choice is COFFEE!"

We head down the red paver-laid path to a little bookshop with a sidewalk sign promoting their pumpkin spice lattes. Once inside, Bash gives me space to do my favorite thing in the world—browse the book aisles sipping my latte without a care in the world. We meet back towards the front of the store after an hour, me with a new romantasy three-book series by an indie author, him with his own small stack.

"Steve Jobs? Really, Bash?" I ask, leaning over to eyeball his top book. He shrugs, "Can't deny the man's success!"

He pays for our books, despite my insistence on buying my own.

I'd have to work on that with him. I've never really been the type of girl who wants the guy paying for everything. It was why I always worked at least part time, even after Rob moved up the ladder at the law firm. Despite enjoying a good romance read, I wasn't a damsel in distress. I related more to the sword-swinging heroines who rode the backs of dragons, at least in my mind. *Meg, he brought you to a real*

Chapter 12

version of your favorite TV show town, buys you coffee and BOOKS?! Quit complaining and MARRY HIM! Back in your box, Margaret.

Out on the sidewalk, he reaches for my hand. I feel like a teenage girl again, marveling at his long fingers threaded between mine. His thumb occasionally brushes back and forth over my knuckle, a subtle way of conveying thoughts I'm not sure I'm ready to hear. *Chicken.* But I can't deny the feelings it sparks in me, all the way down to my toes.

We stop in a local store, full of beautiful handmade items ranging from soaps to hand crushed locally grown herbs to leather, wood and glass goods. I pick up a hand painted unicorn for Daisy and a vintage rattle for Oliver. Bash picks out a hand sewn, buttery-soft leather crossbody for his niece and a soy candle for his sister.

"I can't believe it's already this close to Thanksgiving," I say, as we stroll to the gazebo in the town square, our bags left behind in his car. "I should start working on my menu. Amelia teases me about putting too much time and effort into the holiday but considering her version of cooking is bringing a frozen pumpkin pie to the house and heating it up in MY oven, I don't bother to listen to her thoughts on the matter."

We sit down on a bench together to watch a group of children play hide-n-seek in the bushes and trees of the park. Bash leans back to rest one ankle on the opposite knee. His arm stretches across the back of the bench. *Good grief, just scoot over already. If that isn't an open invitation, I don't know what is!*

I bend forward, pretending to adjust something with my shoe, then slide over as I sit up, hoping that makes it less obvious. *Smooooth.* I can feel every millimeter of contact between us—his arm heavy across the top of my shoulders, his hand brushing my upper arm, the small space where our legs touch. I can't help it, I lean in even further. He smells like the soft leather of his jacket, mixed with spearmint. My lips curve up as it takes me right back to high school. He smelled almost exactly the same then.

Reading my mind, he reaches into his jacket pocket and pulls the pack of gum I already suspected he was carrying out to offer me a piece.

"I knew I smelled spearmint," I answer, taking one. "My favorite! You still carry a pack, like you did in high school?"

"Always," he answers, staring out across the park. He slides the pack back into his pocket without taking one himself.

"So, Thanksgiving. Will you, Rebecca and Scarlet go down to see your folks or will they come up here?"

"Actually, they'll all be in Europe for Thanksgiving," he answers. I look up and see his eyes gleam with pride. "Some of Rebecca's reclaimed art pieces are being displayed at a big gala in Paris that week. She's going early and our parents are bringing Scarlet a few days after to support her. I'd go too but I've got some big meetings in the office and couldn't make the timing work."

Margaret lights up my brain like a Christmas tree. I smack him lightly across the chest in surprise and ask, "And were you going to tell me that you'd be alone for Thanksgiving?"

He smiles mischievously and sneaks a look at me out of the corner of his eye, "I might have been hoping you'd ask…"

"Ok, obviously you'll be coming over to my house then. It's settled. Jared is coming home and, if you're alright with it, I'd love for you to meet him and for him to meet you. Plus, Amelia will be dying to spice things up with inappropriate questions while Mark tries and fails to smooth things over. Oliver may be a little fussy from teething. Honestly though Daisy will be the most important one to impress, so you'd best say yes when she asks to paint your nails bubblegum pink," I say, throwing down the gauntlet.

"Sounds like a good time, what can I bring?" he replies smoothly. Challenge accepted.

Chapter 12

I laugh, and he looks deeply offended. "What? You don't think I can cook? I can cook, Meg. I'm very good at following directions." He says it with a quirked eyebrow that suggests he doesn't just mean in the kitchen.

I blush and swallow to reply, "Hm, we'll see. As for Thanksgiving dinner, how about we keep it simple, and you can bring a pie. Store bought is fine."

He tilts his chin down to bring his lips near my ear where his breath tickles the sensitive shell, "Prepare to be impressed. My made-from-scratch crust is sure to knock your pants off."

My eyes go wide. "Don't you mean socks? Knock my socks off?"

He shrugs, feigning innocence, "I've heard it both ways. Shall we grab some dinner before we head back to the city? How does a local cafe sound? I'm not actually sure there's much more around."

"It sounds perfect," I manage to say, despite the butterflies dancing a jig all over my insides. *You are toast, Meg Franklin. Absolute freaking toast.* Tucking some hair behind one ear, I walk out of the park trying to exude far more confidence than I feel down inside.

Chapter 13

You really should not have had that 4th cup... By 2:00 Thanksgiving Day I am positively vibrating. I think I can feel the caffeine in every cell of my body. But I didn't sleep well last night and got up early to put the turkey in. So those repeat shots of espresso seemed like a good idea at the time.

"Mom?" Jared calls down the stairs. "Have you seen my red flannel anywhere? I know how you like us to dress for the season and all."

"Yep, it's hanging in your closet! I ironed it last night," I call back, my face splitting into an even wider smile. I'd picked him up from O'Hare yesterday afternoon and it felt so, so good to have him home. Even if it was only for a few days. I had been a little nervous to tell him about inviting Bash over for Thanksgiving dinner. But he'd been typical Jare about it. Listened quietly, asked a few questions then responded with kindness and support. This 18-year-old had greater emotional maturity than most people my age.

"We did good, Rob," I whisper to the stove, wiping my hands on my apron.

One hour to go til the guests arrive. Time to put in the casseroles. I'm so nervous my hands are shaking. Or maybe it's the espresso. *Both,*

Chapter 13

definitely both. You'll likely drop the turkey platter carrying it from the kitchen. Won't that be fun!

I smile to myself as I pop one particular dish into the oven, wondering if he'll notice. I've got quite a spread ready for today, so he might not. I've been prepping and cooking all week. But it's my family. They're worth it.

The house smells amazing and, if I do say so myself, looks pretty good too. The table is a beautiful display of my Gram's china, handmade name cards and brass candlesticks positioned in the faux fall foliage. I may not have a natural eye for decorating but I'm well-versed in Pinterest. With it being Jared's first visit back home since starting school and our first thanksgiving without Rob... I just want everything perfect.

Jared comes down the stairs looking like a dashing lumberjack and restores the smile to my face. He lets out a low whistle. "Mom, wow. You've outdone yourself. You know Aunt Amelia's going to rag on you for overdoing it right?"

We both chuckle, knowing its true. She's always teased that I brought the sugar to the family, and she brought the spice. All I know is that my life would be far more boring without her.

The doorbell rings and Jared turns saying, "I'll get it!"

It takes everything in me to not stop him from opening the door. Based on the timeliness, I know it's Bash on the other side. Amelia and Mark will absolutely be late, so it can only be him. My heart is pounding in my chest knowing my son is about to greet the man I was once head-over-heels in love with. A man who now is sparking feelings in me that I've been skirting around in my brain for the past few months. *Deep breaths, Meg. In. And out. Good. Now try not to let your son see you mooning too much over your old boyfriend across the table.*

My face feels so flushed I suspect it matches the cranberry sauce I've just set on the table as voices float through from the entryway. I smooth my hair a little and try to cool my cheeks with the back of my hand as I hurry into the living room to greet our first guest.

"Bash! Er, Sebastian, I see you've met my son, Jared," I say stupidly, interrupting the conversation between the two.

Sebastian's gaze meets mine and his smile washes over me like a soothing bath but is quickly replaced by concern. "You feeling alright, Meg?"

He crosses the living room in a few steps and his hands are on me then, one gripping my shoulder lightly as the other tests the temperature of my forehead. Jared's eyes widen from the entry, then narrow on us. If possible, I flush even brighter and brush Sebastian off with a weak laugh making an excuse about overheating from cooking in the kitchen all day. Jared grabs the pecan pie Sebastian had set down on the table and takes it into the kitchen before returning.

"Maybe you'd better sit a minute, yeah? Jared was just telling me about his first semester. Sounds like his advanced chem class is a real bear. Completely unforgiving professor, you were saying Jared?"

Jared is nodding his head then, gaze darting back and forth between Sebastian and I while his head just keeps on bobbing, the gears of his mind visibly turning. *Well, isn't this just going dandy.*

"I have some last items to pull from the stove. You two can continue getting to know each other. I'm sure Amelia and her brood will be along soon."

Jared snorts and rolls his eyes, "Yeah if 45 minutes late is soon!"

Bash says quietly, "Let me help. Jared, you cool on door duty?"

Jared hesitates before nodding, meeting my gaze for confirmation from me before heading to the armchair closest to the door, pulling out his phone. I sneak out a long quiet breath as Bash follows me through the dining room into the kitchen.

"Hey, the place looks amazing! I guess you found your fall decor after all," he teases with a wink.

Chapter 13

"Oh yes, Martha Stewart herself came over and helped me pull the boxes down from the attic. I thought you'd appreciate the gesture since you'd seen my previous lack," I reply, grabbing a potholder and pulling open the oven door.

I grab the first casserole pan and slide it out of the oven, pivoting to place it on the island behind me. Searing pain registers in my brain mid-turn as the heat of the glass pan scorches my ring finger. "Gah!" I yell, dropping the pan, jumping back out of instinct before it hits the floor and shatters into a festive mix of seasoned stuffing and glittering glass.

Bash is on me in an instant, grabbing me with concerned hands. "Where are you hurt? Did it burn you?"

"Ouch, yes, dang it. I forgot that potholder has a small hole in it, been meaning to replace it," I tell him, pulling in a hissing breath.

Without a word, Sebastian picks me up by my forearms, stepping over the mess on the floor to the sink. Jared skids around the door frame as Bash turns on the water to hold my hand under the cool stream.

"Hey future doc," he calls casually over his shoulder without taking his eyes off the red welt pulsing on my fingertip. "Got any burn cream around here?" Seeing the mess and Sebastian holding my fingertip under the water, Jared jumps into action.

"Let me see. Ooh. Yeah. You got it good. Just first degree though, I'm thinking. Keep holding it under the cool water. Cool, not cold, ok? I'm gonna raid the linen closet medicine basket." I hear him bound up the steps and open the closet upstairs. I move to pull my hand back from the water, but Bash's grip around my wrist is firm.

"Listen," I say twisting my head to look up at him with a frown. "This is not a big deal! It's just a little burn. I don't need the A-team springing into action."

"Meg," Sebastian says, taking the serious tone one might with a small child who is learning how to listen. "When the men in your life want to take care of you, don't resist. Just let us take care of you."

So now he's part of the men in your life? Swoon. As the pain from the burn dulls a little under the water, I notice more than just his hand on my wrist. One arm wraps around my waist, holding me up in front of the sink while the other holds my finger under the water. More than just my finger is burning when I hear Jared pounding down the stairs and jump back, away from Bash before he rounds the corner.

"Got it!" Jared hollers, sliding around the corner into the kitchen. Sebastian backs away to let Jared take the lead on treating my burn, and I feel like that errant child.

"Thanks, Jare," I say, as movement behind him catches my eye. "Oh no, Bash, don't clean that up, I've got it."

He's bent over the mess on the floor scooping the mix of glass and my made from scratch spicy stuffing into a pile for the trash. Grabbing the dustpan, we clear the mess together. I groan in disappointment as we dump all that beautiful dressing in the trash can.

"It smelled amazing. We'll have to live vicariously through its aroma," Bash says with a smile, placing his hand over his heart. "Rest in peace, stuffing."

Twenty minutes later Mark, Amelia and two sleeping kids have arrived. I dug out a box of Stove Top I'd bought as an "emergency backup" in case this new recipe didn't turn out. We're sitting down now piling our plates high with all the goods. My heart is warm as I look around at these people, my family. Well, plus Bash. *Don't you think maybe he...* Nope. Don't even go there. Too soon.

I dish out some of the green bean casserole onto my plate, and pass it to Bash, watching him surreptitiously out of the corner of my eye. He scoops out a large helping and takes a bite after passing it on. His eyes close and he sighs in contentment. Then they fly open.

"Wait a second, this is my granny's green bean casserole recipe!" He

Chapter 13

catches my gaze, shocked. "How?"

I blush scarlet as everyone else at the table pauses to hear my response. I take a sip of my drink and answer, "I, well, I know it's always been your favorite. And I thought since she had passed, that is, I hope you don't mind, I reached out to Rebecca—Facebook you know—and she got it from your mom for me. It's really not a big deal."

Squirming under the attention, I finally meet his gaze. He's staring at me in awe, his blue eyes so... full. I catch Amelia arching one eyebrow out of the corner of my eye, smug as the Cheshire cat.

"Thank you," he whispers, just for me to hear, reaching under the table to give my hand a squeeze.

"So. Sebastian," Amelia says loudly, emphasizing each syllable of his name as she dishes out more mashed potatoes onto Mark's plate while he checks the kids. Oliver is asleep in his car seat in the living room and Daisy is snoozing on the couch beside him. She'd fallen asleep on the ride over, and we couldn't bear to wake her just yet. She had an absolute angelic look while asleep.

I tilt my head and shoot Amelia a warning glare which she promptly ignores. *Buckle up, because here we go!*

"What exactly are your intentions with my baby sister? Again."

I nearly choke on a bite of roasted turkey I just put in my mouth. Thank goodness for that gravy to help it go down. Sebastian just smiles easily at Amelia.

"For pity's sake, Amelia, we just sat down!" I let out a huff of air and bury my face in my hands.

Between my fingers I see Jared smirking at my discomfort and raising his hand like he's in a lecture to add, "Oh yes, I'd like to know too!"

"Ugh, being around your delinquent aunt always brings out the worst in you, son."

"Hey!" Amelia smacks the table in protest. "I'm a reformed delinquent! Look at me now, responsible for creating and maintaining human life and happily married to boot! Who would've thought, honestly."

"Well, that's something we can agree on," I groan and roll my eyes.

Sebastian pats me on the arm reassuringly, "I don't mind you asking, but I'm not sure how to answer either as I'm only one side of the equation. What I can say is that I don't believe we reconnected by chance. That if out of all the conferences in all the world Meg had to walk into mine, it's worth seeing what's here. But I fully recognize she's been through a lot. You all have," he says looking around the table, eyes landing on Jared. "I'm not going to push her into anything she's not ready for. I'm a patient guy."

And with that he returns to his plate, eating peacefully as if he wasn't just put on the spot by my sister and her favorite nephew. I shake my head in amazement. Mark, sensing the need for his calming presence, speaks up with some well formulated questions to Jared about his class load. God bless Mark.

Daisy wakes and wanders to the table rubbing "sleepies" out of her eyes, as Jared used to say. Her curls are wildly tousled and the turkey embroidered on her shirt is wrinkled from the couch. Seeing her come into the dining room, Sebastian stands to pull her chair out for her with a flourish of his wrist.

"Ah," he says with a slight British accent. "You must be the lovely Princess Daisy I've heard so much about! Sir Sebastian, at your service. Pleasure to meet you milady."

Daisy's surprise quickly melts into adoration as she beams back at him.

"Thank you, good sir," she says primly, climbing up into the chair to sit with absolute propriety. "Mom," she whispers toward Amelia, "he sounds like Peppa Pig!"

Dropping her royal manners for a heaping bite of mashed potatoes, she asks with her mouth stuffed, "So, are you my new uncle or what?"

Chapter 13

I choke on my drink, and Bash gives me a few good whacks on the back. Scooping up the closest item in front of me, I stand and hold up the basket loudly asking, "Rolls? Rolls anyone?!" as the rest of the table laughs at me from behind their napkins.

"Ope, looks like we're out. I'll just go refresh this in the kitchen!"

I run out of the room, clutching the basket to me like a lifeline tossed out to a man drowning at sea.

Setting the basket down, I take a few deep breaths and open the freezer door to stick my head into the fog trying to cool down. Big emotions tend to do that to me, drain the blood from my extremities to pump it all into my overheated face.

Closing the freezer after a few moments, I find Sebastian leaning against the counter, arms and ankles crossed, a wry grin on his face. I have the most ridiculous urge to run my fingers through that perfectly tousled dark hair. He'd let it grow a little longer in the months since I'd first run into him again. It now falls on his forehead a bit, more like it did when we were teenagers.

Tipping his chin up to indicate the dining room he asks, "Little much in there for you, Meg? Your Wisconsin always comes out in times of stress. The holidays can be a tricky time, you know."

I turn away to grab a rag from the sink and start wiping down counters. "Oh, no, it's fine. I'm fine! You know, I kind of forgot how you were. In there with Daisy? I remember you being that way with your little sister. The only 16-year-old I knew who would put on his pirate costume and battle his kid sister for the treasure buried beneath the treehouse. It was, um, it was nice to see that side of you again."

I finally gather enough courage to meet his eyes, but he's staring out the window over the sink now, having shifted to stand at the island. Standing closer now to me, while still giving me space.

"You know, I've spent a lot of years in corporate at this point. I'd kind of forgotten that part of me too, maybe. I guess you bring me back. Remind me who I was. Who I still am, somewhere in here."

He meets my stare, then grabs the basket from the counter, eyes crinkling in the corners. "So did you actually have more rolls for this thing or...?"

"Huh? Oh, yeah I do. I was keeping them warm in the oven."

We return to the dining room, basket full. Amelia's eyebrows are practically arched into her hairline at this point.

"So!" Amelia starts again, but Mark swoops in saying, "We're going to my folks' place this year for Christmas. Did Ames get the chance to tell you yet? I hope you don't mind, but my grandmother's health is really declining, and my mom wanted to be sure we had one more Christmas together."

Amelia shoots ocular daggers at Mark, who shrugs apologetically and winces as Daisy claps her hands and squeals "Yay for Grandma Nancy and Pop Pop!"

"*No*, I hadn't had a chance to tell Meg yet so *thank you so very much, Mark*," she says through bared teeth, saying his name like a bad word.

Turning toward me apologetically her eyes soften as she says, "I was going to tell you before we left tonight, I swear. I'm really sorry, I—I didn't want to be gone then. At least not this... well, this first year."

I swallow hard and force a smile on my face, waving a hand in her direction, "Oh, don't be silly. Of course, you should go see your in-laws! I wouldn't want Mark or the kids to miss what could be his grandma's last. I'd never forgive myself if I was the cause. We'll be fine, right Jare?"

Jared must catch the edge of desperation in my voice because he latches on quickly to respond, "Oh yeah absolutely. Actually, Aunt Amelia, I was going to suggest Mom and I take a trip together. Wouldn't that be cool? I could fly out from New York and meet her somewhere exotic, you know? If you're up for it, Mom. I thought..." he pauses

Chapter 13

and tucks both lips in for a moment as he meets my eyes. "I thought it might be easier to... you know, be someplace else."

Someplace else. Someplace other than the house we spent our last Christmas with Rob in. Someplace other than the living room full of memories of us gathered around the tree, Rob wearing that silly Santa hat to pass out presents. Someplace other than the crackling fireplace where instead of three stockings, only two would hang. Someplace that didn't have the same couch where we'd propped baby Jared up in his "my first Christmas" sleeper for Rob to snap a hundred photos as I posed him with fake presents scattered around because we couldn't afford professional photos those first few years. Someplace, anyplace other than here.

I clear my throat to keep my voice from cracking, "That sounds great, kiddo. See, sis? We won't even be here either! Let's hope I can find an opening at this time of year. I've heard holiday tropical getaways are becoming all the rage." I tuck my hair behind my ears and busy myself arranging the now half empty platters on the table.

Amelia's opening her mouth like she's searching for a compromise, when Bash cuts in saying, "I think I know a perfect place."

We all turn to look at him in surprise. "Really?" Amelia asks. "What did you have in mind cyber guy?"

"I've been to this one spot in Dominica that is absolutely breathtaking. I have a connection there. I'll reach out next week and see if I can get you two one of their villas for that week. I bet my guy can make something work."

Amelia arches that eyebrow again and turns to Mark with her glass raised, "Did you hear that, honey? He has a *guy*. With *villas*." She dips her chin for emphasis and takes a drink.

Mark nods seriously and replies, "Remember when I got us moved up in line at the DMV babe, because my old college roommate was working the counter? How about those connections, hm?"

He winks at her as she snorts, "Oh yes, my love, verrrry impressive that was."

Mark turns to Bash, "It's like a resort type place? Beachfront? For being born and raised in the Midwest, these two sure are hardcore beach girls."

Bash sets down his glass and grins at me in an "I know" sort of way that sets my stomach swirling before answering. "Yeah, it's a nice little resort, private villas right there on the ocean. It's very relaxing. Might be the perfect place to do some writing," he adds with a loaded look in my direction.

He's been badgering me to write a book ever since the 10th grade when I first told him my dream was to be a published author. It's still a dream, but one I keep close to the chest. It just feels so out of reach. *Just put it back in your "maybe someday" file, Meg. That's worked out great for you so far.*

"Speaking of writing," my attention shoots back to Bash, wondering where he's going with this. "Has your sister told you about the classes she's been giving at Angel House women's and children's shelter?"

"She told me back in September when she first went... wait, classES? As in, you've done more of them?" Amelia asks, a mix between happy and accusatory that I didn't tell her.

When I don't jump to answer, Bash fills in the details as I feel my cheeks redden with the attention.

"Oh yes, the women enjoyed the class so much they begged her to come back. We usually don't repeat the same class every month, but they insisted. She's already done another class this month and has one scheduled for next, alongside a story session for the children currently in the house. When I stopped by last week, I had a few asking when she's coming again as they had journal entries they wanted to share with her. She's really making a difference. Some of them I've never seen so engaged."

Chapter 13

The way he's looking at me has my heart expanding in my chest followed by warmth pooling in my belly. *That's the look. Remember? Haven't you missed that feeling? Haven't you missed being cherished?*

"Well," Mark breaks the cord of tension between Bash and I with a word. Thank goodness for Mark. "That's positively wonderful. I think Amelia and I will take care of the cleanup since you did all the setup and cooking. Why don't you three spend a little time with the kids? It sounds like Oliver just woke up. He's got a bottle ready to go in the bag, if you wouldn't mind, Auntie Meg?"

I open my mouth to object, but Bash puts a hand on my arm, "That's perfect. I'd love the chance to get to know your children a little better. And I think our hostess could enjoy some time off her feet."

In the living room, I settle into the armchair with Oliver and his bottle while Jared pulls out the dusty Candy Land box from the top of the hall closet. He, Daisy and Bash begin a heated game. Daisy is just as competitive as her mama, if not more so.

I watch the three interact, laughing at Daisy's insistence that she does NOT need to go back because she drew the gingerbread man after she had already drawn the ice cream cone, arguing that the ice cream cone cancels it out. Some kind of rules she'd invented, which felt awfully convenient for her position in the game. With Oliver snuggled up warm to my chest, the happy banter of the game, clinking of dishes in the kitchen to the tune of Mark and Amelia singing *Baby It's Cold Outside*, I take a moment and try to breathe it all in. I'd never imagined that I could feel any peace while celebrating a holiday with a major *piece* of our family gone. But at this moment, I do.

We enjoy far too much dessert and just enough lively conversation for the evening before Daisy's eyes start to droop, despite her afternoon nap. Mark shakes Sebastian's hand vigorously at the door and Amelia, to my surprise reaches up and gives him a hug. Before pulling away she whispers something in his ear, to which Bash replies, "I'd expect nothing less."

"What was that about?" I ask, closing the door behind them.

"Oh, you know," he says, waving a hand, "just the usual barely veiled violence from Amelia. Threatening life and limb should I hurt you."

I laugh as Jared chimes in, "And I'd help!" He bends down to place a kiss on my cheek and whispers in my ear, "He's... alright, Mom. Just. Be careful. Ok? And don't stay up too late." He throws a "good night" over his shoulder and heads upstairs.

Bash and I find ourselves alone in the quiet, soaking in the warm post-Thanksgiving dinner glow that still permeates the room. That's when I remember. I touch Bash's arm gently and point my chin towards the office. Without a word, we slip into the darkened room.

I hesitate as anxiety coils inside, thinking of Jared, how much he idolized his dad. "You—you had texted earlier this week that you had an update about the wire transfers?" It's hard to make my mouth form the question when I'm not sure I want to know the answer.

"Ah, yes," his answer is a little too hesitant for my liking. "We were able to trace where the wire transfers were being sent."

I can feel my pulse in every part of my body as sweat prickles beneath my sweater. "And?" His pause makes my heart clench even tighter. "Just tell me. I can't take the suspense. I'm a wreck over here waiting. I didn't ask earlier because I didn't want Jared to overhear. I need time to process myself before I share with him. So, please, tell me now and give it to me straight. I'm a big girl."

Bash meets my gaze straight on, the blue of his eyes taking on a darker, stormier coloring. His voice doesn't waver as he tells me, "It was going into an account of a woman named Samantha Brenner. She's 35. Works at a restaurant close to where she lives in Rogers Park. Two children. A boy and a girl—ages 16 and 15."

The floors have disappeared from beneath my feet. The earth has disintegrated and I'm falling, falling away into nothingness. My heart

Chapter 13

has ceased its beating, no breath is in my lungs, no oxygen travels my veins. Two strong hands grab my upper arms, shaking me gently and calling my name, pulling me back.

"Meg. Meg, breathe. It's ok. I'm right here. You're ok. Just take a breath, please." The air fills my lungs obediently but it's too much, too quick. The oxygen burns. I bend in half with a hacking cough and go down on my knees on the thick Turkish rug of the office. My fingers grasp at the thick fibers.

The rug. This rug. Rob said he'd found it while on a backpacking trip he took with a few law school buddies after passing the bar together, leaving me home with the baby. Had it shipped back, which must've cost a fortune. Why hadn't I asked where he got that money then? IF that was even where he went. How would I know. Maybe he never even took that trip. Who had I been married to?

"Oh God," I whisper into the dim light of the office. It was all falling apart. That sliver of peace—gone. I felt the ribbons slipping through my fingers, and I couldn't find the strength to so much as grab at them. "Oh God, Rob had a second family all this time."

"What? No, wait, we don't know that. You're jumping to conclusions with this. Let's back up."

My eyes snap up to Sebastian, hovering over me and the panic quickly melds into rage, spilling out toward the nearest bystander. "Back up? You want me to back up? Ok let's back up to the fact that I have no idea who my husband was. Let's back up to the fact that he's been sending $2000 a month to this WOMAN with two kids for who knows how long with no explanation. What conclusion should I be jumping to? If you're such a *genius*, then why don't YOU figure this out? I asked you to HELP me and instead you're tearing my life apart every time you open your mouth!"

A gasping hiccup escapes my chest, choking and burning. Bash doesn't say a word. He doesn't flinch away from the rawness of my pain or my anger. Instead, he joins me on the floor, his long legs bent awkwardly around me to pull me into his chest and holds me. No reassurances. No shushing. No words. He just holds me.

After a few moments, my senses return, and the shame creeps in over my outburst. Untangling myself from him I turn away to grab a handful of tissue from the box on the desk. My face is a wreck. I can feel the swelling around my eyes and know my nose has turned its classic cherry red.

"Bash," I start apologetically, but he holds up a hand.

"Not needed. Seriously, I get it. I can't imagine what you're feeling right now. But I stand by what I said earlier. I know your mind wants to immediately jump to the worst scenario. That's human. Let's just slow down here though. Think. Has Rob ever given you a reason to believe he had kept this kind of secret from you?"

Wiping my face with a fresh tissue and adding it to the growing pile in the trash can, I take a few breaths and close my eyes. Like a string of movie clips, the years flip back from the most recent memories. Standing at the grave watching as they lowered Rob's casket into the ground. Rob shrinking as the cancer took him from us one chunk at a time. Rob making partner at the law firm. Rob whistling loudly from the stands at Jared's basketball games, clapping at his elementary Christmas program, laughing at our adorable son's toddler antics, falling into a deep depression...

There. That was the moment I'd never quite gotten to the bottom of.

"I thought he was going to leave us, once," I admit quietly. "When Jared was two, Rob got his first job as a lawyer. It wasn't the kind of firm he wanted to be in, but we were too strapped for cash for him to hold out for a corporate law gig to open up. He was under a lot of pressure, and it kept getting progressively worse. He was so distant. Wouldn't hardly talk to me. Worked all kinds of hours, barely saw Jared. I thought for sure we'd lost him. But then he got the job at the

Chapter 13

firm he built his career at, and it was like the sky cleared. Even though something still simmered under the surface, he came back to us. He never told me what it was, and I guess I just accepted it, thankful he had stuck around."

"That must've been really hard for you, especially home with a toddler," Sebastian said gently. "I know it probably feels impossible, but don't assume the worst just yet. At this moment, you get to decide. Do you want to go forward in investigating this? I'm sure we can dig up more information, and ultimately nothing is stopping you from knocking on her door if you feel so inclined. I've got her address and would be happy to go with you."

The stabbing in my chest is settling into a heavy ache. I place a hand on Sebastian's chest and meet his concerned eyes with my bloodshot ones.

"I think," I finally say, giving my thoughts and feelings a moment to settle, "that for tonight, I've had all that I can take. I'll ask you for that information, but not right now. Maybe next week. Ok? I just... need some time."

His brow is furrowed as he studies my face, looking for fault lines in danger of another eruption. But I've regained control for now.

I tack on a weak smile and attempt to soothe the concern in his eyes with levity. "Don't worry about me. I'm a pro-level compartmentalizer. I'll tuck this into a filing cabinet waaay back there and it won't see the light of day until I'm ready to pull it out again. And when I am ready, you'll be the first to know."

He smiles a bit. "That's my girl." He says it teasingly, but that doesn't stop the words from curling in my stomach, setting me off balance for other reasons.

Get a grip, girl. One moment you're freaking out over your dead husband's secrets and the next you're mooning over an old infatuation. Which is it? Are you mourning, raging, or moving on?

This really is a confusing mental and emotional mess. But tonight was not the night to untangle and figure it all out. This feels like the next right thing for now. That's all I can say.

When Bash slips on his leather jacket at the door and leans in to hug me, I decide I really don't want to say anything at all and melt into his arms for a moment. For this moment. My body molds into him, his arms wrapping around me in a way that feels so familiar, yet nearly forgotten. An old favorite memory—the warm scent of leather mixed with crisp spearmint. He's even taller now than he was then, and his lithe teenage boy body has filled out into man's. My head comes just to the center of his chest, and he rests his chin on top of my hair.

"Meg," he says pulling back to look at me, but saying nothing further.

We step through the open door onto the stoop. His eyes hold mine with a fierce, unyielding grip that threatens to overwhelm all my rational thoughts and propel my body back into his arms. The depthless blue conveys words that I think he knows I'm not ready to hear, yet find part of myself longing for him to say. I'm cold from stepping out of his embrace. I can still smell him from where it clings to my sweater. *Ugh, that leather jacket, just like back then.* I'd steal it off of him right now if I thought it would hold onto his scent forever.

After a long moment he finally says, "Call me next week."

And I say the only word I can muster right now around all the feelings overwhelming me from the inside. "Ok."

I watch him pull away and stand out in the crisp night until I can no longer bear the cold.

Chapter 14

"Sorry, but are you sure this is the right place?" I ask, gaping at the villa I've just stepped into.

"Yes, Ms. Franklin. Mr. Sylvain requested our larger, two-bedroom villa, but please—deepest apologies madam—this was the only one available at short notice. I can get the manager if you are dissatisfied?"

I peel my eyes away from the accommodations to note the dark-haired man bowing before me in apology. "Dissatisfied?! No! Sorry, no I'm not dissatisfied at all. It's—well, it's a lot nicer than I had expected. This is incredible!"

The small man beams at me, his teeth bright against his golden-brown skin, crisp shirt displaying the resort logo. Secret Paradise was an apt name for this oceanfront heaven the driver dropped me at 10 minutes ago. I fumble with my purse, reaching for cash to tip the concierge who's shown me to the private villa.

"Oh no, no madam," he says, shaking his hands in front of him. "Mr. Sylvain has already covered all gratuity for your stay. Please. No more. It would be too much."

My eyebrows raise in surprise as I tuck the bills back into my wallet.

"Ah, ok then. Thank you for letting me know."

Bowing his head again to me, he gestures at some informational pamphlets arranged artfully on the entry table. "Please, enjoy your stay, madam. Anything you need, just ask. We do it all for you here in Paradise." And with that, he left me to gawk at my surroundings open mouthed.

The resort—if that was even the correct term for such a lavish place to stay—was situated on a cliff overlooking the ocean on the island nation of Dominica. Instead of your traditional high-rise hotel with hundreds of rooms, it was a collection of private villas—around a dozen, by my count. This one was the furthest out from the entrance, tucked far enough apart from the other villas to feel almost completely secluded, yet easily accessible to the rest of the resort. The concierge had indicated a golf cart parked out front to get around the property. Although in this paradise, I doubt I'll mind walking.

The villa was a creamy white stucco accented by a red clay tile roof. The double doors were frosted glass with a dark wood frame around the edges. Inside the light airy pallet was soothing and cool in contrast to the hot, salty breeze floating in from the ocean. It stirs gauzy curtains pulled back from a full wall of glass doors, mostly open to the balcony. A cocoon style chair sat near the edge, overlooking the ocean. A perfect spot for coffee and my latest read. The private infinity pool appeared to spill off the edge of the cliff into the waiting sea below.

I don't think we're in Kansas anymore... And I really don't think Bash is just "a manager" at Guardian. This trip must've cost an absolute FORTUNE.

Tiled floors ran throughout the inside and patio. The small kitchenette was stocked with a variety of coffee options for the French press, some tea bags, and a bowl full of fruit that smelled so fresh it must have been picked that morning. Fresh milk and juice were in the small fridge.

Chapter 14

An intimate seating area with a comfy couch catches my eye. Jared and I could take turns taking the couch, with the one room situation. Double doors lead into the bedroom. A massive bed with dark wood and flowing white linens dominates the space while doors out onto another small balcony with a hot tub overlooking the side of the cliff. I couldn't imagine sitting in a hot tub in this sticky heat but maybe the evenings were cool.

The bathroom off the other side of the bedroom was just as beautiful as the rest of the villa with a deep soaking tub and walk-in shower with more knobs and sprayers than any shower I'd seen before.

Yep, this will do nicely.

I pull out my phone to snap a few pics for Amelia and the book club and realize I'd forgotten to power it back on after the flight. I busy my hands while it restarts—unpacking a few things onto the bathroom counter and hanging the dresses I brought for dinner in the closet.

The screen finally comes to life, and I frown, noting the multiple notifications of texts and voicemails from Jared. He wasn't scheduled to arrive until tomorrow morning, but he should already be heading to the airport for his first flight.

The texts are mostly to the tune of "call me when you get in" and "are you there yet" with the last one "I left you a voicemail, please call me when you get it." Worry seizes my mama heart as I lift the phone to my ear for his message.

"*Heeeeey Mom... listen. Ah, remember that one lab I was telling you about, with the prestigious infectious disease doctor. Well, I'd applied for a J-term project with his team. I didn't say anything because he's never invited freshmen to participate in his lab. I was sure I didn't stand a chance. But he chose me, from a paper I wrote earlier this semester on communicable disease in third world countries. I only found out 4 hours before I was going to leave for the airport. You must already be in the air. I... Mom, I feel terrible. But I also know you. I know if you weren't 30,000 feet in the air and had been* able to answer you'd tell me to take it. You've always pushed me to reach high. You're why I had the guts to apply in the first place.

But the thing is, as you probably figured out, I can't come spend Christmas with you like we planned. The lab starts the 26th, and there's no way I can make it to Dominica and back in that amount of time. Can you forgive me? I hate that I won't be there for you... but please. Please don't leave. You deserve this trip, Mom. I looked up the resort and woah. Looks amazing! Promise me you'll have an adventure? For me? And for Dad. Ok? I love you. Call me when you can."

I sit the phone down on the bed and take a few deep breaths. My heart is swelling with pride. Of course, Jared would be the first freshman to ever make the cut for something like this. He'd told me earlier this year that every student to ever be a part of this particular professor's lab projects always got into the best med schools when the time came. The guy's letters of recommendations were like Willy Wonka's golden tickets. Given sparingly, they opened the gates to your wildest med school dreams.

While the pride overwhelms, a simultaneous ache of dread settles deep in my stomach, slicing at the tenuous grip peace had on my barely healed heart. Christmas alone in paradise. Not just Christmas, but the first Christmas as a widow. I could do it though. I'm strong. But the 26th... The one-year anniversary of Rob's passing. I blow another breath out through puffed cheeks and take a minute to assess if I can do this or not.

If I go home, I'll be alone there too. Or worse yet, Amelia would turn right around from heading to Ohio, refusing to let me be alone, and then Mark would potentially miss the last holiday with his grandma. I'd never forgive myself if that happened. Not to mention the load of guilt it would dump on Jared. *Yeah, that's out.*

I could fly over to Italy to spend the holiday with my parents. *You're PARENTS?! That's the WORST option.* They hadn't even come last year

Chapter 14

for Rob's funeral. The flight's too much for my father, according to my mother. I don't think I could handle being with them anyway. *Which leaves us with...*

Staying is the best choice. Quite frankly the only choice. *Ding, ding, ding! We have a winner! Girl, you're in paradise. Quit moping. Put on your swimsuit and go float for an hour in that pool before the sun goes down.*

I give Jared a call first, spending the majority of the time convincing him I'll be fine and reiterating how very proud I am of him. I follow up the call by snapping a few photos of the place, so he knows what kind of swanky vacation he's missing out on. I include a selfie of me, smiling broadly with the ocean view behind me. The smile immediately drops after the shutter sound, but I zoom in on the image and find it convincing enough.

At least one good thing had come out of this month. After my complete rage-meltdown in front of Bash after Thanksgiving, I'd calmed down enough by the first week of December to think a little more rationally. Deciding to snoop from a distance, I did what every woman in the 21st century does when she wants info on someone. I checked social media.

Samantha Brenner has both a Facebook and an Instagram account but, much to my chagrin, both are locked down pretty tight with privacy settings. Not that I blame her for that. From what I could see in her profile pictures, she looked like a former prom queen whose beauty faded too quickly from too many hard knocks in life. Her eyes didn't hold much sparkle in the photos.

But a public account had tagged her in a recent post. My pulse really picked up when I saw the name—Zach Brenner. Clicking through the photos, I felt like I had my answer. Zach and his sister, who could've been his twin except in size, were gathered around a Thanksgiving meal with Samantha. Their mother. Neither child looked much like her though with their deep caramel skin and shining, tight black curls.

No way could these teens have been Rob's. Bash was right, though I hadn't quite phrased it that way when I told him. Still, the explanation for the money transfers was a complete unknown to me. It still bothered me, but once I realized Rob wasn't hiding a second family all this time, it was more of a frustrating unknown instead of a life-altering secret. So for now, I let it sit.

After a long, meditative float in the pool, I order dinner to be delivered and test out the high-tech shower while I wait. I'm bundled in the world's fluffiest robe towel drying my hair when the doorbell chimes. A doorbell. This place has a doorbell. Chuckling to myself at the novelty, I pad barefoot across the sitting room to open the door.

Mussed dark hair tumbles across a forehead covered in a light sheen of sweat. A muscled chest heaves slightly beneath the well-fitted black t-shirt. No golf cart—he walked up. He sucks in a big breath and says, "Well, hello there. Fancy meeting you here."

The hair towel drops to the floor. I'm frozen, suspended in time. He laughs and reaches over with a pointer finger to lift my hanging jaw up.

I latch onto sanity long enough to say, "Bash! Hi!"

Chuckling again he answers the question my brain can't yet formulate into words. "Jared called. He was really worried about you being by yourself. As soon as he found out he couldn't come, he called my office and my assistant, bless her, had the sense to patch him through to me. I got on the earliest flight I could. I..."

He pauses to search my eyes, still wide with shock as my hands cling to my robe, holding the front closed. *He came. Oh, he came! Meg, he came for you.* A wet piece of hair slips over my forehead, and he reaches out on instinct, tucking it behind my ear.

"Is it ok that I'm here? I'll sleep on the couch. Sergio, that's the concierge who took you to your villa, told me it was a one-bedroom. Sorry about that, I asked for two."

Chapter 14

I'm nodding like a bobblehead doll. "Of course, yes! Oh my gosh, look at me leaving you on the doorstep with your bag. Sorry, I was just so surprised! Please come in."

I open the door wider, and he passes by me into the living room, the subtle scent of spearmint cool on the warm tropical air, flooding me with the sweet ache of nostalgia. For a moment I let myself believe we're those kids again. Two teens, desperately in love and trying to figure out how to be together in a world intent on tearing them apart.

"I ordered dinner already, but I'm sure we can add another entrée to the order if we call now."

He looks up from where he's setting out a few items from the leather duffel he brought. "No problem. I ate a little on the plane. I'm good til breakfast. The room have everything you need?"

I choke on the crazed giggle that bubbles up. "Everything I need? Bash, have you seen this place? It's incredible! I thought there must be a mistake when Sergio opened the door. I can't even imagine what a stay here must cost. You've got to let me reimburse you. Seriously, this is too much."

He waves a hand of dismissal at me. "Don't be ridiculous. I know the owner. He owed me one. No big deal."

It definitely felt like a *very* big deal to me, but I wasn't about to argue with his generosity and make myself out to be an ungrateful recipient. I slip quietly into the bedroom to put on some loungewear, stashing the plush robe back onto its hook in the bathroom.

Glancing into the mirror, I'm somewhat horrified at the wet tangle my hair somehow turned into post-shower and attempt to yank a brush through it before pulling it back into a simple braid. I resist the urge to put on a little bronzer to brighten up my pale face – *or maybe that red lipstick? Nothing says "kiss me" like fire engine red lips...*

After that intrusive thought, at least I don't need to put on any blush. Opting instead for some lip balm I sigh at my 40-year-old face and smile tentatively at the mirror. *Not too bad, Franklin. Not. Too. Bad.* I flip off the light.

Back in the living room, Bash is setting out the dinner that must've arrived while I was changing. He lays the fork meticulously on a white cloth napkin before pouring fresh water from a sweating carafe into the glass. A lit candle flickers, casting a warm glow on the table for two.

"There you are," he says warmly, smiling up at me. "Dinner is served, milady." He makes a show of pulling out my chair for me before settling across from me in the opposite seat.

The chicken and roasted vegetables smell delightful, but I frown at them. "This just doesn't feel right. Eating in front of you while you sit there with nothing. Here," I say, moving the roll from the extra plate. I cut up some chicken and arrange it carefully with a good mix of the veggies on it to pass to him.

He smiles at me, amused. "What?" I ask, feeling self-conscious.

"Oh, nothing really, I guess I'm just seeing your maternal side come out. This is a new aspect of you now that 16-year-old Meg didn't have." He paused before adding, "I like it."

I blush under his observation and turn the scrutiny back on him as we both take a small bite of dinner. "Well, what about you? You didn't want to have kids?"

He makes a thoughtful hm sound in the back of his throat as he chews, considering. "I wouldn't say I didn't want children. I just didn't find the right person to have them with. And now, I'd say that ship has pretty much sailed. I don't really want to be a father who's confused for a grandparent at graduation. You must've had Jared pretty young huh?"

I nod, washing down another bite with a sip of water. Bash had set out a lemon wedge with the glass and I smile. *Always so thoughtful.*

"That's true. He was a bit unplanned. We were going to wait on

Chapter 14

kids until Rob had finished law school to start a family. But hey, best surprise of my life. It was a little hard, juggling new motherhood with Rob finishing his degree. Trying to find side gigs that still gave me plenty of time home with Jared while helping cover the bills. I know to some it would look like I wasted my journalism degree by primarily being a stay-at-home mom. But Jared's the best thing I've ever done with my life. No regrets. You know?"

Bash is leaning forward at the table now, listening intently to me as his food gets cold. I tuck a strand that's loosened from my braid behind an ear and focus on my next bite to get a little space from the closeness of his gaze.

"He seems pretty incredible, no doubt about that. But your life isn't done yet. Still plenty left to live. So, the question is—what now?"

His eyes are so focused on me, as though my words are the most important thing to him in this moment. This is another thing that was so... captivating about Bash. He had a singular focus, always giving his full attention to the things he cared about. *To the things he loves, Meg. Remember?*

I clear my throat and squeeze the lemon wedge into the water to take another drink, not so much out of thirst but to cool the warmth rising in me.

"I guess that *is* the question isn't it. What now? I'm not a wife anymore. Always a mother but not so hands on. I really like what I've been doing at Angel House. Tasha's probably told you—I've taken to going pretty much weekly. But that's not exactly a career. So..." I let the word trail off, shrugging a shoulder.

Sitting back in the chair holding the sweating glass to my cheek, I let my gaze wander to the balcony and over its edge to the darkening sky and sea beneath it. So serene in this moment, but there was power lurking beneath the surface. Power to transport ships and to sink them. Life was strange that way. Sometimes the very force that moves you can become the thing that drowns you.

"Where did you go?" Bash asks quietly, placing a strong hand over mine. Callouses form bumps at the base of each of his fingers, hard against my knuckles. I turn my head back to face him, smiling softly before turning his hand over in mine.

"Tell me," I say, avoiding his question and lightly running a hand over his palm. "How does a guy who works on computers all day get callouses like these?"

He chuckles and shakes his head. "Weights. The bench press is my top stress reliever. I got into it when I was in college. Nothing too crazy like a body builder. Just something to work through frustrations and release pent-up energy. And when you're all alone, you've got plenty of time for it."

That explains the well-defined... I clear my throat loudly over my own thoughts. "But why are you, Bash? Alone, that is. In all this time you never married."

He makes a sort of "ah" sound, and it's his turn to look out over the ocean view. He brings his hands together, one hand enclosing the other fist and leans his chin on them when he turns back.

"I dated a little here and there. Nothing serious. Except for once, when I almost proposed to a girl. About ten years ago," he says finally.

I wait at least thirty seconds until it's clear he needs some prodding. "And?"

Heavy sigh. "Rebecca talked me out of it. She said... well, she said I wasn't being fair to Chelsea—that was her name. That she deserved someone who would love her with their whole heart." He shrugs and picks at his food, poking at the broccoli as though it has done him a disservice by appearing on his plate.

That rational, protective part of my brain wants me to drop it right there. Instead, my mouth opens, and I hear myself ask, "And that was it? There was never anyone else?"

Chapter 14

His eyes lift from his plate, searing and bluer than the ocean crashing on the cliffs below. "No, Meg. There was never anyone else."

A buzzing fills my brain. I stand from the table, unable to sit there a moment more. I've got to put some space between us without looking like a lunatic. *Too late...* The pamphlets across the room catch my eye and I race over to grab a handful.

"So! What do you want to do tomorrow?" I wince at the abnormal volume of my voice, waving the options at him.

Bash calmly wipes his mouth before laying the napkin beside his plate. He walks over to stand beside me, pushing his hands into his pockets—a subtle signal he'll keep them to himself.

"Depends. Are you in the mood to relax or have an adventure?"

I think for a beat. "Adventure. Definitely adventure."

"Alright," he answers smoothly, sweeping the pamphlets from my hand and leaning past me to place them back on the table. The warmth emanating from him sears me through the cotton of my top—like standing too close to an open oven.

"We've both had a long day. Why don't we tuck in, and tomorrow we'll see what kinds of trouble we can get into."

I swallow and pray it wasn't audible. "Sounds great."

Chapter 15

After a breakfast of fresh fruit, toast and bacon on the balcony, the sun rising behind us and warming the ocean with its light, Bash tells me to "dress to get wet" and leaves it at that.

Outside the villa, we head towards a railed staircase at the side of the house. It zig zags down the face of the cliff, ending at a small sandy beach alcove. Two jet skis bob in the water, tethered to the end of a wooden dock.

My face must show how dubious I feel about jet skis because Bash reaches over to squeeze my hand encouragingly.

"Don't worry. If you're not ready to drive one yet, we can ride together until you're comfortable." I pull a grimacing face and nod to his plan.

Once I'm zipped into my life jacket, I turn to find him already straddling the jet ski, waiting for me.

"Wait, where's your life jacket?"

He shrugs and reaches out a hand to help me climb up behind him. "Real men don't wear life jackets."

"Tell that to Jack and don't expect me to make room for you on MY door," I grumble, stepping off the dock and feeling instantly unstable

Chapter 15

with the waves bobbing us up and down.

My hands are shaking a little as I reach them around Bash's waist, his t-shirt already wet from the ocean's spray. I'm too nervous to even admire the toned muscles of his back and stomach. *Liar.* Ok. Almost too nervous. I tighten my grip as he turns the key, the engine roaring to life.

He must feel my anxiety because he looks down at me over his shoulder with a grin and asks, "Do you trust me, Meg?"

Something in me settles as I answer with the truth. "I trust you."

With a twist of his wrist, we're shooting away from the dock, leaving the beach and staircase and all things stable and solid behind us. I squeeze my eyes shut, trying not to squeal. As my body adjusts to the bouncing rhythm of the powerful machine across the waves, I relax enough to peek an eye open. The villa is behind us now as Bash steers us around the inlet. I've seen these things go at breakneck speeds, so I suspect he's taking it easy on me.

He does a couple laps before turning to yell over the noise, "Ready to learn how to drive?"

Back at the dock, I force him to put on the second life jacket. "Listen. If you kill yourself being stupid, that's your business. But I'm not gonna be the one to do it. So put the vest on."

He begrudgingly complies, and it's his turn to climb on the back. I feel the weight of him settle behind me, his hands lightly gripping my waist through the padding, and focus on the thrumming engine beneath me. He attaches the key strap to my wrist, explaining that if we fall off, it'll shut the machine off.

"You think we're going to fall off?!" I squeak. He winks in answer and puts his hand over mine to twist the throttle.

I drive like a granny who can barely see over the steering wheel. Bash is patient, showing me the controls, explaining the importance of slowing down for turns. He also sweetly points out that we just got passed by a sea turtle, which would've earned him an elbow in the ribs from me had I not been too terrified to take a hand off the steering grips.

Eventually I do feel a little more confident and ramp up the speed a bit. Bash guides us, his voice cutting through the wind whooshing in my ears to head around the inlet to a spot he wants to show me. Soon we're flying over the water, my hair whipping so hard I know strands have got to be cutting into Sebastian's face. But he doesn't complain, just squeezes me tighter when I let out a whoop of enjoyment at the thrill.

A sandy beach comes up on our left and he points for me to turn in. Although there is a dock, the little beach is completely secluded, a half moon of sand surrounded on all sides by rainforest. After securing the jet ski, he uses the key to pop open the seat storage compartment and pulls out two sets of snorkel masks and fins. He hands a set to me.

"I found this place a few years ago when I came. Best snorkeling I've found anywhere! And usually no one else is around to muck up this gorgeous little beach. Remember that time we tried to snorkel in Lake Superior without full wet suits?"

"That water was FREEZING!" I laugh, recalling how blue our lips had turned. "But those rock formations were pretty amazing. I swear that one was Elvis' 70's hair. It was that exact swoop."

"You know," he says, holding out a hand to take my life jacket. "I read somewhere that—due to its massive size—when a drop of water enters Lake Superior, it takes almost two centuries for it to flow out. So that means..." his eyes hold a mischievous twinkle and it dawns on me where he's going with this line of thought.

"Oh, no! No, no, no Sebastian Thomas Sylvain don't you DARE finish that sentence!"

"Your pee will still be in that lake for another 177 years!"

I screech at his laughter and reach over with both hands to firmly

Chapter 15

shove him off the dock. Instead of resisting, he lets me and goes tumbling down in a splash laughter.

"I cannot BELIEVE you brought that up! You promised you would never speak of it!" I yell down into the rippling water where he's still laughing, wiping it from his face.

"Aw c'mon, it's not like I posted a warning sign to future swimmers or anything," he says with a devious grin. "Help me up."

I reach down before the red flag has time to wave in my brain. Grabbing my hand, he pulls me down with him into the clear warm water of the inlet. I surface with a gasp and splash him with all my might, trying to act enraged but unable to withhold my laughter.

"There she is." Bash snakes an arm around my waist to hold me up in the water. The clear cerulean waves lap around us, welcome and enveloping, making me forget myself for a moment. "That's the carefree Meg I remember." He says fondly.

I push away with a splash—feeling more than I want to—and ask, "So are we going to snorkel or talk about my bodily functions all day? For all you know, I've already peed in here and now you're just swimming around in it right now."

"Well. You wouldn't be the first," he says good naturedly.

I'd thought the water was fairly clear and beautiful from above. But once the snorkel mask and fins are in place and we dip our heads under the water, an entirely new world blooms that had been invisible from above.

The color of the coral is brighter as the sun's rays penetrate the surface to illuminate the intricate designs below. Schools of fish in all sizes and color dart around, in and out of the coral, swimming in captivating patterns and formations. A perfectly formed starfish is attached to the rock beside me. I resist the urge to reach out and touch it, not wanting to disturb its habitat.

Bash gives wide berth to a sting ray rippling past him and points to a clown fish emerging from an anemone close to me. A tree-like coral formation is home to a family of seahorses, holding tight to the branches as the water moves in and out in the shallow area sending their bodies swaying. The entire cove is breathtaking.

After an hour exploring the inlet, we lay on the dock to let the sun dry the salt water on our skin, talking about the two years we spent together in high school, while diligently avoiding what happened after. At some point, we'll have to. Right? *Let sleeping dogs lie, I say. Be present here. Now.*

I turn down the opportunity to drive back, preferring to relax and enjoy the ride.

After climbing the seemingly 10,000 steps back up to the villa, we find a note has been left on the kitchenette counter, alongside some fresh squeezed juice. The resort is hosting a Christmas Eve dinner tonight with traditional holiday dishes from around the world.

"Christmas Eve. Is that today?" I press the glass of juice against my forehead. The cool sweat from the drink soothes my overly sunned skin. I feel nearly crisp.

"Is this your first Christmas somewhere that doesn't have winter? It's a bit of a novelty, right?" Bash takes a sip from his glass. "Wow, now that is fresh. I'm thinking mango, pineapple and… orange maybe? Yum."

"It really is good," I agree. "And yes, I've always been either in Wisconsin or Chicago for Christmas so more of your traditional cold weather, snow, fire in the fireplace where the stockings are hung with care vibe for sure."

My tone is inadvertently wistful, and he considers me a moment. "You're missing it? Being there?"

I shake my head definitively, the squeeze in my heart confirmation. "No. Not this year. I did not want to be home this year. In fact, I'm considering selling the place."

Chapter 15

I surprise myself by saying that thought out loud. I'd felt it niggling at me a little, but I hadn't even admitted it to myself until this moment. But saying it, now? It felt right. That house had been mine and Rob's. It didn't feel right for just me anymore.

"Sure," Bash responds, gently massaging a small circle between my shoulder blades somehow targeting the exact spot where the muscle is particularly knotted. "If you decide that's what you want, I know a guy who can help."

I roll my eyes and chuckle. "Of course, you do."

That night we don the nicest outfits we brought—that black dress I wore to Jared's graduation with strappy sandals for me and a dark teal button down, sleeves rolled up to the elbow, with black slacks for Bash. The color makes his eyes seem more turquoise than blue, like the ocean in our secret cove. *All that man's clothes must be tailored just for him because they fit him perfectly. Remember to breathe.* I tried to keep myself from admiring his form too long, lest he notice. Although I think the jig might be up as I catch a sly smile lift the corner of his mouth before I look away.

Over dinner, he tells me more about what I missed from his family life—his parents retirement fun, Scarlett and Rebecca's latest adventures. His pride in both of them brings such a light to his face, I'm captivated until it hits me.

"Oh, you're missing Christmas with them! That's terrible! You already missed Thanksgiving, and now I've pulled you away from them for Christmas. Oh my gosh, I feel awful."

"Hey now," he says, reaching over to pull down the hand I was hiding behind. "You didn't do anything. I came here of my own accord, remember? And they'll be fine! I had my assistant get everyone's gifts from my apartment and overnight them to my parents' place for me."

"No, but this isn't right, you should be with your family," I protest, feeling the guilt heavy in my chest.

His expression turns firm. "Meg. There's nowhere else I'd rather be than right here with you right now. Look at my eyes. You know I'm telling you the truth."

I meet his gaze and it's like a little window cracked open again. When we first met, he had been so shuttered and closed off. Then I wormed my way into his heart, and I could see the rawness of his very soul when he looked at me. He didn't trust many, so I'd never taken that trust lightly.

We finish dinner and head back to the villa, strolling in quiet contentment under the glow of the moonlight.

"I brought your present with me," he says sheepishly once back inside. Crossing over to his bag, he pulls a package out and hides it behind his back.

"Oh, you shouldn't have! This trip is already way too much! Plus, I have a gift for you but at home, obviously. Now I feel bad."

He gives me a teasing grin, "Don't worry. It's not a big one. And don't laugh. I wrapped it myself."

The package is a little smaller than a sweater, but soft, like material. I search a moment to figure out where to open it—he's got every seam taped up end to end. Once the paper is ripped and the gift falls out, I burst into laughter.

"Ok, this is a good one. New potholders! Just what I needed, thank you, Bash."

He grins like the teenage boy I knew back then and reaches back into his bag, pulling out a case. "I brought one more thing too, but it's not a gift. Something for us to enjoy together."

"What is it? Is that a movie?"

"You'll see."

After opening an inconspicuous cabinet in the corner to reveal a TV, he fires up the unit and pops the DVD into the player. Turning the couch away from the ocean view to face it, he pats the seat next to him

Chapter 15

and hits play.

As soon as the opening credits blink on I gasp. "You brought White Christmas?"

Bash nods and smiles at me. "Still your favorite?"

Do not cry, do not cry, do not cry. I nod to keep my cool and tuck in next to him on the couch. Reaching behind us, he pulls a soft, silky blanket and covers me with it. Despite the residual warmth of the evening, it feels right. We settle in to watch Bob Wallace fall for Betty Haynes and her for him against their better judgment.

* * *

The next day—a strange version of Christmas Day—Bash insists on sending me off for a day of pampering at the spa. An oddly relaxing mud bath is followed by a deep cleansing facial and the most incredible massage of my life. I return to the villa in late afternoon fully pampered and fairly relaxed, all things considered.

Jared and I FaceTime out on the patio while Bash catches up on some work at the small dining table.

"Mom," he says, his tone serious. "Tell me the truth. Are you ok? Did I screw up by not coming? By not being there for you?"

"Jare, you are the best son a mother could ever ask for. I would've been so angry with you if you had missed out on this opportunity just to be with me for a few days. No way, kiddo, you're right where you're supposed to be. And look at me! I'm in paradise!"

To prove my point, I switch to the front camera to give him a panoramic view of the infinity pool overlooking the ocean.

"Now you be real with me," I say, switching the camera back. "Are you going to be ok tomorrow?"

Jared takes a moment, considering. "I think so. I miss Dad a lot. But I'm keeping busy, and I know he would've been proud of what I'm doing. I know I'm going to be ok. I just want to be sure that YOU are. Was it the right thing to send Sebastian? I just couldn't bear the thought of you being alone. He seems like a great guy. And... if I can say this without it being weird since you're my mom. The way he looks at you? Well, let's just say I knew he would be more than willing to fly down there at the drop of a hat for you. I'm still... still kind of wrapping my mind around it. But I want you to be happy."

I swipe a tear away and laugh a little, avoiding Jared's gaze for a moment. "Thanks, son. It was the right call to send him. I'm not sure I would've done so hot on my own. He's been great."

We end the call a few minutes later so Jared can get brushed up on a few study topics before he starts in the lab tomorrow. Bash and I order in for dinner, neither of us particularly keen on making the effort to go back to the fancy restaurant tonight.

Once the food is delivered, we set up a picnic-style dinner out on the patio, right next to the glass barrier at the edge so we can watch the ocean waves crash against the rocks below in the moonlight.

"So," Bash says after a few minutes of companionable silence. The filet cuts like butter, the beef so tender and juicy it melts in my mouth. "Tomorrow is kind of a big day. Want to talk about it?"

"In some ways, it's hard to believe it's been a year," I say after a few moments. I think I am ready to talk about it with Bash.

"Rob had been having stomach pain off and on for months. I kept pushing him to go to the doctor, but he was stubborn. Adamant nothing was wrong. Finally, one night the pain got so intense I almost called an ambulance for him. But we got through that night, and he agreed to an appointment. After some blood work and scans they found it, but it was already too advanced. Stage IV pancreatic cancer. The oncologist made it clear; the prognosis was grave. It was nonresectable.

"But still we fought with radiation and chemotherapy. Jared researched like crazy. We tried so hard to get him into clinical trials, but his case was so far advanced he didn't qualify. Then last summer a miracle occurred, and he did get into a trial for an immune checkpoint inhibitor in development given in combination with his chemo for unresectable tumors. His oncologist was amazed he got into the study, at his stage. It felt like a Hail Mary pass. We—I allowed my hopes to rally once more. But by November we knew the treatment had failed and hope was pretty much gone by that point."

I pause, needing a moment to collect myself as the weight of all those months—researching, appointments, tests, watching him disappear slowly before our very eyes, disappointment after disappointment—threatens to crush me once more. Bash reaches across the table and squeezes my hand. He doesn't say a word. He just sits with me, present in my grief.

With a sniff, I forge ahead. "So yeah, by the time he passed, we'd been losing him for a full year. That's why in some ways it feels even longer than the year he's been gone. If that makes sense."

"Losing someone you love never really makes sense, Meg. Whatever you feel, it's right."

Sensing our appetites have been suppressed with the heavy conversation, he rises to carry the plates into the kitchen, carefully stacking them neatly for the staff tomorrow.

I stand up too, testing the strength of my legs. I've aged half a century. "I think I'll tuck in early tonight," I say in a small voice.

He looks at me and sees all the way through to my soul. "I think that's a good idea. Just call out if—if you need me. For any reason. I'll be there."

A rumble of thunder rolls out across the inlet. A storm heading this way.

"I'll close up here," he says, motioning to the open back wall. I nod, words all spent, and head to the bedroom.

Pulling on an old t-shirt and sweats from my bag, familiar in their worn comfort, I brush my teeth then close the door to the bedroom behind me, knowing Bash will use the other door off the living space to get ready for bed later.

After tossing and turning for what felt like hours, a loud clap of thunder startles me from the fitful sleep with a cry of surprise. I shoot up in the bed, my heart hammering.

A moment later, a knock at the door. "Meg? I heard you cry out. Are you ok? Can I come in?"

Am I ok? One hand rests on the pillow, the fabric wet beneath my touch. A swipe of my face and I realize it's damp from my tears.

"I—No. I mean yes, please come in." I wipe at my cheeks and flip the pillow over, trying to hide the evidence. My eyes feel swollen and wrecked.

I hear the door open, and he's at my side an instant later, worried hands cupping my cheeks as he looks me over, examining me for injury. But there's no wound to be found, at least not on the outside. As my eyes adjust to the partial light, I meet his worried gaze. He looks as shattered as I feel.

"Meg," he says my name like a plea. "Tell me what I can do. Tell me how to help you."

His hand on my shoulder feels like all that is holding me together in this moment. "Would you hold me? Could you just—would you just hold me? Even if I can't... Even if I'm not sure..."

He shifts beside me, scooping me up in one fluid motion. His arms are strong around me, his chest solid against my shoulder and hip, a forearm under the crook of my knees.

He maneuvers us across the bed, pushing the covers down, until we're in the very center. There he settles me on my side, reaching for the duvet with one hand while the other remains cradled under my head, my body curved like a tight S. He fits himself in behind me, like two pieces of a puzzle, and pulls me even closer with the arm wrapped

Chapter 15

around my middle.

My body remembers, I remember the way he would hold me. Though we've both changed, we'd always fit together this way. Laying on the couch to watch a movie, or on a blanket under the stars. We always just fit.

Without conscious decision on my part, I melt into him. Into his warmth, into his strength, into the deep pool of his feelings for me. Feelings I haven't yet acknowledged. Maybe this wasn't fair, asking him to comfort me as I mourn another man, a life that didn't include him. But if I'm being honest, part of me is also mourning what we had been. What we'd had and then lost. And that loss led to another loss, which led me here today.

I don't regret marrying Rob. He was a good man. A solid man. We'd built a good life together and had the most incredible son. I could never regret the life that gave me Jared. Rob loved me in the straightforward way that came from two people who chose to do life together, who chose each other every day. And we'd lived it.

Yet here, in Sebastian's arms, I'm overwhelmed by the intensity of the feelings we had once shared. Feelings I'm terrified to be feeling again. Because I almost didn't survive the first time things fell apart. I know I'm stronger now, and surely wiser? But I never want to go through that a second time.

For the sake of all that is holy can you just shut up and enjoy being in this man's arms for the moment?!

I take a deep breath in and blow it out slowly. He shifts slightly behind me, molding back into me and whispers "I'm right here. I'm not going anywhere."

I let those words sink into my bones, and with that promise, finally fall asleep.

Chapter 16

"Wait, wait, wait—time out. *Dang it David, tell those kids to go watch their movie upstairs, I can't hear a word Meg is saying and she JUST got to the good part!* Ok, go back. Repeat what you just said," Kristen turns back to me on the couch, as if she didn't just break the sound barrier yelling over top the noise of the combined six kids running around. Even the teens are joining the chaos, not trying to be cool for the last 30 minutes of the year and hyping up the younger ones instead.

"I said we spent the next two days swimming, hiking the rain forest, jet skiing, snorkeling, even tried parasailing. We had massages on the beach and ate dinner by the pool every night, basking in the time and space with just the two of us."

"No dummy," Cece elbows me in ribcage nearly spilling her glass on me. "She means the LAST part. The *sleeping* part," she adds with a huge eye roll.

"Oh." I blush. "We slept that same way for the rest of the nights. Him curled around me protectively until the sun came up the next day, when we'd do it all over again."

"Slept, eh?" Kristen arches an eyebrow at me over her mug. I already

Chapter 16

told her she was going to regret that latte later when she couldn't sleep. She never listens.

"Get your mind out of the gutter," I snag the hot mug from her hands and take a sip so I too can regret it. "Yes, just slept. And we didn't talk about it or what it means or what happens next. We just lived each day in the moment, and at night we slept."

"...and now?" Cece prompts, her eyes gleaming with excitement.

I sigh, somehow both wistful and heavy. "I—I think now I'm ready to make a decision."

Both women squeal and lean in as the kids pound back down the stairs, followed by their dads.

"It's time!" Kristen's oldest yells, passing out the hats, noisemakers and year-shaped glasses from the dining room table. "Countdown time everyone!"

Kristen and David's place feels electric as this part of the world sits, holding its breath on the cusp of a brand-new year. Someone unmutes the TV. The New Years Eve bash at Navy Pier is in full swing, as the announcer begins the countdown.

"10... 9... 8..." *Are you really ready?*

"6... 5... 4...." *Can you take the next step?*

"2... 1! HAPPY NEW YEAR!"

Both the screen and the living room erupt around me in a cacophony of fireworks at the pier, cheers and noisemakers. My best friends' husbands kiss them while their children hug one another. I laugh and smile, wrapping my arms around the middle over my softest oversized sweater, allowing myself to accept the grief that is now a part of me and the joy of having a life ahead of me still to live.

The celebration continues with the kids pulling the strings from those plastic champagne poppers that release confetti. Kristen will complain about the mess later, but she loves making these kinds of memories with her kids. Happy, carefree memories that were so foreign to her own childhood.

My phone buzzes in my back pocket. I pull it out, stepping into the shadows of the darkened hallway.

Happy New Year, Meg. I'd love to spend the first day of the year with you.

I bite my lip to hide my smile and thumb out a response.

Yes. There are some things I'd like to discuss. Us, being the main topic. I pause, considering.

But you know, I still haven't seen your place. Feels like so much has centered around me and my life. I need to see more of you, learn more about your life now. Pick me up at 10 and let me into your life.

I hit send, surprised at my own directness. I didn't even ask it as a question. How very decisive of me. *New Year, New Meg. Atta girl.*

The reply comes before I've even stashed my phone away. *As you wish.*

Another text pops up, a fireworks gif from Jare. I reply with my own of Snoopy doing a happy dance. We frequently use gifs to communicate through the week to check in on one another. On Sunday he called absolutely brimming with excitement over the work he was doing in the lab. It was clear he'd found his passion, and my mama heart is so happy for him.

I head back into the living room to join my friends and their families in celebrating a fresh start, the turn of the calendar, and all the hope-filled possibilities a new year brings.

* * *

"So…" I say, running my hands over my legs to quell my nerves. It feels a bit ridiculous to be so nervous around the man I just spent days alone with absolutely at ease. But we were back in the real world. The noise and grime and rush of the city felt so foreign after the peaceful bliss of paradise.

Chapter 16

Bash glances down at my fidgeting hands and reaches over to grab one, holding it over the center console as he navigates the city streets confidently with the other hand. We stay that way for the drive. The questions between us settling unasked and unanswered for the moment.

"Uh, you live in a hotel?" I ask, gaping as he slows in front of one of Chicago's tallest buildings, built right along the Chicago River. It had to be close to a hundred stories.

"Not exactly," he answers, maneuvering the car smoothly around the side of the building, foregoing the large underground parking for a smaller entrance. The gate slides open and a burly man in the security box waves at him. Bash nods his head in greeting before pulling through. *Ha! Told you he wasn't just a manager.*

This was a smaller parking garage, with space for up to 10 cars, I'd guess. A shiny classic red Camaro is backed into one space, the SS logo gleaming on the chrome grill. What looks to be a refurbed green army jeep sits a few spaces over, the doors and top removed with five-point safety harnesses in place of the traditional seatbelts. My eyebrows shoot up at the sight of the slightly rusted orange pickup truck rounding out the collection as the sleek black sedan pulls into a space two slots over.

Stepping out of the sedan, the garage is warm despite the cold January day. Noting my surprise at the old truck, Bash shrugs nonchalantly. "They each serve a purpose, even if it's a nostalgic one."

His eyes hold mine pointedly, and I can't resist crossing over the open spaces to place a hand on the old truck. Countless hours had been spent together on the worn bench seat inside the cab and on a blanket thrown over the rust-speckled truck bed. Peering through the hand-crank window, I could still picture him—eyes sparkling with laughter, driving with one hand on the wheel and me slid all the way over to sit next to him, bouncing along the dirt roads we loved to explore after school. His hand resting gently on my thigh. My fingers tangled up in the hair on the back of his neck.

"I can't believe you still have this old thing." I say it quietly, more to myself than him.

But he must hear me because he replies just as quietly, "Some things are worth holding on to."

I turn away from the burning in my eyes, the back of my throat, and realize he had moved to stand behind me. My hands go up automatically between us, his chest warm beneath my palms. I tip my chin up to meet the gaze boring into me as though it were a tangible thing.

Longing and desperation thrum through me and have me whispering his name like a prayer. "Bash."

His mouth comes crashing down on mine without warning, without reservation. As if the coals of our young love had merely been banked for all those years and never truly put out. The fire between us reignites in an instant. With a long-forgotten muscle memory, every cell of my body responds. I rise on my toes as my hands lift to grasp the back of his neck, pulling him down to me. Every piece of me fits every part of him.

His lips are as full and soft as I remembered while his hands and body are bigger and stronger. I am swept away powerless in his grasp. As his mouth angles over mine to deepen the kiss and his arms tighten around my waist, my leg wraps around him of its own accord trying to pull him closer.

The alarm on the black sedan suddenly blares, magnified even more by the enclosed concrete space of the garage. I jump, smacking my head on the truck's solid-metal side mirror.

I wince and force a laugh, rubbing the tender place on my skull, pretending an inferno of forgotten passion had not been kindled. Bash's eyes are dark and so full of heat I pull back, lest I burn. *Too late*

Chapter 16

for that, darlin'.

Desperate for a moment to breathe, think, anything, I notice the elevator tucked into the back wall and gesture to it. "So does the tour end in the garage or do we actually get to go up to your place?"

The elevator has just two buttons—Garage and Penthouse. I swallow hard as I recognize the same feeling I had at the villa. Things I feel a little foolish for not seeing sooner. As the doors open to an ornate private lobby, empty aside from the round marble table in its center holding a massive vase of fresh flowers, I state the obvious.

"So... you don't just work at Guardian."

He just smiles and says, "No. I don't just work there."

Placing a warm hand on the small of my back he steers me towards the double doors leading into the penthouse. At the first step in, I find myself blinking repeatedly as my eyes adjust to the enormity and brightness of the space. The living room is modern but cozy with couches arranged artfully around the fireplace to allow for conversation. The ceiling must be at least 15 feet high. But it's the tall bookshelves lining the walls on either side of the mantle that stop me in my tracks.

"Stop. It. You have sliding library ladders?!" I squeal.

He grins widely at my jubilance and nods, lifting a shoulder in a "go ahead, you know you want to" gesture. And I absolutely do. I let out another squeal and climb to the very top of one of the ladders, shoving off the side of the shelving to glide smoothly along the track to the opposite end. Back and forth I go for a solid two minutes, giggling like a schoolgirl while Bash waits patiently for me to get my fill, amusement on his face.

"Well then, if you're done playing," he teases once I've finally climbed down, "I can show you the rest of the place?"

I count five bedrooms in all, one of which is a home gym that rivals the equipment of the fitness place my yoga studio shares space with.

Each room is designed to provide a view featuring the river, Lake Michigan, or the bustling cityscape. Bash confirms we are 89 stories up. The sights are beautiful and slightly dizzying.

After some more poking and prodding from me, he confesses that he built Guardian Securities from the ground up, with very little resources aside from his brains and a lot of hard work.

"But Guardian is one of the most renowned cybersecurity firms in the WORLD, Bash! How could you not tell me it's YOUR company?! I wrote a whole investigative piece on it, for goodness' sake!"

He smiles sheepishly, tucking his hands into his pockets. "Yeah, I knew about the article. It's framed in my home office. I just didn't want to make a big deal out of it. Make you think I was trying to impress you with wealth when I was really just desperate to be back in your life, Meg. That is, if you'll have me."

His honest admission squeezes my heart, and I try to show him by squeezing back with the hand he's been holding for the tour.

In the gourmet kitchen, he makes me a cup of tea with the boiling water tap on a swinging arm over the eight-burner stove.

"Oh, I've always thought those were so cool!" I beam, reaching out to unfold and refold the arm.

He chuckles, handing me the steaming mug, the teabag beginning to darken the water inside. "I've always loved that about you."

I give him a suspicious side eye. "What?"

His smile is open and sincere. "How the smallest things bring you such happiness. Things other people see and think little of, you're enthralled by. I've always admired the way you find such vibrant joy in the little things in life."

I feel my cheeks redden as I look down into the mug, inhaling deeply the spearmint black tea aroma wafting from within. He passes me the sugar and grabs the half-and-half out of the fridge.

"I seem to remember finding a whole lot of joy in life... when I was

Chapter 16

with you." I admit, drawing in a breath to tell him what I came here to say.

But the moment is interrupted by a buzzing from his pocket. After a "go ahead" nod from me, he pulls it out to examine the screen.

"Ah, I need to take this. Please forgive me. You can go check out your work though. It's showcased in the office," he says, jutting his chin towards the solid door that had been left half open. Opening a slider door I'd mistaken for a window, he steps out onto the balcony and closes it behind him before taking the call.

After stirring in the sugar and cream, I mosey down the hall, my interest piqued by the office of the man I'd referred to as the "Mystery King of Cybersecurity" in my piece. I knew there was more he'd been holding back from me. I'd felt it niggling at me in the quiet spaces when we were together. It now seemed so clear I wondered how I'd missed it. *To be fair, you've been a bit distracted.*

The office door swings open easily to the one room without floor to ceiling windows. It must be in the center of the house. Security reasons, maybe. The space has a slight hum to it, as if giant servers lay just behind the dark wood paneled walls. I suppose they probably did.

A large desk dominates the room, four screens facing the high-backed swivel chair. A wave of nostalgia hits me, remembering his teenage bedroom. His was the first computer I'd seen that someone had built themselves. It had glowed blue, with clear panels in the body to show the guts inside. Even back then he'd had two screens.

Sure enough, on the wall to the right of the desk, a large frame had an open magazine inside, the glossy pages filled with words I'd written about Guardian Securities. *He framed your work.* I smile at it, tracing my finger around the frame. Even though I had been unable to unearth the secret of who really owned and ran the company, the article held enough intrigue that it was a big hit. It was the first piece I'd written that had made the cover of our printed magazine. Definitely my best work. And here it was, on display in the CEO's office.

I suppose now I could write a follow-up piece about the actual CEO. Now *that* would really get me some recognition. But of course, I wouldn't. I would never break Sebastian's trust that way.

The wall behind the desk has me laughing a little. It was lined with what looked like dark wooden filing cabinets. Scratch that, they *were* filing cabinets, though if I had to guess, they were likely metal fireproof and faced with a wood finish for aesthetics. I suppose the King of Cybersecurity would have paper files, not trusting the internet to keep his secrets safe.

I circle around, interested in seeing how this space compared to the way the Bash of 20 years ago kept his desk. A sharp pain shoots up my shin as my focus on the desk causes me to miss the partially open filing drawer. The suddenness tips me forward to grab at the pulsing shin and shoot a dirty look at the offending drawer.

Hanging file folders line the drawer, each labeled with Bash's crisp, small caps handwriting. I'm about to push it closed when one of the labels catches my eye. It catches my eye because it's *my* name on the label.

Naturally he would have a file on me, I'd asked him to dig into our lives myself to find out where that money came from to pay off the house. But curiosity has my hand pulling the drawer open further, revealing neatly labeled subfolders: 5277 Berkeley Ave—our address. eTech Magazine. Social media. University of Chicago – where Rob and I both graduated from. Lurie Cancer Center—where Rob had his treatments. Jared. Chase bank. Central High School.

A tiny seed of doubt had been planted back in July when I ran into Sebastian in Prague, and he didn't seem the slightest bit surprised to see me. That seed was now growing rapidly into a raging forest as I stare at the files containing details of my life. Details I had most assuredly *not* shared with him. My heart begins to pound sharply, and

Chapter 16

my fingers tingle hot then cold as I try to make sense of it. I think I might be sick on the floor.

Stay calm, Meg. You've jumped to conclusions before and were way off. I'm sure there's some logical explanation. He probably had to really dig to find out what was going on with the house.

Yeah, sure. That makes sense. I asked him to unearth massive secrets from my life. Now I'm upset because he was thorough? You can't ask someone to investigate, then get sensitive about privacy. I'm just being silly.

Still, instinct has me reaching for the file furthest back. The high school I'd transferred to when my family moved from Wisconsin. Inside I find snippets from the news that mention the high school newspaper staff, of which I was a part. My school photos from junior and senior year. And finally, a physical copy of my high school graduation program.

I jerk my searching fingers back from the program as though it burned me. He had been there. At my graduation. He was there. All those years ago. And I never saw him. My mind is churning at a pace I can't keep up with. Flashes of confusion and doubt flood my senses.

There's a logical explanation. There has to be. He probably came but saw that you were happy. You had ended things on bad terms. He was probably afraid to upset you again. Yeah, that's probably it.

I move on to the file marked Jared. That one certainly seemed out of place. This one is the smallest. Just a few things printed from online news sources. Jared's birth announcement Rob and I put in the paper. A few photos and blurbs that had appeared in the news over the years from sports he'd played, tournaments where he'd made the winning shot, a group photo of his debate team. But why? Why did he have information about my son from years ago?

Determined to find sense in this, I grab the file with our address. Here's where I'm sure I'll find the research I asked him to do. I expect it to be thick. Filled with the information he was digging up. But instead of research, the folder only contains three sheets of paper. A copy of our last mortgage statement from December. A wire transfer agreement. And a payoff receipt. The wire transfer is signed. Sebastian Sylvain.

I feel I am somewhere floating above my body. This isn't real. This isn't happening. Not again.

I watch my hands—detached from my brain—calmly gather the papers back into the file. My legs stand my body into an upright position from the floor, and my feet walk evenly out of the office back to the kitchen. My ears register Sebastian ending his call and sliding open the door, then closing it again. It seems my body is still in working order, even as my soul splinters.

"Hey, did you want to see the bal-..." Sebastian's words cut off as he catches sight of me, standing at the counter with the evidence. He blanches and air hisses out of his lungs like someone has punched a hole right through him. "Meg. I—I was going to tell you. I had just been waiting for the right time."

My voice is low. Dangerously low. "Tell me what, Sebastian? Tell me that you've known exactly where I was all these years while I wondered if you were even alive? Tell me that our 'bumping into each other' in Prague wasn't by chance at all? Tell me that you've been keeping tabs on me, on my family, on my SON for YEARS?"

The pitch of my voice is increasing with each truth flung out like a dagger, aimed straight for his lying bastard heart. "Or maybe it's to tell me that for these last months you've been stringing me along, letting me go through so much grief and confusion and heartache and turmoil believing my husband was some kind of criminal with a dark past when all along it was YOU! YOU were the one who paid off the house, and I bet you opened the account for Jared too. Do you deny it? DO. YOU. DENY. IT?"

Chapter 16

He slumps nearly in half as he absorbs the punches of my words. He can't look me in the eye, but I'm not finished. I shove into his shoulder, daring him to push back. Daring him to say it's not true, it's all a big misunderstanding.

"Oh, NOW you don't want to look at me? After STALKING me from a distance all these years?! Or maybe you *liked* me hurting and confused. Maybe you *wanted* me doubting Rob, so I would turn to you. So I would fall apart just when you were there to catch me. Maybe you like seeing me hurt like I was back when we met. Back when you were the first thing to make me feel like a whole person. Was that it, Sebastian?"

I fling out his full name as though it were a curse word. "Oh, that's right, you were going to tell me. And how did you think that would go? That I'd be so thankful for my knight in shining armor? That I'd be grateful for you meddling in my life without invitation? You haven't changed one bit, have you? This is exactly what drove us apart two decades ago and you're here doing it again! You are UNBELIEVABLE!"

I slam the folder down on the counter and grab my purse, launching my body in the direction I think I remember the door being.

"Meg." His voice is a ragged plea behind me. A haunted, begging whisper that finishes the job of shredding my poor, battered heart to ribbons. "Meg. Please."

I don't even turn around. Punching the call button, I bite back over my shoulder, "Goodbye, Sebastian. Don't follow me this time. Not even from a distance."

As the elevator door glides closed, I allow the briefest look at him, standing there in the foyer. He makes no move to come after me, even as his arms stretch out slightly toward me of their own volition. Frozen in the air. His eyes darker, more broken than I'd ever seen them.

Good. Maybe he can feel what he's done. Let his heart be just as shattered as mine. It had never been fully whole anyway.

The door slides closed with a thud and the elevator glides smoothly down the shaft, away from him. But unfortunately, there was no button to escape from the pain of his betrayal. Burning hot anger holds back my tears until a taxi takes me home where the breaking is complete.

Chapter 17

Twenty-four years ago

I close the bathroom door behind me quietly, not wanting to draw attention to myself. Turning the ventilation fan on, I pull the blanket tighter around me and curl up on the rug in front of the bathtub. The voices from downstairs still carry to here, but with the white noise of the fan, I can almost block it out. Far better than my bedroom. The door is too close to the top of the stairs. I'm too old to be hiding this way, but sometimes it just feels easier. Easier than facing how much their fighting still affects me.

Things were supposed to be better here. That's what they'd promised. Dad would have work again, and we wouldn't be so strapped for money. Amelia could start her classes at U of C so she could live at home. They even lured me with the promise of my own car, so I could drive up to see Bash on long weekends now that I had my license.

Instead, four months later we're living in a dark, cluttered house in an overcrowded, dirty neighborhood. Amelia had gotten a last-minute full ride to the University of Michigan and left for Ann Arbor in August. Money was more of an issue now than ever. Dad did appear to have more work, yet it seemed we'd failed to account for the significant increase in our cost of living by moving from Superior, Wisconsin to a suburb of Chicago.

The yelling was what got to me the most. When we were younger, Amelia got me through it. Amelia could turn anything into a game. We'd see who could find the best station on the little AM/FM radio in our bedroom with music at the closest pitch to drown out the fighting. As we got older, we had contests to see who could burn the best mix CD to sync with the timing and tenor of the fights. Bonus points if you could match a song key to the rising octaves of Mom's voice.

But now she was gone. Faced with the reality of our parents' violent marriage alone, there were no more games. I tried our playlists but listening to them without Amelia just made my chest ache. That's how I discovered the better sound proofing provided by the upstairs bathroom. Tonight's fight featured Mom overspending on groceries and slot machines and Dad's excessive drinking.

And today the last straw broke me. The car they got me—the little red Neon with the tear in the passenger seat and broken stereo that I loved like it was shiny and new—was repossessed in the early hours of the morning before the sun came up. I came out for school to find drag marks in the little gravel parking area in the alley behind the house.

The curses floating up the stairs have me shoving a bath towel along the crack under the door to try to block it out more. I pull out my prepaid phone and checked the time. It was late enough I could call him without wasting my minutes. My finger hovers uncertainly over the green button.

Things had been… weird between us since I moved. I knew long-distance was going to be hard. But Bash only had one year left of school and promised to come here for college next fall while I finished my senior year. Then we could go anywhere together. That was the plan.

But the more time we spent apart, the more disconnected I felt.

Chapter 17

We called each other every night. But more and more the line was awkwardly quiet after the initial "how was your day" topics were covered. Our lives had been so intertwined before, but now I felt like we were on completely different planes.

There had always been stark differences in our family lives. He came from a happy, middle-class home with two parents that loved each other. I came from... well, my family. That hadn't really mattered before. Not when we'd had each other. But with things darker than ever around here, I didn't feel like I could share it with him. He didn't understand. He'd never experienced life like this. And I hated telling him. It made me feel like I was less than. Inferior. We weren't on an equal footing.

I was supposed to go up and see him this weekend. We had Friday off from school for parent-teacher conferences—which I guarantee my parents would not be attending—and the extra day would be perfect to get up there. I was really hoping that seeing him and being together in person would fix everything.

Counting down from ten, I press the button with my thumb and hold the phone up to my ear. It rings only once before he picks up.

"Hey, babe!" He sounds so happy it hurts. "Less than 72 hours until I get to see my girl!" He sing-songs the words, and I cringe. Hard.

"Heyyy, Bash," I sigh. "So, listen..."

"Meg. What's wrong?"

Another long sigh. "I can't come this weekend. It's a long story, but I won't have a car. And since we haven't yet mastered the technology for human flight... well, I just won't be able to make it."

I can practically hear the crestfallen look on his face through the heavy silence on the other end.

"I don't understand, baby, what's going on? What do you mean you won't have a car? Has something happened?"

The nickname grates on my raw, sensitive nerves, and I grind my teeth. "Sebastian, I don't want to get into it. I just needed to tell you I can't make it. Ok? End of story?"

He scoffs, frustration edging his tone now. "End of story? I'm sorry if I'm feeling just a little blindsided by this Meg, but I feel like I deserve to know what's going on with my girlfriend. My mom went and bought all your favorites for the weekend. She even planned a little get-together with some of your old friends from school so you could see everyone while you were here. Rebecca's been chattering my ear off about when you'll be here, all the games she wants to-"

"GOD Sebastian, ok, yeah, I'm SO sorry to let everyone in your perfect, wonderful, precious family down! Is your dad disappointed, too? Did he mow the lawn for me? I'm sorry I've screwed everything up! I'm sorry my mess of a life is really throwing off your weekend party plans. But unless you know how to get my car from the impound lot and make the bank forget how behind we are on payments, then I. Can't. Make. It."

My face is flaming hot. My chest heaves sucking air in and pushing it back out. The phone is silent in my hand until Bash pulls in a long breath too and lets it whoosh back out.

"I—Meg. I'm so sorry. I didn't know."

"Yeah," I answer softly. "Well, how could you?"

The silence stretches again, and I can't bear it.

"So, now you know. I don't really feel like talking any more tonight." I squeeze my eyes closed, the tears slipping out the corners anyway. "Good night, Sebastian."

"Good night, Meg."

***

I haven't spoken to him in three days by the time Friday comes. I sleep in. Late. Finally hauling my butt out of bed around two, I'm

Chapter 17

embarrassed. Ashamed of the way I treated him when none of this was his fault. But also, I couldn't stand his pity. I tell myself I'll call him tonight and apologize.

Downstairs, Mom has the newspaper out to compare her stack of Powerball tickets to last night's winning numbers. She straightens when she sees me stumble into the kitchen.

"Oh, did you just get up? Why aren't you in school?" She eyes me suspiciously and noticeably sniffs the air. For drugs, alcohol, tobacco—I'm not sure.

"No school today, Mom. It's parent-teacher conferences." I bite my tongue to keep from tacking on "remember?" I learned a long time ago that no, she did not remember and saying that word as a question was like lighting a match too close to a box of fireworks. It may or may not go off with a bang.

"Oh right, those silly things. As if parents actually had the time to go to such nonsense."

My lips twitch, biting back a smirk as I note the unwashed dishes in the sink, the basket of dirty laundry sitting outside the laundry room and my unemployed mother talking about not having time.

I've just sat down with a cup of tea to give my murky brain a minute to clear when she twitches back the curtain from the window over the sink. I found it odd the kitchen was in the front of this house. But then again, the whole space was a weird hodgepodge of design, so I guess it was par for the course.

"Now who's this? I haven't seen that car in the neighborhood before." She prides herself on her intricate knowledge of the comings and goings of every resident of our street. She sucks in a sharp breath of air.

"Meg, I think you'd better come over here!"

So much for enjoying a quiet cup of tea. Sighing, I drag my stiff body up from the plastic chair and cross to join her at the window, feeling like a neighborhood snoop.

My heart drops into my bare feet. I don't recognize the black Civic that's parked on the street in front of our house, but I do recognize the dark mop of hair and broad shoulders climbing out of it.

"What's he doing here? I would've thought he'd have lost interest in you by now, since you're not around to give him what he wants."

I ignore the barb that's offensive to both Bash and me and run to grab my jacket from the hook by the door, slipping my bare feet into some old tennis shoes from the rack. It's early November and most of the days already have a distinct pre-winter chill in the air.

The storm door bangs behind me as I fly down the concrete steps. He stops on the sidewalk and holds his arms open for me to jump into, wrapping both arms and legs around him and burying my face into the space between his neck and collar. His leather jacket is unzipped and warm from the car heater. He envelops me into it, into him, and I take the first deep breath I think I've taken all these months. Leather and spearmint. Home.

"Bash." I breathe. "You're here."

"I'm here," he says, holding me until I ease my grip first. He sets me down on the sidewalk and smiles warmly. I feel it all the way to my toes, even though the air moves crisp and cool around me.

When he glances over my shoulder to the house behind me, the warmth turns into a lead brick in my stomach, as I look back and see it through his eyes. The outside is haggard—crumbling brick and peeling paint. The window in my room in the finished attic has a black hefty trash bag and cardboard over it for now. It was broken when we moved in. And the inside is even worse. I don't want him to see it. I grab his arm and turn him back toward the street.

"Ah, my mom's in a mood. Let's go talk in your car."

I propel him forward to the waiting sedan. It isn't until we're seated that it hits me.

Chapter 17

"Wait. Where's your truck? Please don't tell me you traded it in. You know how I love that old thing!"

Bash's eyes sparkle like he's holding a secret. "Nope, I didn't trade in the truck."

"O-kay," I say, emphasizing the syllables. "Why are you smiling like a lunatic?"

He dangles the keys in front of me. "It's for you, silly! And guess what, the stereo actually works AND it can play CD's!"

His face is alight with joy as he completely misses reading my face, which likely looks like I just got steamrolled by a cement truck. My ears burn as my stomach roils.

He finally catches on that something isn't right when I can't smile and don't reach for the keys. "You don't like it? We can trade it in for something else. Is it the color?"

I can't even look him in the eye right now as the shame and embarrassment build within me to the point of combustion. Yanking the door handle, I get out of the car as quickly as possible and start walking. Anywhere but to my embarrassing house on this embarrassing street in this embarrassing life.

The car door slams behind me, and I hear him calling my name. My feet won't stop though, carrying me past the liquor store on the corner across the street to the park. I don't stop til I reach the stale pond at its center. A thick green layer of scum has built up since the fountain stopped working this summer. Even the ducks wouldn't swim on it anymore.

I stand at its banks, chest heaving and each breath burning as I bend in half, supporting myself with my hands on my knees. My father, while not a very wise man, was a very proud man. Maybe that was something I'd inherited from him, I don't know. But what I do know is I can't stand feeling like someone's charity case. I think I might vomit into the cesspool before me.

Bash has caught up to me now and grabs my wrist, whirling me around. I'm surprised by the gesture. He's never once touched me in anger, but his grip right now is bordering on rough.

"Meg, please tell me what is going on! Talk to me! I don't understand what's happening! I know you haven't been happy lately, but I'm here now. We can fix this. Promise me we can fix this."

His grip is too tight on my wrist. His voice is too desperate, too pleading. Some instinct has me ripping my arm away. His face looks as though I've just slapped him. Good. Let him feel a little of my pain.

"Just tell me how I can fix this."

His voice is barely above a whisper and desperate tears pool in his ocean blue eyes. My own are dry and gritty, each blink scraping like sandpaper. Something inside has snapped, and I can't pull the pieces back together now.

"You can't fix it." My voice is dry, hollow, foreign to my ears. "You can't fix it because you don't get it. I don't want you to come in and save me. I know my life isn't as 'good' as yours, but it is mine, Bash. It's MINE. I don't need your car. And I don't need your pity. Just leave. This isn't working. Go back to your perfect family and leave me alone."

His face crumples as my words hit their mark. My heart falls like a glass ball, shattering around me in a million pieces. But I can't take it back. I won't take it back. I'm not his charity case. I won't be the pity girlfriend pulled up from the slums to join his shiny happy family. His breathing is heavier, cheeks reddening as he meets my gaze again.

"I don't understand why you're doing this. All I've ever done is love you," the words come out angry, harsh and jagged. "Don't make yourself some kind of martyr just because your life is hard. News flash, life IS hard, Meg! You're not special!"

He pulls back from his own words, the color draining from his face. "Wait, Meg. That didn't come out right. Just let me explain. I didn't mean it that way."

Chapter 17

I hold up a hand to stop him. "Oh. I think it came out exactly right. Don't call me, Sebastian. We're through."

I turn and walk away as though my chest isn't caving in with the absence of my heart. As though I didn't just ruin the one good thing I had in my life. In typical Grant-family fashion, I hold my chin up high and walk away from the building I'd just lit on fire as though it didn't contain everything good, everything safe in my life. The only thing I get to keep intact now is my pride.

Chapter 18

Amelia's fingers are warm and unflinching as she lightly runs them up and down my back in soothing circles. I'd been crying into her lap for the last 30 minutes. Before Rob died, I never cried. *You really are falling apart.*

Dad always said it was a sign of weakness and told me to buck up any time my lip had quivered as a small girl. I learned quickly to straighten my back and hold my head high, trying so hard to earn his approval. I didn't so much as make a peep the time I flipped my bike, splitting my chin open on the hot asphalt. Twelve stitches later and not one tear shed. It didn't work though—I never did earn his love.

Amelia's favorite phrase was always "screw Dad," so she'd never bothered to seek his blessing for her life. Probably why she was the stronger sister, and I was the one sobbing into her leggings.

The flow of tears seems to be ebbing, so I sit up and reach for the box of tissues on the end table.

"Ok, sis," she breaks in lightly. "Tell me how you want it done, and I'll work out the details to make it look like an accident. I'm leaning towards a stabbing—a mugging gone violent—but I want to hear your preference."

Chapter 18

A laugh bubbles up from the pain, and I have to wipe a fresh trail of snot that comes up with it. Apparently, I'm an ugly crier. Maybe lack of practice.

"Seriously though. What can I do? How can I help?"

I look around the living room, avoiding her gaze and thinking about the next steps.

"Well, I've decided to sell the house. I'd been thinking about it already anyway, and now I can see it's definitely the right move."

Amelia seems dubious but doesn't voice it. "Ok. You can come stay with me and Mark and the kids for a while until you figure things out."

I shake my head vehemently. "No. I've got to do this on my own Ames. I appreciate the offer. I know you'll always be there for me, but this is on me. I will, however, not turn down your help in moving when the time comes."

She smiles at me gently. "Count us in. I'm a wizard with a packing tape gun."

After she leaves to get back to the kids and her life, I start taking control of mine. Just like last summer, I sit down to make a list.

1. Sell the house.
2. Use proceeds to pay HIM back. Every. Cent.
3. Find an affordable apartment to rent. *Good luck in THIS city.*
4. Talk to Frank about going full time with the magazine.
5. Keep volunteering at Angel House, work out a schedule for when HE won't be there.
6. Look for a new career that feeds my soul.

I tack the list on the fridge with a magnet from Salzburg and get to work.

* * *

By the end of the following week, I'm feeling good about the progress I've made. The house officially went on the market Friday. The realtor was very positive about its marketability. The first showing is already scheduled for today while I'm at Angel House.

Pushing through the now-familiar doors, I pause in the foyer. This place just feels… safe. Protected. Nurturing. I love the work they're doing here and am determined to still be a part of it. Despite…

"Meg! Hi!" Tasha's hug is firm and for a moment I feel like she's holding me up. She has a way about her that both strengthens and comforts. She releases and studies me.

"Something is different." It's a statement. Not a question.

I shrug her off for now saying, "I won't say you're wrong, but I promised Brit we'd meet in the garden to go through the poetry collection she's been working on."

She's studying me, peering into my soul. I take a step back for self-preservation.

"But I'll find you after I'm done, ok? I was actually hoping to talk to you."

Tasha's clear gray gaze looks straight through me. No wonder she's so good with these women. She truly sees each one. "Ok. I'll be in my office tending to some long overdue paperwork. Join me when you're finished."

Walking down the hallway I pause to greet Annie and Thomas, working diligently on assembling the world's longest train track, he tells me. Jane watches her children from a doorway nearby, lines of worry etched on her face.

She'd attended some of my group writing sessions before, but I hadn't felt like we'd bonded just yet. I found her even more guarded than most and easily startled. A few weeks ago, Annie proudly presented me with a poem she wrote about how beautiful her mama was. When I'd shown it to Jane, the small flicker of a smile was quickly swallowed by the

Chapter 18

tears in her eyes, but not of joy. They were tears of a deeply wounded soul. I could tell she didn't believe the words her child had written about her. My heart ached, for what must've happened to break her so badly.

I find Brit already settled at a picnic table set up near the garden fountain, winterized now for the season. A radiant heater gives a bubble of warmth to the sitting area. The second journal I gave her after she'd filled the first one is there along with random napkins, receipts, and scraps of paper she's written on. I smile, recognizing the feeling. The need to write in the moment. The drive to get it out on paper and using whatever scraps you can find.

"Oh hey!" she beams, noticing my arrival. "So, I'm trying to get organized here, but I can't wait for you to read this one I finished last night. I think it's my best one yet."

She is a different person, Meg. You got to witness and be a part of that. You can't give this up.

I smile at her enthusiasm and assure her I can't wait to read it. We spend the better part of an hour going through the collection she's been building since our first class. I'm gently encouraging her to consider letting me send it to a website that publishes original poetry, once complete, while assuring her it's her choice if she wants to share. I told her she never knows who might find strength in her words.

She hands me the last poem. Her eyes sparkle as she bites at her lip, both excited and nervous for me to read it. I take the notebook from her, careful not to smudge the penciled lines, and read.

An Ode to My Mother
When I was small and you were tall, you meant the world to me
I'd sail the world, cross deserts bare all for your company
Each scrape you soothed and wound you wrapped with tender loving care
Until that day I needed you most, that's when you were not there

I came to you bleeding, broke and hurt, though not on the outside
You said "he'd never," dismissed my cries and pushed me to the side
You sat a spectator to my pain as my soul shriveled and died
Never said a word, even when you heard, even though you knew he lied
I thought you'd always be there for me, a mother's love is strong
But when you wouldn't stop the hurt I knew then I was wrong
I hope one day I have a girl with shining eyes and curls
And I'll make sure she knows to me she is the whole wide world
I'll slay the dragons, kill the beasts and all who hope to wound
They won't come near my little girl, never make it to her room
I'll be her guardian, protector too, with me she will be safe
Because I won't become you, Mom, my word I'll never break
So Mom I hope you're happy with the monster that you chose
Because I won't be coming back, this is my final prose.

My throat is thick with emotion as I slide the notebook back to her. I swipe away the tears brimming in my eyes and smile up at her, hoping my face exudes the pride I feel for her.

"Brit," I say when I can speak. "What you've done here... it's beautiful. I hope you can see that. You've spoken raw and real and true to your heart. The angry, broken girl I met at that first class has changed so much. You're doing it. You're healing. And it's such a privilege to watch."

Tears welling in her own eyes, she hugs me tightly. And for a moment, we stay there embracing in the cool January air.

She pulls away first, swiping at her cheeks. "I just wish... I wish she had loved me enough to want to watch out for me, to stand up for me. You know? When everything started, I would pray all night for a guardian angel to come stand at my bedside. Tasha has been encouraging us to not spend too much time asking 'why' and instead focus on how we can make a different world for ourselves and those

Chapter 18

to follow. I guess that's what inspired me to write this. To consider what kind of mother I might one day be."

She shrugs, looking a little embarrassed at having shared so openly. I wrap my arm around her shoulder.

"I'm sorry she didn't protect you. You deserved her protection. You are more than worthy," I tell her gently. "And for what it's worth, I think you'll make an excellent mom one day, because of the work you're doing right here, right now."

After wrapping things up with Brit, I head back into the house to find Tasha. She's in the office buried by stacks of paperwork. There is a method to the madness. Each stack is labeled with a sticky note.

She's chewing thoughtfully on a pencil while reviewing a document when I enter. Sticking the gnawed pencil into her messy bun and pushing up her reader glasses onto her head, she motions to one of the chairs in front of the desk.

"Sit, girl, sit! Can I get you a cup of tea? I'd offer coffee, but I never have it made after lunch. Keeps me up."

"Tea would be lovely," I smile.

She flips on the electric kettle on a credenza and readies two teacups complete with dainty saucers. "Chamomile good?"

"Hm? Oh, I mean yes. Chamomile is great." I'm all nerves now. I know Tasha admires and respects Bash. And she's known him longer. I was anxious about our relationship possibly affecting my work here.

Once the tea is poured, she has us settle in the wingback chairs by the bookshelves instead of the desk. A more "cozy" place to sit, she says.

"So," she eyes me over the steaming cup. "What's up?"

Tasha never did beat about the bush. She was both empathetic and no-nonsense. It was an interesting mix.

"I, well, I've been coming weekly for the last few months. As you know…" She nods at me and circles her wrist for me to get to the point.

"I just wanted to ensure I'll still be able to do that. That... that nothing has changed for me here, despite, um, despite Sebastian."

She snaps her fingers. "I knew it. I knew something was going on with you two. But you're not telling me this with happiness. I assume it's not going well."

I take a sip of the tea, counting on the chamomile to do its job. "It's not going anywhere. We're through."

"Ah," she says, taking a sip from her teacup before setting it to rest on the saucer on the small table between us. "Well, I'm sorry to hear that. Ever since he hired me, I'd wondered why he didn't have someone. For a while I thought he was some kind of monk. But then I saw him with you and thought this was finally it. You were the reason why he'd never shown interest in anyone else. Why I never had to worry about him being around any of these vulnerable women."

She makes a hm sound in the back of her throat, rubbing her chin as I take another drink, uncomfortable with her summary.

"Wait. Sorry. What did you say?" I set my cup down next to hers with a light clatter.

She raises a brow. "That I never had to worry about him with any of my girls."

"No," I frown, "before that. You said he hired you."

"Right, when he first opened the place."

Surprise skitters through my brain. "Sebastian started Angel House?"

Tasha chuckles and reaches over to pat me on the knee. "Started it, funds it, operates it from behind the scenes, yep! He does it all."

I sit, speechless, considering yet another thing I didn't know about Bash. Why did he let me think he was just a volunteer here?

Answering the unasked, Tasha says, "You're likely wondering why he didn't tell you Angel House was his."

She picks up her tea and takes another sip. "I never asked him directly, but I think he enjoys a life outside the spotlight. I may not know

Chapter 18

everything, but I do keep the books. I see the financials. He pours a ton of money into this non-profit. So, I know he's got to be loaded. He doesn't seem like the type who wants to be famous. Money like that attracts a lot of attention. I just figured he didn't want it."

"I guess…" I murmur, taking another drink of the now cool tea before setting the teacup down.

"Listen, thanks for your time. And for letting me continue to work with the women here. I—" Glancing down at my hands, I rub the place where my wedding band had been. "I just needed to make a difference. Do something for someone other than myself. What I wasn't expecting was how much these women have done for me, how they've changed me. I feel like I'm seeing the world with new eyes. So many broken people fill this city. How many of them have no one in their corner? You know? So thank you. For letting me be a part."

She smiles at me serenely, knowingly. "There's so much good we can do down here. If only we're willing. And—if I can be so bold—we require a backer like Mr. Sylvain, with funds to make it a reality. Whatever has happened between you two, I won't interfere. But please know that none of this would exist without him. He had his reasons for starting the place, but that's not my story to share."

She starts to rise from her chair but pauses, slightly raised, before sitting back down.

"Dear, I know your life has been in a transitory phase, with the death of your husband and your son off to college. I'll cut to the chase. I'm in need of a temporary second House Mom here at Angel House."

Seeing my confusion, she continues.

"We like to keep a House Mom on staff. Someone who lives on property here with the women so if any sort of issue occurs or if a woman comes seeking shelter in the middle of the night, someone is here to help. The current 'Mom' is getting married in six weeks. I've got an older woman lined up to replace her, but she's taking a 3-month sabbatical after she retires next month. I need someone in the interim. I really had no intention of bringing this up to you but… I guess you'd say it just felt right."

My brain is still working to process this offer on top of the information she's already dumped on me as Tasha pats my hand understandingly and stands. "I don't need an answer today. But think about it, would you? These last months have proven your ability to make healthy connections and real change with these precious souls. The women trust you. And I don't trust just anyone with them."

She moves to stand behind her desk and picks up the document she'd been examining when I'd first come in, pulling the readers down from the top of her head.

"Now scoot, or I'll put you to work updating the department inventory logs for our insurance. Oh, and Meg?"

She peers over the top of her readers as I stand from my chair. "I'm rooting for you two."

She dips her head to study the papers before her, and I turn to leave her office with a heavy, aching heart. There was nothing to root for. It had all come unraveled and there was no putting it back together. Some paths just weren't meant to be taken.

Chapter 19

The Meg in the mirror looks even older than her 40 years. My hair is lackluster. Eyes dull. Skin pale from the long January that turned into February without fanfare. Nothing left of the glow from those days in Dominica. I push the memories of that trip away. I've lost a bit of weight since then. Not in a flattering way but more like a "coming off from a stomach flu" way. I didn't even have the company of Margaret the last few weeks. It seemed she'd given up on me after I let her down.

It had been a month since that day at the penthouse, and I hadn't seen Sebastian once. Not for his lack of trying, though. My phone buzzed so often I left it off most of the day at this point. I knew I was being childish, wallowing in the hurt and allowing more time than I should to feel sad and sorry for myself. I couldn't seem to find the will to pull out of it.

I left work early today, claiming to have a headache. To be fair, I did have a headache. And a heartache. An entire life ache. Shortly after I got home, a text popped up from the front desk receptionist for the magazine. She said someone was there to see me. She didn't catch his name but he was tall, dark and handsome with the most beautiful blue eyes and impeccably dressed in a tailored suit. Her words. It had to be Sebastian. I'd thrown my phone down and not responded.

I was going through the motions. I'd listed the house and already had some interest. Put in more hours at eTech, hovering somewhere between part time and not quite full time. Kept my visits to Angel House weekly as I considered the offer Tasha had made. But inside, I was hollow. Even more lost than before. And I was too exhausted to do anything about it.

My phone screen lights up again now, on the counter beside me. Tasha's name flashes, and I frown. She rarely calls and it seemed extra odd on a Wednesday afternoon. I swipe to answer, and she's talking before I even get my greeting out.

"Meg? Thank goodness. They're gone. Annie and Thomas. They're gone. Their scumbag of a father showed up at the elementary school and took them. It was a new receptionist. She didn't know to check the list and... never mind. It doesn't matter right now. Just. Can you come? We've called the police, of course, but Jane is beside herself. Everyone's in a panic. I just... we need a soothing presence and the girls trust you. I'm going to go with Jane. The police want to take her to their old neighborhood to ask if anyone's seen them. Her ex has moved around so much, there's not a current known address for him."

All self-pity, every ounce of exhaustion evaporates from my body as I'm filled with fear-fueled adrenaline. "I'll be right there," I say into the phone, already halfway down the stairs. Grabbing my keys from their hook, I fly out the door.

The air in Angel House is heavy, thick with worry when I arrive. Tasha and Jane are already gone, so I get busy, moving among the women, trying to offer comfort and encouraging words. Annie and Thomas are currently the only kids living here. The entire house had adopted them as their own.

I find Brit pacing the library, breathing fast, hands clenched into balls.

Chapter 19

She runs at me when she sees me, grabbing my upper arms desperately. "Meg! Did they find them yet? Are Annie and Thomas safe?"

I take a steadying breath and attempt to share some calm. "Not yet, Brit, but remember they've only just begun looking. I'm sure they'll find them. I truly believe they will."

One of the new girls—barely 18—was carefully reassembling the train tracks. She catches me staring and says weakly, "So it'll be ready for them when they get back."

I blink at the tears burning at the back of my throat and nod to her in approval. Some of the older women have formed a circle offering silent prayers, but Brit is too keyed up to be still enough to join them.

She resumes her pacing, punching a fist into her open hand. "Yeah. They'll find them. I bet Sebastian'll find them first. Have you seen that guy's arm muscles? He'll punch that bastard's lights out. I know he will."

My heart drops. "Sebastian? He was here?"

Brit doesn't notice the tightness of my voice, too distracted by the pounding rhythm of her combat boot steps. "He was. He came first. Before the police even. Took some papers from the office and left again. I heard his tires squealing as he went away."

"If anyone can find those kids, it's Bash," a voice says from behind me, and I turn toward it.

A tall, lithe woman walks up gracefully to join us near the windows Brit has been pacing in front of. Clad in a classy dark pantsuit, it's her gorgeous auburn hair that catches my eye first. The spark of recognition hits as I take in her face, although it's much older than the last time I saw her.

"Rebecca?"

"Hey, Meg," she responds with a light side hug, stepping back to tuck her long hands into her pockets. "It's been a while. Sorry our first chance to meet again is under these circumstances."

"Wow, look at you! You're gorgeous!" I blurt, taken off-guard by seeing her here, in this place.

She chuckles lightly. "Well, I don't always don the business look, but I had a meeting today with a local gala. You'll more often find me in a junk yard, jean overalls with burn marks from my welding torch and the world's messiest bun."

"Oh right," I reply. "You're an artist! Ba—ah, your brother told me."

Her smile drops as she nods, her gaze growing serious. "Is there any news? I came as soon as I heard. I can't imagine what Jane must be feeling right now."

I shake my head, a wave of helplessness threatening to pull me under even as a question flits through my mind. "Nothing yet. But... I guess I feel a little out of the loop. I didn't realize you were involved with Angel House too?"

"Oh, Becca comes around," Brit pipes in, pleased to have information to share. "After all, she's the reason this place exists."

I look back to Rebecca, confused.

"My brother... He's very protective, you know," she meets my gaze with intensity, telling me she knows just how much I know that fact. "He wasn't always THIS bad. But when I was in high school, events pushed him over the edge from being protective to being... obsessively so."

A storm of emotion passes over her face. I reach out to touch her elbow, bring her back.

"Hey, you don't have to tell me if you don't want to. It's ok."

She shrugs a bit, scuffing the toe of her kitten heel on the laminate planks of the floor.

"It's not like there's much else to do right now while we wait—the women seem to be supporting each other, which is good to see. I feel more anxiety when waiting silently. Besides, I think you probably should know. It was so long ago, and I've done a lot of work and healing since then. I don't mind talking about it. He probably told you about Scarlett?"

"Yes, your daughter. He couldn't say enough about her. Very proud uncle."

She smiles, leaning back against the window behind her and crossing her ankles, in a move so like her brother it makes me ache. "He is. What he probably didn't tell you is that Scarlett was conceived… against my will. Granted, she's the best thing that ever happened to me, but the way she came into being was not. And Bash? Well. He blamed himself."

My chest aches for Rebecca, my mind reeling and confused for Bash. "I don't understand. Why would he blame himself?"

"He was home from MIT, visiting for the weekend. I'd begged him to go to a football game with me that night. He had a paper to work on for class and said he'd meet me there. He got busy with his research and ended up not getting there until after the game was over. And by then… well, it was too late. I don't remember much of that night, but he said he found me walking alongside the road outside the high school with one shoe, dress torn. What I do remember is him pleading with me to tell him who did it. But I saw the look in his eye. I didn't want him throwing his life away doing something stupid, so I never told a soul. I refused to file a police report. I'm not sure he ever fully forgave me for that.

"And he definitely never forgave himself. After what happened to me, I was in a safe place surrounded by a loving family that helped me down the path of healing. So many girls and women don't have that. He wanted to give as many women as possible a chance. A chance to know what safety feels like. To experience love without manipulation and abuse."

She shifts, crossing her arms to glance at the women gathered, then away.

"As soon as he got his first job out of college, he rented out a room in a community center for rape victims to come and find love and support through weekly meetings, guided by a therapist—which he also paid for. But it grew so much from there, expanding to what it is today—a full-time shelter for survivors of all types of domestic abuse. I still come every Thursday, for the rape survivor support group that gathers. Some of the older women and I have a group of girls we mentor. Plus I lead some art therapy classes here and there. But it's all run on his dollar."

She pauses, looking as if she wants to say more, but unsure if she should. The mortgage. The college account. Guardian Securities. Angel House. It's all been him. A Guardian Angel. With so many emotions running through my heart and mind, I stay quiet processing.

Brit, who'd clearly heard the story before, had turned toward another group, huddled together sharing their favorite stories of the children in the corner. Casting them a glance, Rebecca gently grabs my elbow and steers me in the other direction, between some bookshelves towards the opposite end.

She faces me intently once she stops in a more private space. "I know this isn't my place. But I feel like I should say something. Bash told me what happened. What he did. And please know, I absolutely gave him a piece of my mind, ripped him up one side and down the other about what an absolute idiot he is."

She says it so fiercely, I believe her and find myself nodding for her to go on. She chews her lip for a moment before continuing, blowing a quick breath out her nose.

"He was stupid. Really, really stupid. That story I just told you, what happened to me. It really changed him. He always kind of had that 'rescuer' vibe going anyway, but when that happened, it's like it kicked that personality trait into overdrive. After the attack, he checked on me every single day, sometimes multiple times a day after he found out I was carrying Scarlett. If I didn't answer my phone, he would panic

Chapter 19

until he heard from me again. It wasn't healthy, but I knew it was his way of processing. He got better, with some professional help.

"Now with the line of work he's in... whew. Some of the stuff he does as a contractor for the FBI involves tracking down the nastiest bad guys through dark web activity. I'm talking human trafficking, *child* trafficking. It's so messed up. And I think that made his overprotectiveness even worse. I barely date because I know any guy I show up with he's going to have a full criminal background check and internet activity sweep done on the man before we finish dinner!"

She lets out a laugh at her own joke, which was not really a joke, and pulls out her phone to check for any new messages. Sighing when she finds none, she faces me again.

"Bottom line—my idiot, overprotective brother loves you, Meg. I know you know that. Was he wrong to do what he did and hide it from you? Absolutely. But he's been pining away for you for DECADES. I honestly believe he can and will change for you. Because you're IT for him. You're worth it."

She gives a long sigh and puts a hand on my shoulder. "You look like you could use a cup of tea. Still obsessed with spearmint? I think Tasha has some in her office."

I meet her gaze, surprised. "Yeah, how did you know spearmint was my favorite?"

She lets out a chuckle and rolls her eyes with a smile, "Because it's the only kind of gum my brother has carried for YEARS—ever since he met you! It's never been his favorite. He prefers cinnamon. But he started carrying it in high school just so he could offer it to you, and he's never stopped."

"Are you se—" a commotion at the front door cuts me off with a start. My heart pounds in my ears as we race out of the library to find Sebastian standing in the doorway, the setting sun streaming through the door in a hazy glow around him. In one arm he has a bundle held up onto his chest and shoulder. Annie, I realize with a cry of gratitude. Thomas stands on his other side, holding tightly to his leg.

Sobs of relief and a few cheers go up in the hallway behind me. We hold back from running to him, not wanting to scare the trembling children. Rebecca goes quietly to Annie first, gently taking her out of Bash's arms as the little girl recognizes and reaches for her. Kneeling down before Thomas, the tearful little boy looks up into Rebecca's warm eyes.

"I didn't let him hurt her, Miss Becca. He said he was gonna, but I kicked him real hard, and he got mad and closed us in the dark and didn't come back. But I didn't let him hurt her, I promise I didn't."

The vise squeezing my throat threatens to choke me completely. I take a few steadying breaths to avoid bursting into tears, for the children's sake.

Rebecca calmly takes the boy's hand and tells him, "What a good big brother you are, Thomas. Just like Sebastian. Your mama will be so proud of both of you. Why don't we go see if there are any cookies in the kitchen while we wait for her to get back? She'll be here soon and will be so happy to see you both. Ok?"

The boy nods—never taking his eyes from her face—and follows her to the kitchen, clinging to her hand.

Chapter 20

Sebastian's eyes are dark, haunted pools as they reach mine. I silently reach for his hand, pulling him into Tasha's office and closing the door softly behind us. First things first.

"You called Tasha?"

He nods, throat working up and down as he swallows hard.

"Good. I'm sure they'll be back soon then."

He stands in the middle of the dim room, lit only by the fading evening sun. I walk past him to the desk, turning to face him while leaning on it for support.

"How did you find them, Bash?" I ask quietly, but I know he can hear me. He runs a shaking hand over his face, pulling it through his hair before gripping the back of his neck.

"Surveillance feeds," his voice is low and gravelly. "I had my guys at the office pull footage of the outside of the school. Got the plate numbers and make and model of the car. They were able to follow it pretty closely til they lost it in an alley in West Garfield Park."

A shudder goes through me. That neighborhood was known as one of the worst in the city—the highest rate of violent crimes per capita. A hand goes to my throat, but I stay silent.

"The police were out as well, canvassing the area after we called in the information. I just happened to locate the car first. I had my security team with me and were about to storm the house it was parked in front of, but I had a feeling," he shrugs and studies the hands fisted in front of him, the veins bulging on the back.

"I sent the team in and stayed behind to check the car. I found the kids in the trunk, curled around each other. Thomas came out with feet and fists swinging until he realized it was me. Next week, I'm putting both those kids in karate class."

He walks numbly to slump into the chair that I sat in just weeks before across from Tasha. His dark gaze meets mine and regret fills his eyes.

"I thought I'd protected them, Meg. I took all the proper legal routes—hired a great lawyer for Jane to get his rights removed, filed restraining orders. It wasn't enough." Violence now overwhelms the despair, and his knuckles go white.

"I wanted so badly to go in that house and absolutely tear that piece of scum apart. I was seconds from leaving the kids to do just that. But when I looked into Annie's eyes, buckling her into the back seat, I knew I couldn't leave them alone even for a minute. So, I left the security team and the police that were arriving to deal with the trash. The cruiser with Tasha and Jane was further out, radioed in that they'd meet us here. But part of me wishes I'd had the chance to kill him with my own two hands. Why couldn't I protect them?"

Resting elbows on the chair arms, he sinks further with his head in his hands. Anger and weariness exude from him like steam off a hot spring. I find myself moving toward him, drawn without conscious thought, until I'm sinking down to my knees at his feet. Taking his head in between my hands, I lift it just a bit to meet his eyes. I see the moment he breaks.

Bash's arms come around me, sweeping me into an iron hold that pulls me up and into his lap. His head falls to my chest, and his breath hitches with a gasp, squeezing me even tighter.

The sound is strained, hoarse when he finally speaks. "I just kept imagining finding them broken, hurt, or dead. I—I was so afraid I'd be too late. That I couldn't save them. Like I hadn't—"

His voice breaks and my heart breaks with it. I give him a moment to bury his face in my neck and take some deep breaths before I lift his head again.

"Sebastian. Look at me," I say gently but firmly. "What happened to Rebecca was not your fault."

His eyes widen with surprise, and I nod in confirmation, his pain reflected in my eyes.

"Bad things happen. Every day. We can't possibly protect ourselves and the people we love from all of them. This world has a lot of darkness. But it also has a lot of light, if you know where to look. Like the light I saw in Thomas' eyes—despite the horror he'd just experienced—when he looked up at you. He trusted you. He felt safe with you. To him, you're a light. I see light in Rebecca, despite what's happened to her. She's made something beautiful. And that's in part because you were there for her. Just like you were there for Thomas and Annie.

"I see the light in my son, Jared. Who suffered the pain of losing his father, only to find his deeper purpose in life through it. And—and maybe I'm finding mine too."

I swallow thickly. "You've been a part of that. You helped me find myself again when I was lost. You were the light in the darkness of my grief and lost wanderings. For me... you feel like home."

His gaze wavers, unable to believe what I've just told him.

I clear my throat. "However, I believe we still have a lot to discuss between us. As soon as Tasha and Jane are back and things settle here, my place?"

He nods, and I lean forward to give him a soft kiss on the cheek. A big breath of air releases from his lungs. We stand to rejoin the others and watch as a mother reunites with her children.

* * *

Bash offers to stop for takeout to bring to the house, but neither one of us feel much like eating. I let him in the front door, and we both stand a little awkwardly in the entry for a moment. I finally motion to the dining room, heart and mind too full to say much just yet. We take up seats at the table across from one another. The dark wood feels solid, the grain lines soothing under my unsteady hands.

He clears his throat and laces his fingers together atop the table before meeting my eyes. "I am so sorry, Meg. I went too far. I know I did. I won't excuse it. Sorry feels like a weak word, but it's what I have. Would it be ok if I explained… tried to explain where my head was at? I just—" His gaze drops to the table, sorrowful. "I just want you to see me."

I nod and take advantage of his pause to really look at him. His white shirt is unbuttoned at the collar, the gray tie hanging open down the sides peeking from under the black jacket. Even with the haunted look in his eyes, he was still the most beautiful man I'd ever known. Dark circles shine under his eyes. His cheeks seem little hollower than I remembered, as though he too has lost some weight.

"When your family moved away, it was like my world stopped turning. I felt like I was suspended in time, yet everyone else moved on around me. I was just waiting, counting the minutes—*the seconds*—until I graduated and could come be near you again. Then that day, when I came down thinking I could surprise you…"

He chews the inside of his cheek as the hurt plays out over his face. He looks like that 17-year-old boy all over again, and I just want to

Chapter 20

wrap my arms around him. I don't know if my heart is ready to forgive him, but the rest of me yearns to reach out.

"After graduation, I was dead set on coming to Chicago, even though you didn't want a relationship anymore. I just wanted to be near you, in case we had any kind of chance. But I'd gotten a scholarship to MIT and my parents—you know how supportive they always were—they told me I was making a mistake throwing away this opportunity. That if we were meant to be together, it would work out, even if I went away. So, I went. Begrudgingly."

My heart squeezes, thinking of him almost coming to Chicago right then. Could we have worked it out at that point? I'm not sure. My family was still in a pretty dark place, and I was suffering too. I push away the "maybe" trains of thought from my head.

"Once I finished school though, I knew I would move. I knew I would have to find you. It wasn't hard to follow your path. The graduation announcements from your high school had little blurbs about each grad, including where they were heading for college. I—I hope that's not too weird that I came for your graduation. I was already home for summer break from MIT, and it's not too far of a drive. I didn't want to interfere with your life or mess with your path forward. I just wanted to see you. And I was so incredibly proud to see you walking that stage, wearing your honors cords with your head held high. You've always been a marvel to me. But I let you go, again, because what did I have to offer anyway? A long-distance relationship? I still had a few years left at MIT.

"So, I went along, biding my time through college until I finished my last exam. I skipped graduation and headed to the U of C campus to look for you. I don't know why I was expecting some movie-scene reunion where I present myself to you, ready for forever," he scoffs at himself, picking at a knot in the wood of the table.

"After half a day of wandering around, I caught a glimpse of you walking across campus. I was headed right for you when a guy appeared out of nowhere, throwing his arm around you. You smiled and kissed him before walking into your dorm building together. I was crushed, but you seemed happy. I… I wanted you to be happy."

Revisiting these memories must rile something in him because he stands from the table to pace the dining room floor. He tosses his jacket and tie onto the back of the chair in a fluid motion. As he paces, his hands alternate between shoved into his pockets and running through his hair. He stops in front of me, bracing his hands on the table and meeting my gaze.

"Meg, I have never forgiven myself for that day. For not walking up to you, telling you how I felt, that I still loved you more than anything. For not sweeping you into my arms and kissing you senseless. But I didn't know what you wanted. I didn't know if you still wanted… me. And that fear kept my feet glued to the sidewalk as I watched you walk away with him."

His pacing resumes. Nervous anxiety rolls off him in waves. But I sit statue-still. Reeling. Absorbing. Processing.

"You know about my company, Guardian Securities."

"And Angel House," I add.

He stops, brow furrowed. "You know about Angel House too? Tasha?" I nod in confirmation.

"I don't know whether to fire her or give her a raise," he mumbles, running a hand over his face. "So, you probably know then, doing what I do involves digging up a lot of dark, twisted stuff. Getting to know those women at the House, what they've been through. Nightmare is too tame of a word. The more I saw, the more I worried.

"I started watching out for you, from afar. I'd seen your marriage announcement in the paper. Then Jared's birth announcement. Eventually, I set a Google alert with your name, Rob's and Jared's, so anything mentioned I'd know. I'd see it. It made me feel like I

Chapter 20

could... like I could know you were ok."

His eyes meet mine, desperate, begging for understanding. His hair is tousled and unkempt from where he keeps running his fingers through as though he can pull the thoughts from his mind to convey.

"I get it, this is where it starts sounding creepy. This is where I cross the line. But I swear, all I ever wanted was for you to be safe and happy. I never ever followed you or drove by your house or work. I know you mentioned Prague that day at my house. I promise you, that was a complete coincidence. You said I didn't act surprised. But I heard you tell that other writer your name at the beginning of the talk. I heard your voice, and it took the remainder of the hour to settle my heart and breathing rate down enough to appear cool and calm when we finally spoke. That's why I didn't seem surprised.

"As for the money... when Rob died, when his obituary notice posted, I didn't want you worried over the financial impact. I assumed you'd put your career on the back burner for Jared. I just wanted you and your son taken care of. I—I did some adjustments on the bank end to backdate the payment to before he passed. I didn't plan on running into you again. I never planned on you knowing. But I didn't realize how it would affect you emotionally, how it would mess with your mind," his voice is weighted down with regret.

A creeping understanding is working its way into my brain. But something more edges into the corner of my mind. One of the files I'd found.

"Ok, Sebastian. Let's assume that I can somewhat understand this. I don't agree with your methods, but I can *maybe* see where you were coming from. But you even had a file for the hospital where Rob's cancer treatment took place. Why would you have that?"

He makes an "ah" sound and pushes back from the table to shove his hands deeper into his pockets. "I... well, I have connections at the cancer center he was being treated at. A good friend of mine is on the board of directors. I found out through some digging that Jared had tried everything to get his dad into a clinical trial to no avail. So, I pulled some strings, trying to give him his best possible chance."

He shrugs, turning away, fully aware he's blown through every privacy boundary in my life. I can't stay sitting at the table anymore. I stood silently and round the table to come to him. Placing a hand on his shoulder, he turns, torment clouding his blue eyes into a stormy sky.

"You did that for Rob? You tried to save him?" My voice is barely above a whisper.

His is equally as soft as he lets down the last of his defenses and says, "I did it for YOU, Meg. Because you loved him. And because I would do anything for the people I love. For you."

Love. He said love. There it was. Still. He loved me still. He never stopped.

He reaches up, hesitantly, giving me the chance to pull away. When I don't, he gently tucks my hair behind my ear, letting the back of his knuckles trail down my neck.

A few more thoughts invade before I can feel resolution. Pulling back slightly I say, "Two more questions. First, what was your plan when you showed up at my office today? That was you, wasn't it?"

"Oh," his cheeks flush a little his eyes dart to the side. "It's probably stupid. But I was there to offer you an exclusive exposé article on Guardian Securities. On me. Unveiling me as the CEO after I've spent years in the shadows. It was dumb."

My heart pounds in my ears at the thought, watching color creep up his cheeks before he meets my gaze straight on.

"I know it wouldn't make up for what I did. But I thought since I had invaded your privacy, I could give you the chance to expose me and provide a big boost to your career. It might be at least a start to reestablishing some trust between us."

Chapter 20

Something inside me crumbles, some walls I'd built up around myself, around my heart. Some that had been newly erected this year and last, and some that had been there for decades. I wrap my arms around his waist, resting my cheek on his chest.

"It's not stupid. And I would take you up on it except I like people not knowing who you are. If they had known, some Victoria's Secret model would have definitely scooped you up by now. Which brings me to my second question."

I tip my chin up toward him, meeting his eyes with intention. One last question. "What happened with Chelsea? Why didn't you marry her?"

He blinks, surprised, and glances out the glass garden door, peering into the darkness a moment before returning to my gaze.

"I think you know the answer to that."

I rise onto my toes, putting myself closer to his eye level. "I want to hear you say it."

His chest heaves and both hands rise to my shoulders, then my face, cupping my cheeks. Gently first, then a little fiercely.

"Because she wasn't you. Because I could never give my heart to her, not when you still held it completely. Because every girl I tried to make myself interested I was comparing to you, and it wasn't fair to them." He dips his forehead down to rest on mine and takes a deep breath.

"It's you, Meg. There's no one else. It's always been you for me. And it always will be."

I tilt my chin up until our lips finally meet again. This kiss is softer, a little tentative, but even more true with no more secrets between us. He whispers my name on my lips, and I open my heart to him. Choosing to believe in him, in us. Taking that next step in faith.

Chapter 21

"Meg, that guy is here for the desk!"

Kristen's voice carries up the stairs, reaching me in the dark recesses of my closet where I found yet another shoe I hadn't seen in years. The second I've found missing its mate. Brushing the closet dust from my hair, I wipe my gritty palms on my back pockets and holler, "Coming!"

Just a week away from the big move and my girlfriends and sister had been in and out helping me list furniture in our local buy/sell page, making donation box runs and packing things in between. I'd always prided myself on being able to "do it alone." I didn't need anyone's help. But the truth was, these past weeks I'd realized how much better I felt with my people around me. When the shadows crept in, their support and presence shone a little more light. It was nice not feeling alone.

Today's buyer was frowning at Rob's old desk, running his hands over the sides and testing the drawers when I rounded the corner to the study. It was the last big item I needed to downsize before the movers came.

"They just don't make 'em like that anymore!" I say brightly, trying a salesman tactic.

Chapter 21

The man harrumphs and glares at me under bushy eyebrows. Ok, that's how we're going to play it. Buckle up, sir. I've been doing this for weeks.

"Yep, she's a pretty solid piece. My late husband, may he rest in peace," I don't miss the surprised glance he shoots me as I flash my widow card, dabbing a bit at the corner of my dry eyes, "he paid a fortune for it when he became junior partner at his law firm. He said it exuded power, that's why he bought it. Gosh, I almost wonder if I should even sell... she really is a one-of-a-kind piece..."

I pull a long, thoughtful face with just a touch of sorrow creasing my brow. The man coughs into his fist and digs into his jacket pocket.

"I'll take it," he says gruffly. "I brought a van. Can you help me load it?"

I try not to brighten too much as I stuff the cash into my back pocket and answer, "Absolutely!"

Unfortunately, it was NOT just salesmanship when I said the desk was solid. The thing weighs a ton! I feel the sweat breaking out on my forehead as we each lift an end to set it on a thick moving blanket, intending to pull it to the front door. That part goes fairly well until we reach the entry and I realize there's no way to get around lifting and carrying the massive thing out the door.

With him on one end, I focus on lifting with my knees on the other end as we maneuver towards the doorway. Somehow, I end up on the down end of things as we start to descend the stairs. The entire weight presses on me. I try using my shoulder against the side panel for support.

Once we straighten out again at the walkway and my shoulder lifts from the panel, I hear a click. Papers flutter over my feet. A hidden door has popped open in the desk, and a file full of documents has fallen out, littering the sidewalk around me. Papers that had been hidden. Papers I hadn't seen before.

Setting down my end rather quickly, based on the choice words coming from my buyer, I snatch up the papers quickly. Shoving them back into the folder, I run back up the stairs to put them safely in the house.

After the cantankerous man and his new desk are gone, I race back in, heart pounding, to take the papers to the office. I spread them out on the rug to examine.

The documents appear to be dated about 15 years ago and are an assortment of corporate memos and safety standards for a company called Great Lakes Freight. They're filled with technical ship jargon I don't understand. There are a few emails too, and some documents printed on Nelson & Nelson Law's letterhead.

There was a name I hadn't heard in a while. Nelson & Nelson was where Rob had landed his first attorney role. It was a bit of a slimy firm, but he needed the job. We needed it. He'd been an associate there six months or so when we hit that rough patch in our marriage. Jared was a toddler, soaking up all my attention with his adorable mischievousness. But Rob had been so disconnected from us. He was barely home, working massive amounts of overtime at his firm, trying to find a position at a better firm, while I took on as many freelance jobs as possible.

Why had Rob hidden these documents, keeping them all these years later?

A newspaper clipping slips out from between the pages, settling into my lap. A bright smiling face shines up from the ragged-edged page, young and full of hope. The photo caption identifies him as "Charlie Brenner, age 23," while the accompanying article references an untimely death aboard the freighter ship on which he worked. A flicker goes off in my brain as I read on. The article states the courts had found his employer, Great Lakes Freight, not responsible for Brenner's death on grounds of the employee's repeated failure to follow company

Chapter 21

safety regulations. It included a canned statement from Brenner's legal team, the jerk that had been Rob's boss. He'd hated that guy. The closing sentence was what caught my eye.

"Brenner is survived by his wife Samantha, his son Zachary (age 1) and his unborn daughter."

"Oh my God..." I whisper, reaching for my phone.

* * *

One hour later, Bash's sedan is parked outside an older but well-kept apartment building in Rogers Park.

Bash reaches across the console to squeeze my hand with a steady grip. "Ready?"

I nod, my eyes not leaving the building face as they rove over each window, wondering which one belongs to a single mom and her two teen kids.

The March day carries a nip of winter's chill despite the sun shining warmly, evaporating the early morning's rain off the sidewalks. Fifteen steps to the entryway. Bash waits quietly behind me as I read through the panel of residents. There it was. S. Brenner. Apt 3C. When I hesitate, his hand comes to the small of my back. Solid. Reassuring. Present. With a deep breath, I press the buzzer with my thumb.

A few moments of silence and then a crackle. "Yes?"

I clear my throat. "Hi, is this, um, is this Samantha Brenner?" A bead of sweat trickles down my spine inside the fleece I threw on before leaving the house. It felt protective at the time. Now it just served to seal in my own body heat.

"Yep, who's this?" the voice crackles back.

"Er, I, uh, Meg. I'm Meg. And I think you knew my late husband. Rob Franklin?"

The pause has me holding my breath. I jump as the door buzzes suddenly, loud and long, unlocking the heavy entry door for us to enter.

I attempt a weak smile at Bash and say, "Here we go," as we enter and start the climb the stairs to her floor. The building feels a bit historic, but with modern touches like fresh lighting and neutral colors on the walls, contrasting with the rich dark woods of the banister and risers. The third floor hallway stretches long before us as we start down it. When we stand outside the door marked 3C, I count ten deep breaths before raising my hand to knock.

Samantha Brenner opens the door. She's a little taller than me, with curly brown hair piled on top of her head. Her features are petite—small button nose, slightly pointed chin, tired gray eyes, dark shaped brows, one of which is particularly arched in a questioning look. She crosses her arms over her Navy Pier sweatshirt, paired with black yoga pants and fuzzy purple socks. She doesn't say anything. She just stares at us until I snap out of my feature-cataloguing brain mode and remember to speak.

"Hi. This is probably weird that I'm here. I mean. I feel weird. Not that you're—ok. Let me try this again. I'm Meg Franklin. My husband was Rob. He died about 15 months ago, and I found some things in settling his affairs that brought up some... questions. Would it be ok if we talked for a minute? Oh. And this is my friend, Sebastian."

Samantha waits another moment, really letting me sweat it out there in her doorway before shifting to the side just enough to indicate "enter if you must." Bash twists slightly to get around her into the apartment.

It's a nice place inside. It has the high ceilings of the older buildings with big windows facing the street. The furnishings are simple, and the place is clean, not an item visibly out of place. Unsure what to do without a verbal invitation, we take our chances and settle into the brown microsuede couch.

Our hostess sits across from us in a burnt orange armchair. Arms

Chapter 21

still crossed, eyebrow still raised, mouth still silent.

I clear my throat to indicate my intention to speak. "I'm sure you're wondering what all this is about..."

"I'd say you're probably wondering why your husband has been wiring money into my account every month for the last 15 years," she says in a low even voice with stunning calm. "It's guilt money. He felt bad he couldn't prove my husband's murder was covered up."

Bash nudges me gently in the ribs with his elbow, and I realize my mouth is hanging open. I snap it shut so hard I wince at sound of my molars smashing together.

"Ah. Yep. Ok. I guess you're not wondering then. I guess maybe I'm the only one wondering. So... uh, Samantha, if you wouldn't mind... Take me from the beginning?"

I try to school my face into a calm expression even as my heart races. I wipe my clammy palms on my jean-clad thighs and consciously stop my knee from bouncing. Bash calmly reaches over to take one of my hands and hold it in between both of his. It settles me some.

Sam—she clarifies—lost her husband Charlie while he was working on a freighter that transported goods across Lake Michigan and the other Great Lakes. On his last visit home, he'd been increasingly concerned over some safety issues onboard the freighter. Charlie told his wife he'd filed a couple of reports but, after getting his wrist slapped by his supervisor on the boat, felt he couldn't say any more without risking his job. They had a toddler at home with a baby on the way. It just wasn't worth the risk, he'd told her.

Three days into a week-long job, Sam got a phone call from Great Lakes Freight's lawyer. Charlie had been in an accident. According to the captain's report, he'd been drinking heavily after his shift and had come above deck, stepping into the restricted zone during a night-time cargo load. He was killed in the incident, and his body was so mangled that they suggested cremation as an open casket was out of the question.

"At the time, eight months pregnant and struggling to get through the day-to-day, I was so hormonal and overwhelmed by the reality of raising these kids alone, I couldn't think straight. They'd already cremated the body by the time my brain finally kicked in and thought to question what I'd been told. Charlie barely had more than 2 beers at a time at home. The story didn't line up, but it was too late for an autopsy. Plus, I knew he'd been filing safety reports that weren't well received."

My heart ached for the woman across from me. I could certainly relate to losing your husband, but facing having to raise your kids alone with little help or resources? I could only imagine.

"I didn't have much money. His company life insurance had barely covered the cremation and funeral expenses. But I figured some lawyers don't require payment until they win a case. That's how I found Nelson & Nelson. I didn't really realize what I was getting into with them. I was young and stupid and trying to survive. Rob was assigned my case and helped me file a lawsuit against Great Lakes. Next thing I know the company's high-priced corporate lawyers are all over me. Rob seemed inexperienced, but he looked like he cared. Which is more than I can say for his boss.

"In the end they offered me $100,000, two years of Charlie's salary, half of which would go to the law firm as their cut. I said I'd take it, because I was desperate. But the day before I signed, Rob came to me upset, asking all kinds of questions about the safety reports Charlie had filed. He asked me if I had any proof, if Charlie had stashed any copies at home I could present. I told him no but Charlie had for sure filed them with the freight company. Rob said there were none filed with Great Lakes. The way he held my gaze though, it was like he was trying to say more without saying it, you know? The whole thing stank of coverup."

Chapter 21

The pit in my stomach was growing with each word she spoke. I could see where this was headed. But I resisted interrupting. People need to be able to share their story.

"But I had nothing. Nothing but my word of what Charlie had told me against theirs. Rob tried his best but was clearly way out of his league. He was being pressured by his boss to close this thing. So, I settled. The price tag on his life a measly $100,000. My half got us through the first year anyway. At the one-year anniversary of his death, I started getting these wire transfers into my account. I didn't know where they were coming from, but I was an exhausted, single mom trying to survive on tips alone. I wasn't going to look a gift horse in the mouth. They started small and grew over the years.

"After the sixth payment hit, an envelope was slid under our door one day with a note that said, 'I'm so sorry. His life was worth so much more.' I guess I didn't know for sure it was Rob til you showed up today, but I always had a gut feeling. He had looked at me so urgently, so desperate for me to say I had proof. Had Charlie's death been proven a result of safety violations, the payout would've been... substantially more."

Sam purses her lips to one side, looking toward the window contemplatively a moment before continuing.

"Honestly, I'm not sure we would have survived the first five years without Rob's help. Things are better now. Eight years ago, I got promoted to manager at the restaurant, and we're good. Since then, I've taken the money he sent and put it into college savings accounts for the kids. Give them a better life than Charlie or I had a chance at. They've got a good chunk of change for when the time comes. So, I guess in a lot of ways it worked out. I had wondered what changed when the deposits stopped, but like I said, we're ok."

She's stated the entire story very matter of fact, without any signs of anger or even detachment, simply acceptance. My entire body has been clenched throughout her story, leaning forward from my seat on the couch in anticipation.

"I'm kind of processing here, forgive me fumbling for words. I'm so sorry for all you went through. I guess I'm surprised you seem so... accepting of it. You don't seem bitter at all."

Sam shrugs nonchalantly. "Charlie and I both grew up attending the school of hard knocks. Absent parents, drugs, gangs, dropouts and the like were common in our neighborhood, in our families. All we really wanted was something better for our kids. That's what brought us together in the first place."

She motions to the apartment around her, "And we have that, even if he's not here to see it. We did ok. We got out of that mess. Our kids are growing up to be decent humans who have a real chance at a good life. I like to think he knows and is happy about it too."

Now that sentiment I truly understood. But her direct summation leaves me stunned. I can't help but admire her attitude, her outlook on life. Bash brings me back with a light squeeze to the hand he's still holding. I take that as my sign and stand to my feet, pulling him up with me.

"Sam, thank you for sharing your story. I'm so sorry for all you've experienced and really glad life has worked out for you. I hope your kids realized how lucky they are to have such a strong mom in their corner."

It's the first strong emotion I've seen from her as a blush creeps up over her cheeks and she stands, tucking her hands behind her and giving me a small smile.

"Yeah, well, I'd do anything for 'em. That's for sure."

"The heart of every good mother," I respond gently.

We thank her sincerely for her time and close the door quietly behind us. When we reach the sidewalk again, I feel some of the pressure inside my chest easing. It rained again while we were inside. Just a

Chapter 21

quick spring shower but enough to re-dampen the small plots of grass along the urban neighborhood. I love the rain. Breathing deeply the petrichor fills and soothes me like a long conversation with an old friend.

Bash is still beside me, holding my hand. Quietly nearby, just as he's always been. Watching. Waiting to see what I need to offer what he can.

Looking back over the past twenty years now feels different than it did before. I can't look back through the scrapbook of my mind without picturing him there too, just outside the edges of each picture. When my fifteen-year-old-self imagined the future, Bash was always in it. Without question. When I'd gone off to college, I forced myself to stop looking for him. Waiting to see if he'd turn back up in my life. I had told myself that it was a silly schoolgirl's dream, convinced myself he was gone. These last months have slowly wiped the fog from the rearview mirror, showing me that he hadn't left at all, just taken a backseat.

I squeeze his hand. "Let's take a walk."

Chapter 22

We walk a full city block before Bash breaks the contemplative silence. He'd been giving me space with pressure-free support for the move since our all-cards-on-the-table talk last month.

"I just want to say again, how incredibly sorry I am for all the ways I overstepped with you. I rationalized somewhat in my mind that it was no different from creeping on someone's social media accounts without sending a friend request... Except that my version of social media contains ALL the data out there."

He stops, shaking his head down at the ground. "I knew I was going way too far, and I let myself do it anyway. It was the one thing that let me stay... connected to you. Be a part of your life. But I know it was wrong. I'm so sorry for violating your privacy and shattering your trust."

I bend my knees a little to duck into his line of sight until he's forced to meet my eyes.

"Thank you. It helps to hear you say you know you were wrong. You know I love being right," I add, hoping to bring a smile to his face. It does, and my own stretches cheek to cheek.

Chapter 22

"I don't need you to continue begging me for forgiveness. But true remorse means change. Saying you're sorry, even feeling sorry, is important. But how are you going to show me you've changed? How can I be sure I'm not going to find more secret files later containing all my coffee shop receipts or the number of reels I watch at midnight?"

"Seventy-four reels on average, more on Friday nights..." he says under his breath. My eyes widen as my jaw drops, and he bursts into laughter.

"I'm just messing with you! I swear I have NEVER once dug into your online activity. So, your reel addiction is safe. At least from me," he adds with a wink.

As our laughter dies down, I take a minute to think about what I really want as we resume our stroll. Approaching the coffee shop on the corner, I smile at the couple sitting at an outdoor table. They're laughing and clapping at the chubby baby toddling shakily back and forth between them, clapping for himself even when he misses a step and his diapered bottom plops on the patio. The dad swings him up onto his lap and the little guy rewards him with a sloppy kiss. Joy is around the corner, if we keep taking that next step.

"I think—in addition to rebuilding my trust in you—I think I need to know that you trust me, too. That you trust I'm smart enough, capable enough and strong enough to make my way in the world. I want you to support my dreams the way I promise to support yours and believe I can achieve them on my own, like I always believed in you. I want you beside me, instead of standing in front of me. I don't want a guardian; I want a partner to go through life with. Side-by-side and watching each other's backs."

I lace my fingers through his, marveling at the butterflies that still flutter all these years later.

"Quite frankly I never did go too hard for the whole damsel in distress fantasy. I prefer to fight the monsters alongside my beloved, instead of watching from my ivory tower while he does all the slaying."

"I like the sound of that," Bash replies quietly, the pad of his thumb brushing over the back of my hand. "I can change, Meg. For you, I will. I've already started. I cleaned out all the files I had and deleted the alerts I'd set. And just to be clear—you've always been the heroine of my story."

I pause and pull his face down until his forehead rests against my own, breathing in his cool scent coupled with that soft leather jacket.

"Are we ready to take this next step then?"

"Together."

Then I kiss him with all the love that's been hidden in that deepest corner of my heart, waiting to be released again. I kiss him and he kisses me, and we're swept away in each other's arms. It's then I know we've found our way back.

Epilogue

"No, I've already told him that he can choose to support what we're doing here or not, but he's not getting a tour. This is a safe haven for women who have been hurt. It's not a zoo, and they are not on display for him to come in with his camera crew and get his PR opportunity. Non-negotiable," I tuck the phone up onto my shoulder to free my hand and finish applying one more swipe of mascara.

"Mm hm. Yes, that's what I thought. Well, we certainly do appreciate the governor's support, and I'll get back with you in two weeks to sort out the details. Yes. Two weeks because I'm out of the office as of yesterday. Right, thanks again."

I hit end and drop the phone into my lap, letting the full skirts of my dress catch it so I can focus on finishing my face before I forget and go out with one eye done, the other bare. *You're doing it, Meg.* Margaret's voice was only an occasional whisper in my mind now. I supposed I didn't need her as much anymore since I'd found and embraced my full self.

A light rap at the door has me calling "come in" with minimal movement of my face. Jared leans in around the door and lets out a low whistle.

"Wow, Mom. You look amazing. I thought I heard you in here talking to someone?"

"Oh," I wave him off with the mascara wand. "Just finishing some last calls for work. I didn't want to dump it on Tasha, not when she's busy setting up the new Angel House location in Indianapolis. Just securing a few more donors. Gotta reach those goals, you know!"

He smiles at me in the mirror as I hold up my pearl necklace, a silent request for him to help me put it on. He takes the necklace and lowers it over my head, careful not to disturb the half up mound of curls atop my head.

"Of course, the big expansion plan! Four new Angel Houses a year until every major city has one. I gotta say Mom, I never doubted you had it in you, but it sure has been cool seeing it come out."

The color rises in my cheeks, reflected in the vanity table mirror at his admiration. I turn toward him as he kneels next to the stool I'm perched on and place a hand on his cheek, the glittering engagement ring still catching my eye, even after months of wearing it.

"Thank you. I couldn't be prouder of you, son. Freshman year under your belt and already top of your class. No surprise for me either because I knew *you* had it in you too. I can't wait to see how you're going to change the world."

He gives me a peck on the cheek and says, "How WE are going to change the world."

Holding an arm out to me, he asks, "Well? Are you ready for this?"

Yes. I was ready. We exit the dressing room, going down the historical house's wide staircase to head toward the crowd filling the garden outside. The sweet strains of a string quartet waft through the open doors. I take my place in line behind Scarlet, Rebecca and Amelia. All three gather to fuss over my dress and hair a moment before giving their best wishes and then, one by one, stepping through the garden

Epilogue

doors.

Only Jared and I remain. I take a deep breath. Not because I'm nervous. I'm a 41-year-old woman who got a second chance at her first love. What was there to be nervous about? No, I wasn't nervous. But the breath reminds me that I'm alive, I'm here and this moment is real. And I am so ready for it.

As the music swells, we leave the covered doorway to pass under the floral archway. Each step down the aisle feels like every step since I was 15 has led me to this moment. It's all been as it should have been. Every joy, every pain, every gift, every loss has led me to this place. Has led me back to him.

Nearing the middle aisle, one guest in catches my eye. Lime green silk dress. A halo of brown curls. Eyes sparkling with delight. Smile stretched mega wide. Bouncing on her toes, Johanna waves excitedly from her seat, then points repeatedly at Bash and gives me two big thumbs up.

Bash's eyes gleam as I meet his gaze. Eyes wide, I nod my head toward Johanna questioningly. He winks and nods with a grin. I should've known when he acted interested in seeing the online photos of the apartment I stayed at in Salzburg that he had ulterior motives. He'd brought Johanna to our wedding. For me. Oh, I love this man.

We reach the final arch where we're to stand before the minister. Sebastian is there. Waiting for me. Just like always. Jared presses a soft kiss to my cheek with an approving squeeze to my hand. I pass my bouquet to Amelia behind me, and Bash takes both my hands in his own. The minister begins speaking but I'm not sure I hear any of it over the beating of my heart, overwhelmed by the love I have carried for so long for this man.

"Together?" he whispers so only I can hear.

"Side-by-side," I whisper back, "for every step after."

Acknowledgments

This story idea came to me all at once as we tucked into bed one night in August 2023. After tossing and turning for over an hour, I finally got up and outlined the whole thing in one go. I didn't return to bed until well after 5 am, about an hour before our children had to be up for school. It was worth it. After the initial outline, the story poured out of me—sometimes in sips, sometimes in long gulps. Parts of the story stuck to the outline. Other chapters took on a life of their own, and surprised even me.

Despite the ease of how this story came to me, at my core I am a people person. If it hadn't been for my people standing beside me and cheering me on, you wouldn't be holding this book today.

To my husband who tells me often, "I love to hear you talk," your love and listening ear have never failed to get me through the hardest times these past 16 years together. Thank you for enduring patiently when I talk endlessly about my stories. Every good idea I have you make even better. You are both my Rob and my Bash—both my dependable and my passionate forever love. I choose you and our girls every day.

My beautiful girls, your joyful existence has given me the courage to do so many things I never thought I could. You are the lights of my life!

Thank you to my parents for raising me to believe I could do anything

I set my mind to. My sister, Emily, is my real life Amelia (minus the kids) who really does kick corporate butt and has ALWAYS made space at the table for me.

Thank you to my very first reader—Elizabeth. You let me send you this book chapter by chapter as I wrote, which I now realize must've been an incredibly annoying way to read. But you did it anyway with so much encouragement and support. I hope everyone has a friend like you in their corner!

To my Beta readers—Heather, Erica, Dad and Daniel—thank you for your excitement and love for my story. Rhonda, my volunteer editor, I couldn't have made a good final copy without you!

Finally—but really first in my heart—I'm so grateful to my Heavenly Father for gifts far more important and more eternal than a story I can write on a page. In you, I find myself, my strength, my purpose.

And you, reader, thank you for buying this book! I wrote it because I had to. Because it lit up my mind so many nights that I couldn't sleep. But writing is even more fulfilling when shared. Thank you for letting me share my heart with you.

About the Author

Kate Goodwin is currently living out all her childhood dreams and couldn't be more thankful for it. When she's not plotting out her next novel or writing life science news, you'll find her enjoying her children or laughing with her husband. Her biggest dilemma in her spare time—read the next book or write one?

You can connect with me on:

https://www.facebook.com/KateGoodwinWrites

Made in the USA
Monee, IL
26 January 2024